Advance praise for *Jenny's Choice* by Patrick E. Craig...

"From the first page I felt a tender compassion for Jenny, the young woman in this novel. Her story unfolds with a gentle hand and a lyrical tone that leads to an ending filled with hope. As with the other books in the Apple Creek Dreams series, you'll want to read this book in one sitting. Preferably with a cup of tea."

Robin Jones Gunn,
bestselling author of the Glenbrooke series and the Christy Miller series

"Patrick Craig's Apple Creek Dreams series is both poetic and sincere. Strong characters who deal with the grief and joy of everyday life make these stories you'll remember long after you reach the last page....*Jenny's Choice* is a tender story of grief, restoration, and grace."

Vannetta Chapman,
author of the Pebble Creek Series

"Patrick Craig's artistry is like a buggy ride across the Amish countryside. It's a gentle, bouncing journey through bucolic farmland blended with a compelling story of family, romance, and faith. Delight yourself to the perfect escape with *Jenny's Choice*."

Michael K. Reynolds,
author of the acclaimed Heirs of Ireland Series

Harvest House books by Patrick E. Craig

◇◇◇

A Quilt for Jenna
▶ http://bit.ly/QuiltforJenna

The Road Home
▶ http://bit.ly/RoadHome

Jenny's Choice

Jenny's Choice

PATRICK E. CRAIG

HARVEST HOUSE PUBLISHERS
EUGENE, OREGON

Cover by Garborg Design Works, Savage, Minnesota

Cover photos © Chris Garborg; Bigstock / robhillphoto.com

Author photo by William Craig-Craig Propraphica

Patrick E. Craig is published in association with the Steve Laube Agency, LLC, 5025 N. Central Ave., #635, Phoenix, Arizona, 85012.

This is a work of fiction. Names, characters, places, and incidents are products of the author's imagination or are used fictitiously. Any resemblance to actual persons, living or dead, is entirely coincidental.

JENNY'S CHOICE
Copyright © 2014 by Patrick E. Craig
Published by Harvest House Publishers
Eugene, Oregon 97402
www.harvesthousepublishers.com

Library of Congress Cataloging-in-Publication Data
Craig, Patrick E.
Jenny's Choice / Patrick E. Craig.
    pages cm.—(Apple Creek Dreams Series ; Book 3)
ISBN 978-0-7369-5109-8 (pbk.)
ISBN 978-0-7369-5110-4 (eBook)
1. Amish—Fiction. 2. Farm life—Pennsylvania—Paradise—Fiction. 3. Life change events—Fiction.
4. Homecoming—Ohio—Apple Creek—Fiction. 5. Authors and publishers—Fiction. I. Title.
PS3603.R3554J46 2014
813'.6—dc23

                                                2013023639

Printed in the United States of America

13 14 15 16 17 18 19 20 21 22 / LB-JH / 10 9 8 7 6 5 4 3 2 1

Dedicated in loving memory to Fred and Alice Niemi:
To Uncle Fred for being a second father to me
and giving me an undying love for fly fishing,
and to Aunt Alice for giving me an undying love for writing.

Acknowledgments

To my wife, Judy,
for her tireless efforts in proofing and editing *Jenny's Choice*.

To Amish author Sicily Yoder,
for her advice and counsel on all things Amish.

To Lindsay, Sarah, Jane, Ashley, Julie, Laura, and Jill
for their extremely helpful advice and critique.

Contents

A Note from Patrick E. Craig

◇◇◇

WHEN I FIRST STARTED WRITING the Apple Creek Dreams Series, I was amazed at the way my characters seemed to spring from the ground, fully developed, letting me see and record all of their strengths and flaws as though I were writing their biographies. First, I wrote about Jerusha Springer and her encounter with God in the Great Storm of 1950 that paralyzed Ohio. Then, I shared the story of Jenny Springer, Jerusha and Reuben's adopted daughter, and her impassioned search for her own identity, which threatened to take her outside the Amish community of Apple Creek.

For the third book, I fully intended to write the story of Rachel Hershberger, Jenny's daughter. But when I finished *The Road Home,* I was startled to discover that I had come to love Jenny Hershberger—her strength, her passion, her mind, her love for God...she had captured my heart. I kept trying to move on to Rachel's tale, but I could not. So I asked my publisher if I could continue with Jenny's story, and Harvest House graciously gave me permission to do so.

So here is the rest of Jenny's story. For the romantic, it's the story of true love. For the pragmatist, it's the story of a gift given and a gift received. And for the one who longs for adventure, it's the journey of a tiny girl who is found beside a frozen pond in the heart of a blizzard, the road a young woman travels to find her way home, and the coming to fruition of the gift that God placed in her heart.

Part One
PARADISE LOST

◇◇◇◇◇◇◇◇◇◇◇◇

Sometimes I think life is like a rushing river that begins its journey high in the mountains, tumbles down over jagged rocks, rushes headlong over cliffs, and pours booming through nameless chasms until at last it escapes the harsh stone walls to the broad plain spread before it, flowing deep and quiet through lush meadows between banks that hold it tenderly.

On the way to this place, we usually make choices quickly and without thinking, like those a boatman makes as his vessel poises on the brink before it plunges headlong into the rapids. We look back on these instantaneous choices and understand, with a quiet shudder in our soul, the eternal enormity of a moment.

But even so, the choices we make as we drift in the place of safety and security can be the most consequential. For every soldier knows that in the lush growth beside a quiet river, or beneath the deep underbrush of a peaceful forest, the enemy is most likely to be hidden.

"Choices"
from the journals of Jenny Hershberger

CHAPTER ONE

The Departure

◇◇◇

NOVEMBER 1978

JENNY HERSHBERGER WALKED SLOWLY INTO the room and surveyed the piles of boxes waiting to be moved out to the wagon. Her eyes turned to a heap of clothing spread across the bed. With a weary sigh she brushed back an errant curl that had escaped from her *kappe*. Each item she looked at seemed to have a mouth clamoring for her attention, each with a story to tell or a memory to unveil.

This will be the hard part.

She went to the pine dresser—the first big project Jonathan had undertaken after Grandfather Borntraeger began to teach him woodworking. The detailing was coarse and the lines of the piece a bit awkward, but she had loved it from the moment Jonathan moved it into their room. She remembered him standing proudly beside it as she ran her hands over the top and opened each drawer as though it were a treasure trove. She loved the smell of the linseed oil he had rubbed into the wood, and when she had spread a lace piece over the top and placed her things there, it had become a symbol of all that Jonathan had left behind from his old life and all that he had become to be with her.

Now she picked up one of the objects on the top of the dresser, a small box. A sharp, almost physical pain touched her heart as she opened the lid. Inside were several folded pieces of paper. She took one out, slowly spread it open on the dresser, and began to read.

My precious Jenny,

It's the end of another long day here in Paradise. I've been in the fields since daybreak with Grandfather Borntraeger. As soon as the thaw came and the soil started to warm, we began preparing the ground for spring planting. This is the hardest work I've ever done, yet at the same time it is the most fulfilling. Your grandfather is a kind man, but he's very strict and doesn't put up with any complaining or questioning of his methods.

Since I'm so new to this, he must teach me as we work. I feel like a little boy all over again, but he's very patient with me even when I make mistakes.

I'm beginning to comprehend so many things, especially about God and His Son, Jesus. The Bible is a wonderful book. Did you know that God made the first man out of dirt? I wonder if that's why I feel so at home on the land. When I'm out in the fields with Grandfather Borntraeger, walking behind the plow, I feel as though my life finally means something, as if this is the most natural and real way I could ever be. As I work, I remember the words of a song I heard the Amish men singing when I first came to Apple Creek.

Let him who has laid his hand on the plow not look back! Press on to the goal! Press on to Jesus Christ! The one who gains Christ will rise with Him from the dead on the youngest day.

That's who I want to be—the one who lays his hand to
the plow and doesn't look back!

Jenny didn't finish reading, but folded the letter and placed it back
in the box. Tears formed in her eyes as she stood alone in the room,
lost in her sorrow.

"Mama?"

A quiet little voice spoke from the doorway. Jenny turned to the
young girl who stood there. She was small, with dark hair and deep,
sea-blue eyes.

She has his eyes—she's so much like him.

Jenny went to the girl and stooped down as she took the little one in
her arms and lifted her into a hug. The girl softly touched Jenny's face.

"Why are you crying, Mama?" she asked.

"It's nothing, my Rachel," Jenny answered. "I was only reading
your papa's letters, the ones he wrote to me before we were courting,
when he lived here with your great-grandfather and learned the Amish
ways. He wrote to me every day of the two years we were apart. I kept
the most special letters in this box so I could read them now and again
and let *du lieber Gott* remind me how much He blessed me by sending me your papa."

"Is Papa happy in heaven?" Rachel asked.

"Oh, yes, my dearest; Papa is very, very happy with Jesus and all
the angels."

"Why do we have to move to another house, Mama? I like our
house. What if Papa decides to come back from heaven and he can't
find us? Won't he be sad?"

Jenny sat on the bed and set Rachel down beside her. "Papa won't
come back from heaven, darling. Heaven is so *wunderbar* that once
you've gone there, you don't ever want to come back. And we wouldn't
want to call him back to this world once he's been with Jesus. He will
wait for us there, and one day we will join him and be with him again.

"In the meantime, we're sad that he's gone…very sad. We must move because it's very hard for your mama to live here without Papa. There are so many things that make me remember him, and my heart breaks again each time I see them. I need to go back to my old home and be with my mama and papa so they can help me not to feel this way. And they will help you to be happy again. Your *grossdaadi* can't wait for you to come, and Mama, my mama, has prepared a special room just for you. You will love being with them. Thanksgiving and Christmas will be here soon, and it will be comforting to be in Apple Creek with our family and friends for the holidays."

"Oh, yes, Mama, I love *Grossmudder* and *Grossdaadi*. It will be nice to see them. But won't we ever come back to Paradise?"

"Only *der vollkluge Gott* knows the answer to that question, my darling. Now, do you have all your things packed up like I asked you?"

"Mostly, Mama. Can you help me with the rest?" Rachel asked.

"Yes, dearest. I'll be there in a bit, when I finish here. Run ahead."

Rachel bounced off the bed and ran from the room. Jenny smiled as she watched her go.

She has her papa's eyes and my bounce!

Jenny sighed again as Jonathan crowded back into her thoughts. She stood up, grabbed an empty box, and quickly put the letter box and the rest of the items from the dresser top into it. Then she folded up the lace piece, placed it on top of her other belongings, and closed the box. She set it with the others, piled the clothing on a chair by the door, and then pulled the quilt and the linens from the bed. She folded them and put them into the last remaining empty box. She surveyed the stack of boxes and then went to the closet and took out her suitcase. Carefully she packed her clothing in it and snapped the latches shut. The click of the latches echoed in the room like tiny gunshots. Finished.

She took a deep breath.

There, I'm done. That wasn't so bad. Cousin Borntraeger can carry all this out for me and take it to the storage place. Mama said to just bring our clothes for now.

She heard boots on the front porch, and her heart leapt. Then just as quickly, reality dashed her hopes. Another deep sigh. How many times had she heard Jonathan coming up the front stoop and walking across the porch to the door? It was always such a comforting sound at the end of the day. But now…

There was a knock and then a voice calling. "Jenny? Are you ready, then?"

"I'm here, Cousin, in the bedroom. Can you help me with these boxes?"

Lem Borntraeger walked down the hall and into the room. He glanced around at the emptiness and pulled his black hat from his head.

"Jenny, are you sure this is what you want? We all want you to stay. I know it won't be the same without Jonathan, but you have family here."

Jenny looked at her tall cousin. He had been one of the blessings God bestowed on Jenny and Jonathan when they had come to Paradise ten years before. He had taken her into his heart from the first day they met, and after she and Jonathan married, he became their good friend and helper. She reached over and patted his arm.

"I have to go home, Lem. I need to be with my mama and papa. You will run the farm, and it will prosper in your care. For me, there are too many memories. Sometimes my remembrances of Jonathan and our days here feel like cobwebs that stick to me and hold me fast. They keep me from going on with my life. And I need to go on now or I'll die inside."

"Will you ever come back?" Lem asked.

"Right now I would say no," Jenny answered. "But who knows the road ahead? We may come back someday when I can be in this house without weeping every time I turn around." Jenny managed a weak smile. "I need to go, Lem."

"All right then," Lem said. "I understand."

He stood for a moment with his hat in his hands. "Jonathan was a good man, and he was my friend. I will miss him deeply." Then Lem put his hat back on and smiled. "It's enough. Now let me load these boxes."

Jenny watched him as he picked up two boxes and went out. She took one last look at the room and then turned to go.

"Jenny…"

She stopped and turned, thinking she had heard Jonathan's voice. But it was only the echoes of unspoken longings that filled her aching heart. She went one last time to the bed and touched it softly.

"Jonathan, oh, Jonathan. You are my true love. There will never be anyone like you for me. Thank you, my dearest, for loving me so deeply. Thank you for being a good man, a wonderful husband, and a loving father to Rachel. May *Gott* be with you on your journey."

Jenny stood silent for a moment and then picked up her suitcase, turned, and left the room. She went into Rachel's room, gathered up the few remaining things that were still unpacked, and laid them in her daughter's suitcase. Then she took Rachel's hand, and together they walked down the hall, through the empty front room, and out onto the porch. A buggy waited for them in the driveway. She boosted Rachel up as Lem put the suitcases in the back, and then she climbed in. She nodded to the driver, who clicked his tongue and set the horse in motion.

The buggy rolled slowly down the driveway. Jenny looked straight ahead. She would not look back. But then just as the horse turned onto the main road, her resolve crumbled, and she turned. The blue two-story house stood in the middle of the harvested fields. As she looked she could see Jonathan behind the plow, waving to her as the rich soil turned and broke beneath the sharp blade. She could see his smile and his blue eyes. She could feel his strong arms around her as they stood together on the porch, looking out over the land—their land—in awe of the blessings of God. She put her face into her hands and silently began to weep. The clopping hooves beat out a slow and mournful cadence—"He's gone, he's gone, he's gone."

CHAPTER TWO

The Journey

◇◇◇

SIX MONTHS EARLIER

IT WAS EARLY SPRING IN Paradise, Pennsylvania. The plum trees were clothed with the first blossoms of the year, and the pink blaze of color added the promise of new life to the otherwise still-dreary landscape. The fields lay fallow around the blue farmhouse, awaiting the cut of the plow and the planting of the seed. The snow had melted only a week before, and patches were still here and there where the shadows kept the sun at bay. The grass in the front yard still wore winter's brown, and the flower beds around the house had not yet felt the touch of Jenny's loving ministrations.

Jonathan stepped out onto the porch, his breath frosting as he walked. The sun peeked up over the eastern hills, and the few song-birds that had bravely returned to Paradise lifted a hopeful melody, urging on the warmth of spring. Jenny followed Jonathan out the door, her best woebegone expression still masking her lovely face.

"Why must you go, husband? Is it really so important to you? We haven't been apart in all the ten years we've been together."

Jonathan turned and smiled at Jenny. "God is giving me this

opportunity to be a strong witness to my parents. It's a miracle that they even asked me to come. And with Dad so ill, this may be my last chance. If I'm to see him, now is the time. Besides, if I wait, I'll have to delay my planting. I'll only be gone a week. I'll be home before you know it."

Jenny added petulance to her woeful countenance, and Jonathan laughed. "One more expression on your beautiful face and you'll twist it beyond all recognition."

Jenny laughed and gave up trying to win him by that means. Instead she moved closer until Jonathan put his arm around her.

"If it was summer, I'd take you and Rachel with me, but I don't want to take her out of school. If we wait till summer…well, Dad may not be alive by then. So if I'm to see him I must go now."

"Oh, I know, Jonathan," Jenny said softly. "But ever since the letter came, I've had a strange feeling. What if something happens to you? What would we do without you?"

Jonathan pulled her even closer. "Nothing will happen. I'm going to take a train ride to Long Island, visit my parents for a week, and then come home. I'll be here in time for the planting, and hopefully my dad will see how my faith has changed me for the better. If he dies without Jesus, he will…well, he'll be separated from God forever, and yet it's God's will that all men should be saved and come to the knowledge of the truth. I have the truth, and I believe it's in God's timing that I should share it with Dad."

"But he's been so judgmental since you converted," Jenny said.

"Yes, in the beginning he thought I was just on another 'hippie trip,' but as the years have passed and after he met you and Rachel and watched my life change, I believe he's softened. In one of his recent letters he said that my religious affiliation seemed to have changed me for the better. He actually said he was proud of me. That was a first.

I'm hoping that with his illness, Dad has begun to think about his own mortality."

Jenny knew she wouldn't change his mind, so she let it drop. But she still couldn't get over the uneasiness she felt. All she knew was that the day the letter came, a warning bell rang inside her. Still, she trusted Jonathan to do the right thing, so she did her best to hear what he was saying and accept that the Lord had arranged this visit home.

Jonathan finished packing the last of his clothes in the suitcase. He closed the lid and looked around the room. Jenny's words had given him a sense of uneasiness he couldn't quite shake off. But he had prayed about this decision when he got the letter from his dad, and his course seemed set. He sighed and shut the suitcase as Jenny came into the room.

"Did you pack some long underwear and extra socks?" Jenny asked. "It's still cold and wet out on Long Island."

Jonathan heard the note of uncertainty in her voice, and he did his best to present an assured front.

"Yes, dear," he said, "I have everything I need. My plain clothes are going to look a bit strange to my folks, but they'll have to put up with it. I know my mom will try to take me shopping for something she thinks is more suitable to Long Island, but it's not going to happen."

"She won't make you shave your beard, will she?" Jenny asked.

"No, but if she tries, that won't happen either," Jonathan answered with a laugh. "Where my parents live, there are a lot of sailors with beards, so I should be able to blend in without too much trouble. Hopefully we'll be spending most of our time at home. Mom says Dad has good days and bad days, so I don't expect he goes out much."

Jonathan took Jenny by the hand and led her out to the front room. He set his suitcase down by the door and looked around the room. As he did, he remembered the early days when they had first come to Paradise to live with Grandfather Borntraeger.

He thought back to those wonderful days when he had convinced Jenny they should take over running the farm, much to *Grossdaadi's* relief. Together they pitched in and spruced up the old place with a fresh coat of paint and some new furniture, and soon Jenny had put her own stamp on the house.

Jonathan looked around the room that held so many memories. He thought of all those nights he had studied the Bible late into the night as Grandfather had helped him to discover the wonder of God's Word. When *Grossdaadi* passed five years ago, he left everything to Jenny and Jonathan, and gradually the place had become the Hershberger farm. Jonathan's favorite times had been spent in front of the huge fireplace, sitting with Jenny before a roaring blaze and reading the Bible or just being together after Rachel was in bed. There were so many things about the farm and their life there that had impacted him deeply. He recalled the day he had taken Lem Borntraeger on as a partner, and from that day, the two of them, with help from the community, had made the farm prosper.

As he stood in the room with Jenny, a strange feeling came over him, as if he were seeing this place for the last time. Without thinking, he pulled Jenny close to him and held her tightly.

"What is it, Jonathan?" she asked.

He couldn't voice his fear without alarming her, so he pulled her close and held her.

"I love you so, dear Jenny. You've been proof to me that there is a God and that He loves me very much, for He gave you to me for a wife. I will always love you."

Jenny's arms slipped up around Jonathan's neck, and she held him as though she would never let him go.

Chapter Three

The Homecoming

◇◇◇

Jonathan watched the countryside roll by. He had left Paradise on Monday morning, endured the long bus ride from Lancaster to Penn Station in New York, transferred by subway to the Hunters Point station, and from there boarded the Montauk train. Now the coach rumbled up the south shore of Long Island, headed east.

When he stepped on the train, he felt out of place among the hundreds of commuters in their suits and ties, so he tried to read his Bible and blend into the background. The train was crowded, and several young kids were running up and down the aisle while their parents slept, so he gave up and watched the fields and towns roll by. After a while he remembered that New Yorkers kept pretty much to themselves, so he put aside the fact that he was dressed in Amish clothing and began to take in the surroundings outside. It was planting season, and trucks, tractors, and other pieces of farm equipment were out preparing the land. When the train passed Hempstead, something caught his eye that made him sit up and look. Out in a large field were a group of Amish men on a horse-drawn planter. They had cultivated a large part of the field and were planting something. Jonathan looked closer.

They're planting potatoes!

Somehow it was very comforting to Jonathan to catch even a glimpse of them as he passed, and after that he relaxed a little.

Maybe this won't be such a bad trip after all.

He read the signs for the towns they passed: Lynbrook, Rockville, Freeport, Merrick...

Every town has a memory. How many times did I ride this train when I was a kid?

He remembered visiting friends, going to the city to see a favorite band, or just jumping on the train to escape the monotony of his home. He remembered his family's old house in Levittown and was immediately flooded with unpleasant memories of his absentee father and his alcoholic mother. No, he remembered his youthful home, but he did not miss it.

The only place I've ever really felt at home is on the farm in Paradise with Jenny and Rachel.

Now he was headed to the end of Long Island for what he hoped would be a short, uneventful visit. He just wanted to see his dad and mom for a few days and then get back home to Paradise. He thought about what he wanted to say while he was there, and as he did, he prayed a simple prayer.

Lord, give me an opportunity to share the gospel with them before I leave.

Two hours later the train rolled into Bridgehampton. A slight drizzle had misted the windows, and Jonathan had gone back to reading his Bible. As the train pulled to a stop, Jonathan stood up, grabbed his suitcase from the rack, stuffed his Bible in his knapsack, and headed for the exit. He climbed down the steps and looked around. At first he didn't see them, but then, as his eyes swept the platform, he saw his mother waving next to his dad.

"Johnny, Johnny, over here," his mother called as she waved again.

Jonathan debated for a moment whether he should ask his parents to call him by his real name, but he decided that was a battle he didn't need to fight.

Show them the love of Christ; let them see Him in me. Christus in mir, die Hoffnung auf den Ruhm.

Jonathan walked up to his parents and let his mother enfold him in a hug. Right away he noticed that she didn't exude the familiar sickly sweet smell of gin and vermouth. He looked at her face. The old anger was gone from her eyes, and she seemed genuinely glad to see him. He looked over at his dad.

"Hello, Dad," he said as he put out his hand. "How are you?"

His father reached out and grasped Jonathan's hand. "Hello…son," he said. "I'm fine. I'm having a good day today."

He held onto Jonathan for a moment and then awkwardly took his hand away and let it hang by his side. The two men looked at each other, neither knowing what to say next. Jonathan's mother jumped into the silence.

"Let's get your things into the car, and Gerald can drive us home."

"Gerald?" Jonathan asked.

"Yes, he works for us. He helps your father, drives us when we need to go out, and runs errands for us. He's by the car, over there."

She pointed to a tall, athletic-looking black man in a dark suit standing by a Lincoln Town Car. He waved to them, and they all started toward the car. Jonathan noticed his father had a slight limp and that the skin on the back of his hands had large purple bruises. When they came to the car, Jonathan's parents climbed in the back, and Jonathan sat in the passenger seat next to Gerald.

Jonathan's mother filled the otherwise awkward silence with chatter about her club and their new home. As Jonathan listened, his thoughts drifted back to his childhood and the hours of his mother's drunken ramblings.

Not everything has changed, but at least she's sober today.

"I hope you brought some warm clothing," his mom said.

"Warm clothing?" he asked.

"Yes, for the boat trip," his mother answered.

"Mom, you didn't say anything about a boat trip," he said.

"Oh, we just decided yesterday," his mother said. "Your father wanted to take you on the boat, and it's a fairly short cruise down to the Outer Banks. Then we can stay in the condo at Oracoke Island for a couple of days. We already bought you a train ticket back to New York from there so you can catch your bus back to Pennsylvania when you're ready to go home."

"I haven't been on a boat since I was a teenager," Jonathan said hesitantly.

His father was dozing off, and his mother leaned forward and whispered in his ear. "Please, Johnny. Your dad really wants to take you, and it may be the last time you will ever be with him. And it would give us a chance to talk. I want to tell you about…well, about some changes I've made in my life since your father got sick. We have a great crew, and the boat is wonderful. It's more than just a boat, it's a yacht. You'll enjoy yourself. Please."

As his mother spoke to him, Jenny's words came back. *"Ever since the letter came, I have had a strange feeling. I don't have peace in my heart. What if something happens to you? What would we do without you?"*

A chill swept down Jonathan's back, and he recognized an unfamiliar sensation in his stomach—fear.

The next morning dawned dull and gray. As they drove to the dock, Jonathan's dad pointed out the boat. It was enormous. He noticed the name painted on the bow—*Mistral.* His father brightened noticeably as he surveyed the magnificent yacht.

"Quite a boat," he said proudly. "She can accommodate up to ten people overnight in four double staterooms and one twin cabin. She has three four-stroke engines that produce 2400 horsepower each, and her top speed is around 45 knots. She cruises at 35 knots."

Jonathan stared in awe. "Dad, this boat must have cost a fortune."

"Well, when I sold my business, we had quite a windfall. We moved out to the Hamptons, and then when I got sick I figured I might as well splurge and buy the one thing I've always wanted. So I got the boat at a distress sale. Some sheikh from Dubai needed some cash and let it go for a song."

They climbed on board as Gerald grabbed the suitcases and carried them aft toward the staterooms. Two men came out of the wheelhouse. One was tall and clean-cut, and the other looked more the sailor. He was shorter with a blond beard and wore a red striped pullover.

"Johnny, this is Jack and Terry," his dad said. "Jack's the captain and Terry is his mate, mechanic, and cook. How's the weather look, boys?"

Terry started to reply. "Well—"

Jack cut him off. "There's some weather out to sea, but the Coast Guard says it turned south and headed toward Barbados. It won't even make landfall in the U.S. If we stay close in, we should be down to Oracoke by about five tonight. Might be some onshore swells, but this baby cuts right through."

He turned to Jonathan, who had on a yellow slicker and a watch cap in place of his black jacket and broad-brimmed hat. Jonathan had made the concession at his mother's urging when he realized that the first gust of wind would probably carry his hat away.

"Ever been on a boat like this?" Jack asked.

"No," Jonathan said. "I used to do a little sailing when I was a kid, but nothing bigger than twelve feet. And for the past ten years I've been living on a farm where we don't use any motorized machinery, so I haven't really been around anything like this before."

"No motorized machinery?" Terry asked. "Are you Amish or something?"

"Yes, I am," Jonathan said.

The two men looked at Jonathan with surprise.

"That's interesting," Jack said. "Your folks aren't Amish."

"No," Jonathan said, "but our family was originally Amish until the 1700s. My father's great-grandfather left the faith to become a frontiersman. Eventually he married an Indian woman, and that's where our side of the family comes from. I only found this out about ten years ago when my Amish wife helped me trace my roots back to the first Amish that settled in Pennsylvania. My wife and her family were instrumental in my coming back to the faith."

"Sounds like an interesting story," Jack said. "Maybe you can tell us a little more about it after we get underway."

"I'd be happy to," Jonathan said, casting a glance at his father. Sharing his story was something Jonathan had hoped for…especially in the presence of his parents.

Jack grabbed Terry and pointed him aft. "Okay, let's get the diesels fired up. I want to make sure that new crankshaft in number two is running smoothly."

He nodded to Jonathan, and the two men went inside. Gerald returned and helped Jonathan's dad go aft, leaving Jonathan and his mother alone on the foredeck.

Jonathan's mother reached over and took her son's arm and led him to a seating area on the front of the boat. A crisp wind was blowing in from the sea, and the smell of the salt water rode on it like the gulls circling above.

"Johnny…Jonathan, I've wanted to tell you something for a long time now." She seemed to gather her courage and continued. "Let me start by telling you how sorry I am—"

"Sorry for what, Mom?" Jonathan asked.

"For all the years I wasn't a very good mother because…of my drinking."

Jonathan looked at her with surprise. She had always been so good at denying her problem and blaming others, especially his dad, so the admission was startling. "Mom, you don't have to—"

She put her fingers to his lips. "Yes, Jonathan, I do. I hurt you terribly. I know that. And I blamed your father, I blamed his work, his affairs— I blamed everyone, even you. But I never was willing to admit that it was me. I was the one with the problem. So I kept drinking. When your father got sick, he had to stop traveling, and he gave up his girlfriends in his other 'ports of call,' so to speak. I think he was really sorry for all the years he was unfaithful, and when he changed, I realized I didn't have an excuse to stay drunk. I started going to AA and got some help. When they talked about turning my life over to a higher power, that wasn't enough for me. I wanted to put a name and a face to it. And I saw how you turned your life around with your new faith, so I started looking. I found a pastor who helped me see the truth about who God really is and what His Son did for me and I…well, Johnny, I'm a Christian now."

Jonathan looked at his mother in complete shock, and then the reality of what she had just told him sunk in. He reached over and took his mom into an embrace and held her tight.

"Mom, that's wonderful. That's amazing!"

They stayed like that for a long moment, and then she pulled back and reached for a hanky in her jacket pocket.

"What does Dad think?"

"Well, he's glad that I've found something that works for me, as he puts it, but he's never gone further than that—until the last few weeks," she said as she dabbed her eyes. "I think he's staring his own mortality in the face. He knows the cancer is going to kill him in a few months, so he's been asking me to pray for him. There's so much between us that it's hard for me to broach the subject to him, so I was hoping you could talk to him."

Jonathan looked at her and then silently thanked the Lord. *You are the One who answers prayer!*

Down in the engine compartment, Jack and Terry listened to the number two engine.

"Does she sound rough to you?" Jack asked.

"Yeah, but it could just be that the new shaft needs to seat itself," Terry said.

"Well, keep an eye on it. I don't want anything to spoil this trip."

The two men turned out the light and climbed out of the hold.

Deep in the heart of engine number two, the new crankshaft continued to rotate with the plunging of the pistons. The tiny crack on the shaft, unnoticed at installation, began to open a millimeter at a time, distorting the shaft and throwing the assembly slightly out of balance. As it did, the minor vibration became more noticeable.

CHAPTER FOUR

Lost

◇◇◇

THE GREY-GREEN SEA ROLLED IN long smooth swells beneath the *Mistral* as the boat powered out around Montauk Point and headed south toward Cape Hatteras. They passed Gardiner's Island well before dawn and now, three hours later, a gloomy, dark morning had arrived. A slight drizzle drifted in off the North Atlantic. The chill of a winter not yet dead bit Jonathan's face as he stood on the foredeck watching the gulls circle behind the boat as it raced through the waves. Their plaintive cries whirled away on the wind, and the sea looked ominous and dead.

How did I end up on a yacht headed for the Outer Banks of North Carolina? This wasn't in the plan. I was supposed to spend a week in Sag Harbor and then go home.

Suddenly a great longing to see Jenny and Rachel swept over him like one of the swells rolling endlessly by. Lost in his thoughts, Jonathan didn't hear anything until he felt a hand touch him on the shoulder. He turned to see Gerald waiting solicitously.

"We have some breakfast ready, Mister Jonathan," he said. "Eggs, bacon, and pancakes, orange juice, and coffee."

Jonathan hadn't thought he would be able to eat much when he first came aboard, given the constant motion of the boat, but the fresh air and the biting sea breeze had done their work.

"That actually sounds good, Gerald," Jonathan said. "Tell my mother I'll be right in."

As Gerald headed back to the galley, Jonathan once more pondered his circumstances. He thought of his long, strange, wonderful journey since leaving Long Island eleven years before—the season in San Francisco trying to find himself, the unfulfilled dreams of success in the music industry, the death of Shub Jackson in that seedy motel in Pacifica, California, and the flight across country from the drug dealers that led him to Ohio. *And then I met Jenny in Apple Creek, we found her grandfather, and I became Amish!*

Jonathan smiled. It was definitely the stuff novels were made of—certainly not real life. There were just so many coincidences! But then he remembered something Jerusha had once told him: Coincidence is just God choosing to remain anonymous.

"So true," Jonathan said as he made his way amidships.

Terry listened to the number two engine. It was definitely running a little rough. He thought about shutting her down but decided against it. It would add a couple of hours to the trip, and he wanted to get into port as quickly as possible. The last he heard on the radio, the weather front was turning again and heading toward New Jersey. That was not welcome news. The *Mistral* was seaworthy, but he didn't want to be out in a gale. And the vibration from number two bothered him. *The new crankshaft probably just hasn't seated right. I'll check it again in an hour*, he thought as he climbed the ladder out of the hold and turned off the light.

Inside the engine, the microscopic crack opened another millimeter, throwing the shaft slightly further out of balance. The distortion caused the ramps on the shaft to rub against the valve lifters unevenly, and after a while, a tiny red spot developed in the metal as the shaft heated up.

Jonathan sat with his father at the table. They had eaten quietly with little small talk, and now they drank their coffee. Jonathan's father stared out the curved window at the sea. Jonathan was about to say something to break the silence when his father spoke.

"Has your mother talked to you about her…conversion?"

"Yes she has, Dad," Jonathan replied. "I think it's great."

"Well, it seems to have made a difference, that's for sure," his father continued. "For one thing, she doesn't drink anymore. But the thing that amazes me is that she found it in her heart to forgive all my indiscretions. That's what I can't figure out. She should hate me after what I put her through. Maybe you didn't know, but I—"

"I knew all about it, Dad," Jonathan said quietly. "It was pretty obvious. I think it was the main reason why you and I didn't really have a relationship. I saw what it was doing to Mom, and I guess I hated you for it. You were gone, enjoying yourself, and I had to stay home with a mother who got drunk and fell asleep in the middle of the kitchen floor with the food burning on the stove."

"I know, son," his father said, tears forming at the edges of his eyes. "And I want you to know how sorry I am. I hope you can forgive me. When you're staring death in the face, your past has a way of slapping you around."

"Dad, I forgave you a long time ago," Jonathan said. He hesitated and then went on, watching the look on his father's face. "When I became a Christian, I learned that forgiveness and grace are the most important qualities a man can have in his life. I found it out when I discovered how much I needed to be forgiven."

"What did you need to be forgiven for? You were always a pretty good kid."

"The Bible tells us all have sinned and fallen short of the glory of God," Jonathan said. "All you need to do is look at the Ten Commandments, and you'll understand."

"What do you mean, son?"

"Well, for instance, I would be willing to bet that everyone I know would confess to stealing something."

"Sure," his father said. "I know I have."

"If you have, what does that make you?"

"A thief, I guess."

"Have you ever told a lie?"

"Yeah, well, I had to tell a lot of lies when I was cheating on your mother."

"And speaking of that, have you ever committed adultery?"

His father's face flushed, and he looked away. "You know the answer to that."

"So, Dad, by your own admission, you are a thief, a liar, and an adulterer. You've broken at least three of God's laws and deserve to be punished. Now if God is a just God, which He is, He can't let you off the hook until the penalty is paid. So that means you'll be kept out of His heaven until your debt is paid off."

"That's what bothers me about this, son. With all my faults, it seems like there's no way to get out from under it."

"That's the amazing thing, Dad." Jonathan was warming to his task. "God loved you so much He became a man and died in your place. When Jesus went to the cross, He carried every sin ever committed to the cross with Him. And if you believe He died for your sins, that He rose from the grave because He had no sin and death couldn't hold Him, and if you believe He is alive today, you can be forgiven. It's that easy, and the truth is, it's your only hope."

"But don't I have to join a church like you did and become a holy Joe?"

"The Amish church doesn't save me, Dad. No church can do that. I'm saved by faith in Jesus Christ alone, not by any works. I love the Amish faith because the *Ordnung*, the rules, give me reference points by which to steer my life, like stars in the night sky for a sailor. I love the simplicity, the separation from what's becoming a truly wicked world. But it doesn't save me. Only Jesus can do that."

"That makes sense," Jonathan's father said. "A lot of sense."

In the wheelhouse, Jack and Terry watched as the storm clouds began to bear down on the *Mistral*.

"I knew that front wasn't going to keep going south," Terry said with a scowl. "In about fifteen minutes we're going to be in the middle of it."

Even as he spoke the first heavy drops of rain splashed on the windshield. The pennants on the running gear flapped and twisted in the stiff wind that had sprung up. Jack looked to the west. The Jersey shore was just visible on the horizon.

"We need to get in closer to shore."

"Yeah, but it shoals up as we head down to the Banks," Terry replied. "We'll get into a bad chop when the waves start piling up in front of this wind."

"I know, but I don't want to be too far out if we need to get into a harbor. Stay up here and let's both keep our eyes peeled for shallow water."

Terry pulled out the navigation maps as Jack turned the boat west and headed in toward the mouth of the Chesapeake. Every other concern was forgotten, including engine number two.

Down in the hold, a strange glow illuminated the darkness. A small spot glowed red on the side of engine number two where metal rubbed on metal inside the crankcase. The engine whined as the distorted crank wore against the restrainers that held it in place. The temperature of the hot spot climbed above 200 degrees centigrade, and the lubricating oil splashed on this hot spot and vaporized. The oil vapor circulated to a cooler part of the crankcase, where it condensed into a white oil mist. The oil droplets in the mist were very small and very explosive. As the *Mistral* labored through the growing seas, the temperature inside the engine climbed steadily higher.

Topside, the boat moved up and down with the surging of the swells that now pounded through in front of the coming storm. Spray flew up as the bow lifted on the crest of each wave and then splashed down into the following trough. The wind picked up and the rain poured down. White foam formed on the tops of the swells as the wind and the waves collided. Inside the galley, Gerald quickly picked up the remaining breakfast dishes as the boat's motion caused them to start sliding about on the tabletop.

Mr. Hershberger looked up from his newspaper at Jonathan. "Looks like we've been caught by a bit of weather. Well, we needn't worry. Jack and Terry are seasoned hands, and they'll get us through."

Despite his father's calming words, a deep sense of uneasiness filled Jonathan. For some reason a verse from Jude came to his mind: "…raging waves of the sea, foaming out their own shame; wandering stars, to whom is reserved the blackness of darkness for ever."

Jonathan felt a sudden quickening of his heartbeat. *Something's going to happen. What is it, Lord?*

Jonathan went to the door of the dining area and stepped out onto the mid-deck. The rain poured down and the wind howled. He watched as the boat plunged through the surging seas. She was seaworthy and making good headway.

Get us through this, Lord! I need to see Jenny again.

Jack and Terry steered the boat toward the Jersey shore. Jack looked over at Terry, who called out navigation points.

"The storm is getting stronger. We have to take her in. What's the closest harbor?"

Terry looked at the map. "Longport."

"Okay. Set a course for Longport. And get on the horn and call the Coast Guard. Let them know we're well north of where we expected to be and coming in."

Terry picked up the radio and switched it to the Coast Guard band.

"Hello, U.S. Coast Guard, this is the yacht *Mistral* out of Sag Harbor, New York. We are—"

Just then, the weakened crankshaft finally gave way and broke inside the crankcase with a grinding thump. The *Mistral* gave a lurch and swung to the right. In the wheelhouse, Terry looked over at Jack.

"What was that?"

"I think we just lost number two," Jack said. "We're in for it now."

Terry took two steps toward the door. Just at that moment, the temperature inside the engine climbed to over 900 degrees centigrade, and the oil mist ignited and exploded. When it did, a flame front traveled down the crankcase with a pressure wave in front of it. The turbulence caused by the moving engine components churned and mixed the vapors, increasing the speed of the flame front and its area, which blew the crankcase doors off the engine.

Topside, the explosion threw Jonathan to the deck. As he lay there, stunned, he saw his mother come out of her stateroom and try to make her way forward.

At the same time, the initial explosion vented through the engine's relief valves and the blown-off crankcase doors and sent a large amount of oil mist into the engine room, where it was ignited by a hot exhaust manifold. The explosion of oil mist inside the closed space blew a huge hole in *Mistral's* side. Immediately she heeled starboard and started taking on water.

The explosion and the sudden listing of the boat threw Jonathan off the deck and into the churning waves. Burning diesel fuel filled the surface of the water between him and the boat. Jonathan saw his father lurch out onto the deck.

"Dad! Dad!"

From twenty feet away his father looked straight into his eyes and reached his hand toward Jonathan and cried out. Jonathan couldn't hear him over the wind, but he saw his father's mouth forming words. "Son, I believe!"

In the wheelhouse, Terry grabbed the radio as Jack struggled with the boat. *Mistral* was listing badly as water poured into the hold.

"Mayday, Mayday," he shouted. "Yacht *Mistral* just experienced engine explosion and taking on water. Position is—"

At that instant the flames from the burning diesel below deck ignited the propane tank, and the *Mistral* exploded with a huge roar. Jonathan struggled in the water. He felt burning oil on his face. He looked up as the broken radar mast came flying toward him. He cried out Jenny's name just before the mast crashed down on top of him and he sank into blackness.

The grey-green waves rolled over the wreck as *Mistral* sank. Within seconds there was nothing left except some floating pieces of wreckage driving west before the howling wind.

CHAPTER FIVE

News

◇◇◇

JENNY WAS UP AT FIRST LIGHT, making her morning coffee after another troubled night. She still hadn't heard from Jonathan. Before he left he promised he would call the General Store and leave a message for her to let her know when he would be arriving home, but when Lem had checked there was no message.

Jenny sat at the kitchen table sipping her coffee and reading her Bible when she heard a car pull in the long driveway. She went to the living room to look out the window. Fear clutched at her when she saw the boxy white car with the red light on top and the state police lettering on the side. The car came to a stop in front of the house, and two uniformed troopers climbed out. Jenny watched as they came across the lawn and up on the porch. There was a knock on the door.

No! I'm not going to answer it! I'll stay inside, and they'll go away and everything will be fine. Jonathan's just fine.

Even as the terrible thoughts crowded in on her, she walked to the door and opened it.

"Mrs. Hershberger?" one of the officers asked.

"Yes…"

"Are you the wife of Jonathan Hershberger?"

"Yes. What's this about?"

"Was Mr. Hershberger recently in Sag Harbor, Long Island?"

"Yes, he was," Jenny said. "Officer, please—"

"Wait just a minute, ma'am," the other officer said. "We just have to confirm that we're talking to the right person before we can give you any details."

"What details? Has something happened?"

"We're not sure, ma'am," the first officer said. "It seems that Ronald and Francis Hershberger left Sag Harbor early Tuesday morning headed for North Carolina on their boat, the *Mistral*. They were supposed to check in with their housekeeper Tuesday night to let her know they had arrived, but they never called. The Coast Guard station in Beach Haven, New Jersey, picked up a distress call from the yacht *Mistral* out of Sag Harbor around three p.m. Tuesday afternoon. It seems there had been an engine explosion, but before *Mistral* could state her position, the radio went dead."

The second officer continued. "The Coast Guard checked with the harbormaster in Sag Harbor. Jack Clarkson, the captain of the *Mistral*, filed a cruise plan, and their destination was Ocracoke Island in North Carolina. It seems the Hershbergers had a vacation place down there. The *Mistral* was a fast boat and could cruise at thirty-five knots, so the Coast Guard plotted a course and they have planes and boats out looking in the area where they should have been."

"But what about Jonathan?" Jenny asked, twisting her hands in her apron.

"Ma'am, they wouldn't have even known about him except that the Hershbergers' housekeeper told the local police that the Hershbergers had taken their son, Jonathan, with them. She said it was a surprise for him that his parents planned. The housekeeper told the police Jonathan had come from Paradise, Pennsylvania, and he was a member of the

Amish church here. Local officers contacted us, and we've been looking for you since Wednesday. It wasn't easy to find you without a phone."

Jenny suddenly felt her knees almost give way. She grabbed the doorframe to hold herself up. The state trooper stepped forward and took her arm.

"Are you all right, ma'am?"

"I need to sit down," Jenny said. "Please come in."

They went into the front room, and Jenny sank down onto the couch. The two troopers looked at her with concern in their eyes.

"Have they found anything?" Jenny asked. "I mean, what's happening with the search?"

"As of now, the Coast Guard has nothing to report," the first officer said. "A storm moved through the area, and it was difficult for the rescue teams to even get out to where they presumed the *Mistral* was. As of last night they hadn't found anything."

Jenny sat on the couch, her mind reeling and her heart pounding. Her whole body felt numb, and the troopers seemed to be talking to her from a long way away.

I knew something would happen. You showed me. I should have screamed and begged and held onto him and never let him go.

"Ma'am, are you all right?"

Jenny looked up at them, and then she burst into tears. "I told him not to go. I begged him. I just knew…" Then sobs overcame her, and she could speak no more.

It was Sunday afternoon. Jenny sat at the kitchen table staring into space. She had sent Rachel outside to play earlier. As she buttoned her daughter's coat, Rachel touched her mama's face.

"I've been praying for Papa," she said.

Jenny pulled her daughter into a long hug and then brushed an errant curl back from Rachel's forehead.

"I know you have, my darling, and I have too," Jenny said, "Now we must put Papa in the Lord's hands."

"Okay," Rachel said, bounding out the door.

Now Jenny sat numbly in the kitchen, thinking. *I've been praying and praying. Will You answer me, Lord? Will You bring my husband back?*

Just then Jenny heard footsteps coming across the front porch and Lem's voice calling her.

"Jenny! Jenny!"

Jenny jumped up and ran to the front door, thrusting it open.

"Lem! What is it?"

"They found a raft, Jenny. There was one survivor from the *Mistral*."

Jenny's heart leaped into her throat. "Jonathan?"

"I don't know, Jenny. All I got was a message from the state police saying that one survivor had been found on a raft."

"How can we find out? Oh, Lem, I have to know!"

"I asked Karen Jamison—you know, the owner of the store—if she could have her son come out and take us into Lancaster. He was making deliveries for her, so he'll be here in about an hour."

"Oh, Lem, it has to be Jonathan, it just *has* to." Jenny burst into sobs.

◇◇◇

Two hours later, Jenny and Lem were in the office of Sergeant Mike Johnson of the state police. He was going over a file. Finally he looked up. Jenny felt as if she couldn't breathe.

"What can you tell us, Sergeant?" Lem asked.

"All I have so far is that there is one survivor. He was found on an Avon raft, but he was far to the north of where the rescue teams were searching. It seems that one of the Coast Guard planes was called back to look for some other missing boats near the New Jersey shore, and the pilot flew north and west to get there. As he looked, he spotted the raft about a mile off the coast. They thought the raft was from another boat, but the cutter that went out radioed in that the raft had *Mistral* stenciled on it and that there was one survivor aboard. That's all we know."

"Can we wait here until you hear more?" Jenny asked.

"Sure, Mrs. Hershberger. We have a break room just down the hall, and there's a cafeteria if you're hungry."

Jenny and Lem left the sergeant's office and walked down the hall. Lem had his arm around Jenny protectively, but they didn't speak. The past several days had taken their toll, and Jenny was ready to collapse from the strain.

"Lem, if it's not Jonathan…what will I do?"

"Let's just take it one step at a time, Jenny. Let's think the best and not the worst. I'm trusting *unser liebender Gott* to bring Jonathan home. So let's just rest in Him and pray."

Jenny and Lem sat in silence in the break room drinking coffee Lem had gotten from the cafeteria. Jenny alternated between great leaps of hope and horrible plunges into despair.

I've got to know, Lord. One way or the other, I've got to know. This waiting is killing me.

After what seemed an eternity, a girl came into the room, saw Jenny and Lem, and came over. "Mrs. Hershberger?"

"Yes…"

"Would you come with me, please? Sergeant Johnson has some news concerning your husband."

Jenny looked at Lem. "Oh, Lem…"

"All right, Jenny, let's go find out."

They walked into Sergeant Johnson's office. The trooper looked up at them.

"Please sit down, Mrs. Hershberger," the sergeant said as he pointed to the chair opposite him.

"What is it, Sergeant?" Jenny asked as she sat down.

Sergeant Johnson looked down at a piece of paper in front of him and then back at Jenny.

"This just came in on our teletype," he said.

He paused and then went on. "The man they found is a black man named Gerald Sanders. He was Mr. Ronald Hershberger's caretaker and valet. He's in a hospital in Atlantic City. From this report, Mr. Sanders is sure there were no other survivors."

Jenny gasped and buried her face in her hands as the sobs came without restraint.

Three days later, Jenny sat in a hospital room in New Jersey with Gerald Sanders. He had a bandage around his head, and his right arm was in a sling. He turned his head and looked out the window when Jenny asked him about Jonathan.

"Like I said, Mrs. Hershberger, I'm certain no one else got off the boat. I was down in the galley cleaning up. The last time I saw Mr. Hershberger and his son, they were in the dining room. They had finished their breakfast and were talking. There was a storm coming up and it was getting pretty rough, so I cleaned all the plates off the table and took them below. I had just finished doing the dishes when there was a terrible thump and the boat skewed to the right. I went out on the aft deck to see what was happening, and then there was a big bang and the boat lurched over on its side. I tried to get up to see what was happening but something else blew and there was a big ball of fire that went right up through the dining room and the wheelhouse. The boat just came apart in the middle."

Gerald took a deep breath and passed his hand over his eyes.

"Stuff was flying all over. A piece of the boat hit me on the side of my head, and then something smashed into my arm. I was still on the back half of the boat, and there was an Avon up on the wall, so I pulled it off with my good arm and jerked the inflator. I pushed it over the side and climbed in just as the boat went down. There was stuff all over the place…and then the waves just swept me away. Right after I got into the raft, I passed out. When I woke up, it was dark and I was freezing cold and soaked. I tried to get the Avon cover on, but I couldn't manage it, so I just rolled up in it and waited. They say I was out there four days, but I don't really know."

"And…my husband?"

"The last I knew, he was still in the dining room with his father. That fireball went right up through there. I'm sure they…I don't think they could have made it, ma'am."

Gerald paused and then looked back at Jenny.

"I'm awful sorry about Mr. Jonathan, ma'am. He was a nice young man."

Jenny looked out the window, but she didn't see the plum tree with its pink blossoms. She didn't see the lawn or the street with cars going back and forth. All she saw was a long black tunnel with no light at the end, and she knew she was seeing her future—a future that she would walk without her beloved Jonathan.

Chapter Six

Dark Days

◇◇◇

The months following the disaster passed in a blur. Jenny had much to do to keep the farm going, and the sheer weight of her responsibilities kept her days in order. Lem helped her, as did other members of their community, and with taking care of Rachel, planting, and caring for the livestock, there was enough to do to keep her mind occupied while the sun was up.

It was the night that she feared—that time when the darkness closed in on her spirit as she lay alone in her cold bed. Images of Jonathan and impressions of their life together drifted in and out of the restlessness of her half-sleep—his wonderful smile, the feeling of his strong arms around her, the look of love in his eyes. But then the sweet memories were joined by terrible visions of Jonathan wrapped in flames or thrashing desperately in the water, his eyes locked on hers, his lips forming her name—"Jenny! Jenny!"—as he disappeared into the swirling maelstrom that sucked him down, down…

The awful visions rushed at her out of the darkness like furious demons. Sometimes she lay at the edge of consciousness, knowing she needed to wake up but helpless to move while the apparitions swirled and danced before her. Then with a tremendous effort of her will, she shuddered awake as a scream pushed its way out of her throat. Mornings finally arrived with the sheets damp from night sweats and her mind and body utterly exhausted.

Little Rachel couldn't seem to grasp the fact that her papa was gone. Every morning she would bounce into Jenny's room with a look of anticipation on her face, just as she had done since she learned to walk. She would stop at the foot of the bed and look wistfully at the empty place beside her mama.

"Where's Papa?"

Each time it happened, Jenny's heart broke.

"Papa's in heaven, darling. Don't you remember?"

"But why did Papa go to heaven? Didn't he like it here with us?"

Then Jenny would lift her daughter up on the bed and pull her close.

"I don't think Papa chose to go to heaven right now. I know that he loved us more than anything and that it would be very hard for him to leave us. But when *der Gott, der klug ist* decides it is our time to come be with Him, then we must go."

"But I miss my papa! Why did God tell him to come to heaven?"

Jenny had to search her own heart every time she had this conversation with her little one.

"I don't know, Rachel," she replied truthfully. "I have asked *du lieber Gott* so many times since Papa went away, but I have never received an answer."

Rachel snuffled against Jenny's shoulder. "But I miss Papa. Why would *Gott* want me to be sad?"

Jenny pulled Rachel closer and almost shouted aloud, but she kept it in her heart. *Rachel's right. Warum würden Sie wollen, dass ich jämmerlich war?*

◇◇◇

The days had crept into weeks, and then it was the end of August. Harvest was in full swing, but there was no joy in it for Jenny. Instead she felt that being in the home that once brought joy to her heart was beginning to wear at her like the tiny drops of water that fall silently on a great stone until finally nothing is left but tiny grains of sand. She could no longer sit in the kitchen—where Jonathan's laughter had once rang out—without weeping. The touch of the quilt her mama made for their wedding no longer brought joy, only melancholy.

In September a difficult truth became apparent to Jenny, and at last she reconciled herself to the reality that she must leave Paradise. One morning she sat down and wrote a short letter to her mother.

> Dearest Mama,
>
> Since Jonathan has gone, it has become plain to me that being here in Paradise without him is killing me just as surely as if I had taken poison. I need to be in a place of love and hope. I need to feel Papa's arms around me. I need to lean against your breast and hear the strong beating heart that carried me through the storm so many years ago and that (aside from Jonathan's love) has always been my surest place of refuge.
>
> May I come home?
>
> Jenny

When the letter was written, Jenny quickly folded it and pushed it into an envelope. Then she walked down the lane to the mailbox. She reached for the handle and then paused. Everything came rushing in on her.

In my heart I've held on to hope that Jonathan may still be alive. If I send this letter, I'm admitting he is dead and my life here in Paradise is over. Oh, Jonathan! I want to be true to you, but I can't walk this road alone anymore. I have to go home—home to Apple Creek. Goodbye, my love.

Then the grief that had remained hidden in a deep recess inside her came like a flood, and Jenny leaned against the mailbox and cried. After a while, she opened the box and placed the letter inside. The closing of the wooden door was like a coffin lid slamming shut.

In a week the answer came.

> Dearest Jenny,
>
> You and Rachel have a home with us for as long as you want. Your papa and I want you to come as soon as you can so you will arrive in time for the holidays. I know it may be hard without Jonathan, but you will be with us, and we will love you both through the hard times. We are waiting for you with open arms.
>
> Mama

Later that day, Lem dropped by to tell her how everything was going. They sat together in the kitchen and drank hot cups of coffee while he talked.

"Potatoes are good this year, we have good corn, the beans and tomatoes have done well, and the cows are producing much *milch*."

Jenny listened while Lem shared, and then she spoke quietly to him.

"Lem, I've written my mama, and she has invited us to come live with them for a season. I don't want to leave Paradise and the farm, but my heart is heavy, and I need to go home to Apple Creek. I will stay until the crops are in and we've finished putting up the winter food and sold the rest to the market. Then I will go. I know you count on me to do the books, and I will take care of that this year. But I'm putting the farm in your hands. I haven't decided what to do with it yet, but if I decide to sell, I will only sell to you."

She could see he was crestfallen.

"I would love to have the farm," he replied. "But more than that, I want you to stay. This is your home now, and we love you and Rachel. If you go, this house will be without life."

"Lem, you are my mother's cousin, my closest blood kin. When I came home, you took me into your heart and have been like a brother to me. I love you too, and I will miss you. But without Jonathan, I'm withering away. I can't stay here."

And so it was decided. Jenny and Rachel would stay until the harvest was in, and then they would go. When the decision was made, it seemed like the memories returned in full force. Not only the *wunderbar* years spent here but even the earliest memories of Jonathan came in like a flood.

Jenny remembered the day they had met. She had been standing on the corner across the street from the Wooster library, lost in thoughts about her birth mother. Without looking at the light, Jenny stepped off the curb. She didn't see the vehicle making a right turn onto Walnut Street from Liberty. The driver honked his horn and swerved to avoid her. The van screeched to a halt, rammed one of its tires into the curb she had just been standing on, and lurched partway up onto the sidewalk. The driver leaned out the window and yelled at her. "Hey, watch where you're going! I almost hit you!"

"Well, if I remember correctly, pedestrians have the right of way!" Jenny called back.

"Yeah, they do if the light is in their favor," he said, pointing toward the signal.

The right turn signal was green. Jenny flushed with embarrassment and started to walk away.

"Wait!"

He opened the door and got out. Jenny stopped and looked at the driver. He was tall and trim, and his long hair was pulled back into a ponytail. He wore a leather jacket with fringe hanging down, bell-bottom jeans, and some kind of green boots. He was very good looking, but his most striking feature was his eyes. They were deep sea-blue, just like her papa's, and she could see a hint of a smile behind them. She felt herself drawn into those eyes and had to pull herself back with a start.

His eyes, they were just like Papa's!

The young man had stared at her *kappe*. His eyes traveled down, taking in her face, her plain wool coat with the hooks instead of a zipper, and then the high-top laced shoes. Finally he spoke.

"Excuse me…are you in a play or something?"

"What?" Jenny asked.

"A play. You're dressed like you're in a play."

"Right," Jenny retorted, feeling both a blush and an irritation rising up within her. "I'm one of the starving pilgrims and you must be Squanto, the Indian who saves us. But wait! The Indians didn't wear green boots and clown suits or drive decorated trucks, so you must be one of those beatniks. But I don't remember any beatniks at the first Thanksgiving, so I guess you're not in the play…"

Jenny smiled at the recollection.

I was so mean to him. He was driving that silly van and wearing that…that outfit. He thought I looked funny.

After the smile came the tears.

Now the buggy carried them away to the train station, where they would climb aboard and wave goodbye to Lem. The train would carry them over the hills and mountains to Apple Creek, but the whistle wouldn't be the paean of joy that had summoned Jenny to her new home ten years earlier. Instead it would be the keening of a mourner, following her away, to be lost at last in the chill autumn wind.

As she looked at Paradise for the last time, she turned her thoughts toward home, toward Apple Creek. Jerusha would be waiting at the station with her papa. Reuben would take her in his arms and hold her close while Mama fussed over Rachel. Then she would be in her mama's arms, and if ever comfort was to be found again in Jenny's life, she would find it there in the beating of Jerusha's heart.

Chapter Seven

Safe Haven

◇◇◇

Jerusha Springer stood on the platform at the Depot Street station in Apple Creek, Ohio, glancing down the tracks to the east. Reuben stood beside her with his arm on her shoulder.

"Looking won't make her come any sooner, wife."

"I know, Reuben, but my heart is anxious for our poor girl. I'm so glad she's coming home. Her letter was so sad. She's heartbroken."

"As are we, wife. Our son-in-law is gone, and our girls are left without a husband or a father. It's a dreadful thing. Jonathan was a good man. He was selfless in his concern for Jenny and so respectful of us. *Ja, es ist ein schreckliches, schreckliches Ding,* a terrible thing."

Then the morning stillness was broken by the faint sound of a train whistle. Jerusha leaned forward again and looked down the tracks. In the distance she could see the train coming—yellow against the harvested fields that were slowly browning as deep fall approached.

"She's coming, Reuben. She's almost here!" Jerusha clutched her husband's arm as the train began to slow for its final approach into the village.

Diesel engines hummed, wheels clattered over tracks, and then the train pulled slowly into the station. Two conductors swung down off the platforms between cars and began to assist people off. Jerusha scanned the faces of the people clambering down off the train.

There! There they were—Jenny in her white *kappe*, her face pale and sad against her dark dress. Jerusha waved and then waved again. Jenny looked up, and a wan smile broke the stern set of her face. She turned to the steps and lifted Rachel down.

Jerusha watched as Jenny pointed Rachel toward them. A big smile crossed Rachel's face, and then she ran to them.

Grossmudder! Grossdaadi!

She bounced into Jerusha's arms as her grandmother covered her face with kisses.

Jenny walked up to them. She was tired, and her face was drawn. Reuben took two steps forward and wrapped Jenny in a hug.

And then it was as Jenny had foreseen it. Her mama fussed over Rachel while she surrendered to the safety of her papa's strong arms.

"Oh, Papa," she said, her voice breaking.

"I know, Jenny…I know."

Reuben held his daughter close, his love for her warming Jenny's very soul, as though she had been wandering out in the cold for a long time and now finally found her way to a fire that began to thaw her frozen heart. She stayed there for long moments. Then there was a light touch on her arm. She turned to Jerusha while Reuben reached down and picked up Rachel. The little girl squealed with delight as her grandfather swung her in the air and then pulled her close. Reuben walked away a few steps and talked with Rachel while Jenny stood close to Jerusha and held her hand. Her mama's face worked with emotion as she reached up and softly stroked Jenny's cheek. Something released deep inside her as she felt the gentle touch. She choked back a sob, trying to keep her composure. Then the love in Jerusha's eyes broke through her shell of grief, anger, and fear, and she collapsed into her mother's arms.

"Mama! Mama!"

Convulsive sobs shook her body as Jerusha pulled her close and began to cry with her. Jenny pulled herself as close as she could. And then she was in her place of safety and salvation—the place that had been her refuge since the night Jerusha held Jenny against her in the heart of the storm so many years before. And Jenny felt her mother's heart—the strong, sure beating that spoke to her without words and told her she was home.

The two women stood together for a long time as Jenny's grief ran its course. Then Jenny reached into her pocket and pulled out a handkerchief.

"I've been carrying these with me for times like this."

Jerusha pulled out one of her own and dabbed at her eyes as she smiled through her tears.

"I know."

As they stood together, a police cruiser with the Wayne County Sheriff's emblem pulled into the lot close to the tracks. An officer got out. He was a well-built, stocky man with a thick shock of sandy hair. He walked toward them with the upright bearing of a soldier and waved at Jerusha and Jenny.

"Uncle Bobby…" Jenny said. "I should have known he would come to meet us."

Sheriff Bobby Halverson walked up to Reuben and smiled at the little girl in his friend's arms. Rachel looked at him shyly and hid herself against Reuben's chest. Reuben stuck out his hand and said, "Hello, Bobby. Thanks for coming by."

"Well, I haven't seen Jenny for a long time, and…say, who's this little one?"

"This is Rachel, our *grossdochter*…our granddaughter. Rachel, this is our friend Sheriff Bobby. I've known him for a long time."

The two men exchanged a glance that was born in hard times and deep friendship. Bobby held out a hand to Rachel, but she shyly snuggled closer to Reuben, so Bobby turned to Jenny and pulled her into a hug. As he held her he spoke quietly into her ear.

"How are you?"

Jenny hugged Bobby back. Then she looked up into his caring face.

"I'm doing all right, Uncle Bobby. It's hard, but the Lord is with me, and I'm home now with Mama and Papa…and you."

"I'd like to take you all to lunch if you'd like."

Jenny looked at Jerusha and then turned back to Bobby. "If you don't mind, I think I'd just like to go home. It's been a long ride, and I need to get unpacked."

"Why don't you come join us for supper tomorrow night, Bobby?" Jerusha asked. "That will give us time to get our girls settled in."

Bobby smiled and said, "I was kind of hoping to get an invite to partake in some of your home cooking, Jerusha. An old bachelor like me can only take so many meals at Eileen's on the Square. What time?"

"Make it about seven," Reuben interjected. "I'll be home from the fields and have time to get cleaned up."

"I thought you folks had finished the harvest," Bobby said.

"We have," Reuben replied. "But we have a new *bisschop*, and he needed help adding a feed storage room to his barn, so we've been working on that."

"Well, okay. I'll see you there at seven. Do you need a ride home?"

"No thanks, Bobby. I've got the big buggy, and Jenny doesn't have that many suitcases. We're fine."

Bobby gave Jenny another hug and then chucked Rachel under the chin. She grinned but ducked away.

"I'll see you later, little one. And I guarantee that you won't be shy with me much longer."

Rachel peeked out curiously from her *grossdaadi*'s arms as Bobby turned and walked away.

"Where are your things?" Reuben asked.

There were a few bags still stacked on the platform, and Jenny saw her trunk and her suitcase among them. "Over there, Papa," she said.

Reuben handed Rachel off to Jerusha and picked up Jenny's luggage. He led the way off the platform to the buggy parked at the depot's hitching rack. The black horse looked up and snorted as the family climbed into the buggy. Reuben strapped the bags to the back. Then he untied the horse, got in, and gave the reins a shake. The horse started off slowly down Depot Street, headed for the Springer farm.

"He knows the way home," Reuben said.

"I wish I did," Jenny said.

Jerusha glanced at Reuben and then pulled Jenny close.

The sun was high up in the sky when the buggy turned into the drive leading to the Springer house. Jenny looked around her. Everything was exactly the same as the last time she had visited—the little white house looked clean and neat, the green lawn was edged by her mama's rose gardens and hydrangeas, the front porch held the white swing where she sat with Jonathan many years before, wondering if they would ever be together…nothing had changed, and that felt safe to Jenny.

She got out of the buggy and walked across the lawn to the front porch. Off to the right of the porch was the path that led to the bridge across the small creek that flowed between the Springer farm and the Lowensteins' place. As she looked, she saw a familiar figure crossing the bridge. The tall man waved to her.

"Hello, Jenny! Welcome home!"

The words pierced Jenny's heart like quick pinpricks, but she smiled bravely and waved back as Henry Lowenstein climbed up the steps.

"Hello, Henry. Good to see you. Is your family well?"

"Well, my pop's getting up there, but he still goes to work every morning. He's going to be around for a long time…" Henry paused. "I just came by to see you and to tell you how sorry I am about your loss." He pulled his old baseball cap off and stood awkwardly, holding it in his hands.

Jenny touched Henry on his arm. "Thank you, Henry. That means a lot to me. You've been my friend ever since I was a little girl, and I know how much you care for our family."

Henry shifted from one foot to the other. "If there's anything I can do, Jenny, you can count on me."

Jenny gave Henry a quick hug and a kiss on the cheek. Henry blushed and looked down at his feet.

"Henry, you've been helping my family for as long as I can remember, and I love you for it. Your friendship is what I need the most right now. Just to be home among people I love and who love me…that's what will set everything right with me. Now come and meet Rachel."

Rachel was standing on the porch, looking at something up by the ceiling.

"Look, Mama. A pretty butterfly," she said, pointing up.

And indeed, a large yellow butterfly was struggling in a spider web in the corner of the porch roof.

"Can I help him, Mama, before the spider gets him?"

"I don't know how to get up there, Rachel."

"Oh, yes you do, Jenny," said Henry.

He reached down and picked up Rachel and lifted her high over his head. "Up, Rachel, up we go."

Rachel reached up and gently extricated the butterfly from the web. Henry set her down gently, and she walked to the porch rail and released the beautiful little creature.

"Henry, you used to do that with me when I was a little girl," Jenny said, remembering.

"And with your sister, Jenna, too," he added.

"I remember, Henry," Jerusha said with a smile as she walked up on the porch. "Jenna loved it when you put her up to the ceiling. 'Up, Henny,' she would say."

"That little girl would have kept me out here all day, putting her up and down, if I would have let her."

Rachel was listening and she looked up at her mama. Then she smiled and took hold of Henry's hand. "Up, Henny," she said with a grin as she lifted her arms.

Henry smiled too, and took the little girl in his strong hands and lifted her up. Rachel shrieked with joy as she soared toward the ceiling.

Jenny felt disconnected as she watched Henry with her daughter. Some things never change. But some do.

She sighed and walked into the house. *Through the front door, past the fireplace, down the hall, and into my room...I've walked this way a thousand times before in happier days.*

Jenny stood in the doorway and looked in. This room had been her refuge all her life, the only place on earth where she felt totally safe. Every night when she was growing up she knew that her big, strong papa was right in the next room, and her mama was only a call away. That knowledge had kept her secure through all her years. But she didn't feel secure now. She felt as if she were standing on a slippery slope with nothing to hang onto as she slid toward an abyss.

Jenny put down her luggage and knelt by the oiled oak chest that her papa had made. He had rubbed it with mineral oil, and the smell was woven into the fabric of her childhood.

Like the linseed oil smell that permeated our bedroom...

She put her head down on the wood and closed her eyes. If only the familiar smell of the chest could somehow take her back in time to the small world of childhood—those wonderful days of innocence when life was Apple Creek and the barn and the land and this house, when her mama and papa and Jesus were the center of all things and life passed not in days and hours but in smells and discoveries and colors and seasons, and all her life was surrounded by joy and peace and love.

She got up, went to the window, pulled the roller shade down, and then rolled it back up again. She flung herself down on the bed, buried her face in the pillow, and groaned. She needed Jonathan. But there was no Jonathan, no way to retreat to her childhood, and all she had was the awful, piercing pain in her heart.

O Gott, make this cup pass from me!

Chapter Eight

Grief

IT WAS A COLD, BITING day in late October. The weather had been stormy off and on since Jenny's arrival in Apple Creek, and everyone at the Springer house had been forced to stay inside. Jerusha cared for Rachel with a grandmother's joy and helped to lift that responsibility off Jenny's shoulders.

For the first two weeks after her arrival, Jenny just stayed in bed most of the day. She slept fitfully at night, and when she was awake she was irritable and had no appetite. She spent hours crying quietly under her covers. She felt as though every ounce of energy had been drained from her body, and it was all she could do to get dressed in the morning. On many days, she just didn't. In the mornings, Jerusha brought tea and some of her wonderful biscuits, but Jenny ignored them.

This morning, when Jerusha came into the room, Jenny was sitting in her rocking chair, staring out the window. The wind pushed the branches of the hydrangeas fitfully against the panes. Large drops of rain were running down the glass. The gray clouds obscured the morning light. Jenny sat with a shawl wrapped around her shoulders.

"Good morning, *dochter*," Jerusha said as she set a tray down on the dresser. "I brought you some tea and biscuits…if you want them."

"Mama, I'm sorry."

"Sorry for what, Jenny? Sorry that your heart is broken? Sorry that you're grieving?"

Jenny thought for a moment. She wanted to apologize for being so useless, but she hadn't even connected what was happening to her with the reality of her grief. She looked up at Jerusha.

"Is that what's happening? I thought I was reconciled to Jonathan's death months ago and moving forward, but now it's like I'm having a relapse. How can that be?"

And then, as if to answer her own question, she continued. "When he…when he left us, it was planting time, and the farm demanded so much from me that I had to work. My nights were terrible, but I could turn the sadness off during the day and plunge into the tasks that had to be done. Since I've come to Apple Creek, I feel like my body won't do anything I ask of it, even if I order it to."

Jerusha sat down on the bed across from Jenny. "This is why we wanted you to come home. So we could help you bear the burden of your sorrow. Your papa and I want to help you through this, but it will not be an easy time for you, and it may go on for longer than you think. Jonathan was a special man, and you two had a special kind of love. I know because it was the same kind of love that your papa and I share. It's not possible to forget a man like Jonathan."

"What can I do then, Mama? I feel so helpless and useless…and even faithless. I don't know where *Gott* is in all of this. I reach out to Him, but I can't hear Him speaking to me or feel His presence. Rachel asks me why *Gott* would want us to be so sad. I don't know…"

"These are the hard questions of life, Jenny. Is it any wonder we call this the vale of tears? All we can do is rejoice in knowing that Jonathan is beyond this wicked world and that he is with Jesus. We can never understand why *Gott* would allow such a thing, but sometimes understanding Him and trusting Him can be two different things."

Jenny was silent again. Jerusha reached across and put her hand on her daughter's shoulder as Jenny stared out the window. The two women sat like that for awhile. Only the rustling of the branches against the pane and the wind whispering against the eaves disturbed the stillness of the room.

As they sat, the wind died down and the rain ceased to beat against the window. The clouds started breaking up, and a ray of sun broke through. A hush fell on the day, and peace crept over the land. Outside the window, one of the last songbirds of the receding fall season picked up a cheery melody. The gray clouds began to disperse, to be slowly replaced by cotton balls drifting through an azure sky. Bright sunlight poured into the room as they sat, and Jenny felt a stirring in her heart.

"I don't want to go on, but I will," she said softly.

Jerusha knelt by Jenny's chair and lifted her hand to Jenny's face. Gently she stroked her daughter's cheek and pushed the errant curls back out of her eyes.

As their eyes met, Jenny knew that God hadn't abandoned her. As she saw the love in Jerusha's eyes and felt it in her touch, Jenny grasped the totality of His presence in her life. When she was a little girl, lost and dying in a snowstorm, God sent Jerusha. Jenny's birth mother had died, and *du lieber Gott* had given her another mother—a mother who took Jenny into her heart completely and without reservation. God gave her a home and a new life and then unveiled the secrets of her past. And then He brought her Jonathan—a precious gift indeed. And from Jonathan, Jenny received her beautiful daughter and ten wonderful years.

"I will be thankful for what I have been given," she said quietly, taking her mother's hand to her face. Jenny could feel the beat of Jerusha's heart in the tips of those fingers. And in that moment Jenny heard a voice within her that she had not heard for a long time.

I will never leave you or forsake you.

◇◇◇

In the days following, Jenny found she was able to begin moving again. It wasn't easy but somehow she found the strength. In those moments when the shock of Jonathan's accident and the numbness of being without him assailed her senses, she would lift up a small prayer of thanksgiving for all of God's blessings in her life. If she found herself despairing or starting to spin out of control, she recited the words of her mother's favorite hymn out loud:

"*Loben wir ihn von ganzem Herzen! Denn er allein ist würdig.* Let us praise Him with all our hearts! For He alone is worthy."

Step-by-step Jenny experienced the healing she needed. The progression could be brutal at times, but Jenny's will was strong. At other times in her life, that had been to her detriment, but now at last it began to serve her. And as she made choices to go on with her life, she felt her faith rising slowly but surely. It was as though she had fallen from a high precipice into cold, deep water where all was dark and she could not breathe. But as she began to move toward the dim light above her, she knew that she would eventually come back to the surface and live again.

Often she would wrestle with many emotions at once: shock, denial, bargaining, anger…and at those times she would feel as though she would never escape the traps they set for her. But Reuben and Jerusha would be there for her, lifting her arms in the battle just as Aaron and Hur lifted Moses' arms, and the enemy of her soul would be pushed back.

Jenny's greatest joy in those days came from Rachel. Rachel was a resilient soul, and she had accepted things being the way they were long before Jenny could. In her *grossdaadi's* arms Rachel had found the male presence she needed, and so she became reconciled to the idea that Jonathan had gone ahead to be with Jesus. For Jenny, Rachel became like a light before her feet on a dark and toilsome journey. When she wanted to stop, Rachel was there with a smile or a hug. When she needed a touch from the Lord, it came through a snuggle or a kind word from her little girl. And as the darkness was pushed back, Jenny began to find herself.

Jerusha and Reuben encouraged her to begin taking part in the daily life of the farm, and the old ways of her childhood helped her to build a structured schedule into her days. As she did, she could see herself developing an identity that no longer included Jonathan. At times this was the hardest part of the process, but eventually she recognized that this was the only way she could recover.

Ever vigilant, Reuben stepped in during the hard times and encouraged Jenny to take part in the church or the Amish school, where she soon served as a helper and eventually as a teacher. And so the days passed, and as the deep winter gave up its icy grip on Apple Creek and the first touch of spring began to melt the morning frost from the etched glass of the window in her room, Jenny slowly began to come back to life.

Then came a day when Jenny awoke to a soft dawn that crept into her room like a mischievous child, softly kissing her awake with the delicate touch of a rose-colored morning. Jenny opened her eyes and saw the pale colors blushing in the fresh sky. She rose, wrapped a shawl around her shoulders, and slipped outside. The day was fresh and clean and warm, and the grass felt cool and damp against her bare feet. Above her head the plum trees were just sprouting the tiny pink buds that would soon burst into brilliant color and paint the world with God's palette. A single wren twittered its call, and stillness lay on the land.

Jenny's heart stirred within her at the unexpected beauty of the morning. An old barn cat came around the side of the house, meowed loudly, and bunted her head against Jenny's leg. Jenny smiled and reached down to scratch the cat behind the ears.

"Hello, Perticket."

The old cat stayed for a moment, enjoying the attention, and then wandered off. Jenny took a deep breath, and the fresh air tasted sweet. The sun began to peek up over the hills to the east, and bright rays of sun shining through the trees cast easy shadows across the fields. A little breeze sprang up, and the air stirred around her, gently lifting the curls from her face. Above her a formation of Canadian geese flew north, honking as they went. Jenny was touched by the wonder of the day, and a thought rose in her heart like a small trout rising for a fly in a still mountain lake.

I'm still alive. This didn't kill me, and I can still find joy and wonder in a day.

The screen door creaked behind her, and she looked around to see her papa coming out on the porch. He was dressed for work, and his handsome face broke into a smile. Reuben stepped down from the porch and came over to Jenny.

"You have a glow about you this morning, *dochter*. It's good for my heart to see life creeping back into you."

Jenny stepped into the circle of Reuben's arms.

Yes, I do feel life coming back into me. It's as though I have been raised from the dead!

"Papa, thank you!"

"For what, Jenny?"

"For not giving up on me, for walking beside me, and for being my rock when the storm raged most fiercely about me."

Reuben's arms tightened around her. Then he spoke, and she could tell the words were difficult by the way they seemed to be pulled from him, syllable by syllable.

"When our Jenna died, I wanted to die too. I felt so helpless, and I believed that but for my wrongheadedness, Jenna would have lived. If *das Vollkennen des Gottes* hadn't sent someone to help me, I would have died by my own hand. And then *Gott*, in His infinite mercy and grace, sent you to us. I can't explain how it happened, but when I saw you for the first time, I knew you belonged to me and to your mama forever. I knew I had been given a second chance, and I loved you with every bit of the love I had for Jenna. And so when I see you suffer, I suffer too."

Jenny looked into her papa's eyes, the deep sea-blue eyes with the smile behind them, and saw home and safety in them.

"And so I would do anything to see you happy again. You make *sonnenschein in meinem Herzen*. And now you have given us Rachel, and the joy she brings with her is beyond our understanding. I can't give Jonathan back to you. If I could, I would give my own life to do so. But that's beyond me, so I give you my love and this place and whatever you need to be happy again. That's my prayer."

And as the bright spring sun warmed the earth, the winter of Jenny's great sorrow began to melt away. The icy stronghold that had imprisoned her dreams and hopes crumbled under the warmth of her father's love, and the river of life began to flow once more in her heart.

Chapter Nine

Healing Words

◇◇◇

What words can I find that describe Jonathan or serve his memory as they should? Kindness? Compassion? Wisdom? Self-sacrifice? Joy, gift, safety…love? Somehow I can't seem to capture the essence of Jonathan with mere words. He was my true love, my best friend, my companion, my coworker, my true yoke-fellow…all of these things. And yet, I still haven't arrived at the heart of the matter. Maybe I'll never be able to describe him or what he meant to me until I, too, have crossed over and my Lord explains it to me.

Jenny put down her pen and looked at the words in the journal. She gripped the edge of the page, ready to tear it out, but something held her back. Then she carefully closed her journal and stood it up in an alcove of the small desk that Reuben had built for her. Her journal—Jenny smiled at the notion and the amazing thing that had happened to her in the past few months. In the depths of her sorrow, Jenny had discovered a desire and possibly a gift for writing.

It had begun not long after the early spring morning her papa helped her find joy again. As she walked in the fields on a clear May morning, taking lunch to her *daed*, time seemed to shift. For a moment it seemed she was back in Paradise, taking Jonathan his lunch and hearing his clear, beautiful voice drifting across the farm to her on the wings of a song. He sang as he walked the rows, top-seeding last fall's oat field with legume seeds. The seeds flew out of the hand-cranked seeder as his strong hands turned the handle, keeping time with the words that floated out of his mouth.

> *"Lassen Sie ihn, der gelegen hat, seine Hand auf dem Pflug nicht sehen sich um! Presse zur Absicht! Presse Jesus Christus! Derjenige, der Christus gewinnt, wird sich mit ihm von den Toten am jüngsten Tag erheben."*

Jenny remembered the words and sang along in English.

> "Let him who has laid his hand on the plow not look back! Press on to the goal! Press on to Jesus Christ! The one who gains Christ will rise with Him from the dead on the youngest day."

Jenny was lost in her memory. Jonathan had been a wonderful singer, and she loved his voice…

Then the moment passed, and she paused and looked around. She wasn't in Paradise; she was back in Apple Creek, taking lunch to her papa instead of her husband. For a moment the familiar sadness engulfed her, and then she had an inspiration. After she gave Reuben his lunch, she ran back to the house and found a scrap of paper and a pen. She sat down at the kitchen table and wrote a note to Jonathan.

> Dearest Jonathan,
> Today I heard you singing as I walked alone in the fields. I love your voice. I am glad you never became a successful musician when you lived in San Francisco, for if you had we

never would have met. Instead you sang your songs to the Lord, and I was blessed to hear your gift. By the way, I kept your guitar. I don't know why, since you put it away when you joined the church, but for me it is part of who you are. I remember when you sang a song for me long ago, and the beautiful sound of the music and the words enthralled me. You said you wrote the song for me. I remember it so clearly.

> Tonight, I whisper in your ear,
> I always want you near.
> Tonight, kiss me tenderly,
> Come so easily,
> Into my heart tonight.

Your songs—how I miss them.

Jenny

Jenny stared down at the note and realized that for just a moment, as she wrote, the weight had lifted from her heart.

Maybe if I write down my memories of Jonathan, it will help me to fend off this loneliness. If I can't have him to hold, I can have him to remember.

The next time Jenny was at the General Store, she looked for something she could use to write in. She found a plain, lined notebook with a black-and-white speckled cover and a place to write on the front cover. She bought it and took it home. She sat at the kitchen table and wrote simply "Jenny Hershberger, Journal 1—1979" on the cover. And that is how she began. At first she wrote only about Jonathan, but as she emptied out the hurt and the pain on the pages, she found there was room in her heart to write about other things too. She wrote about Rachel and the funny or wonderful things she did and said.

> Tonight we asked Rachel to say grace at dinner. She prayed, "Dear *Gott*, thank You for these pancakes." When she

finished, Mama asked her why she thanked *Gott* for pancakes when we were having chicken. Rachel smiled and said, "I thought I'd see if He was paying attention."

One day Jenny wrote a short poem about Reuben.

> Safe in loving arms I rest
> My cares away on spirit wings
> And here my aching soul caressed
> By loving words the angel brings
> To whisper in my papa's ear
> His strength for me breaks all my fear
> And love with gentle voice can sing
> And tell me how my life is blessed
> My papa's arms shall hold me fast
> And bring me safely home at last

Her interest in the history of her people reawakened, and she started visiting the Wooster library once a week. Her old friend Mrs. Blake was still the librarian and welcomed Jenny back with open arms.

From then on there were many nights when Reuben came home to find Jenny lost in thought at the kitchen table, sucking on the end of her pen as she stared down at the words she had written. Jerusha cooked dinner around her and Rachel asked for her mama's attention, but Jenny would be lost in thought. It was on one of these evenings that Reuben realized that Jenny was finding healing in the words she wrote. The next morning Jerusha found him in the woodshop, laying out some of the choice pieces of wood that he kept for his projects.

"What are you making, husband?"

"I'm going to make a desk for Jenny that she can put in her room. Her writing takes her mind off her sorrow, and after she writes she's so much more with us. But she needs a quiet place away from all the hubbub."

Jerusha smiled and laid her hand on Reuben's arm. "You are a good papa."

Reuben spent a month making the desk. It was crafted from birch and lightly sealed with a clear stain—a simple design but beautifully made, with two drawers in the front and a small set of shelves on the back edge to hold her journals. One day when Jenny was out, he moved it into her room. He stood it by the wall close to the window so she could look out on the world as she wrote. When she came home and went into her room, she came straight back out and gave her *daed* a long hug. No words were necessary.

After that, Jenny made a short time for herself each day to sit alone in her room and write. Soon she had filled five notebooks. As she wrote she sensed that perhaps God had a blessing for her in the writing, but it was not something that came to her easily. When she read her words back, she could see that she was still an awkward writer, and it bothered her, so one day when she was at the library, she shared her frustration with Mrs. Blake. Her friend smiled at her.

"Writing is like any creative craft," the librarian said. "It takes time to develop your skills. You have a gift, Jenny. I remember the work you did for me when you were an intern and an assistant here. The research was always so complete, and your writing was clear and concise. The best way to improve on that is to just keep writing. There are also some excellent books I can recommend that will point you in the right direction."

Mrs. Blake selected a few titles for her, and Jenny checked them out and took them home. As she read through them, she could see some of the common traps she had fallen into. Use the active voice. Get rid of the "hads" and write in the present. Show, don't tell.

Then she went back to her entries and began reworking them. She labored over them and sometimes made corrections late into the night. After a while, she could smile as she read her first awkward attempts.

As her skill developed, she realized there was still much to learn. One day when she was at the library, Mrs. Blake directed her attention to a flyer posted on the bulletin board. It was for an adult-education creative writing class to be held at the library on Tuesday evenings, starting in two weeks. She thought about it, and when she got home she went to her *daed*.

"Papa, there's an adult-education class at the library I'd like to take. It's a creative writing class, and I think it could help me with my writing. I want to ask your permission since I am living under your roof and you're caring for me."

Reuben looked at his daughter. "You are old enough to make your own decisions, *dochter*. I've been watching you find joy in your writing, and I want to encourage you. I would only ask one question. Do you know where this is leading you?"

"I'm not sure, Papa. Mostly I write about Jonathan. But at some point I think I would also like to try my hand at chronicling the history of our family. I've been going through the old books at the library, and my interest in history seems to have been rekindled…but not for the same reasons."

Jenny smiled at the memory of her obsessive search for her birth mother and the part her papa had played in it, although reluctantly at first.

"I want to be sure you can stay within the *Ordnung*, Jenny, and yet I know that times are changing. I don't want to limit something that *Gott* may be doing in you."

Jenny looked at her papa in surprise. "Why, Papa, I believe, as Jonathan might have said, you're 'loosening up' a little."

"Youth has a way of making a fool of a man. And old age can sometimes bring wisdom."

"Is that from Proverbs, Papa?"

"No, that's from a little book called *Reuben Figures It Out*."

They both laughed. Their merriment brought Jerusha and Rachel into the room.

"What's funny, Mama?" Rachel asked.

"Papa and I were just laughing about the things we learn as we grow older, Rachel."

Reuben picked up Rachel. "We're finding out somehow we don't get smarter as we go along, little one. We just discover how foolish we always have been."

"I don't understand, *Grossdaadi*."

"You will, Rachel. You will. Just give it time."

With Reuben's blessing, Jenny continued to write. She signed up for the class in Wooster and arranged a ride for herself every Tuesday evening. And that is how the Lord led her to the day that would forever change her life.

CHAPTER TEN

A Helping Hand

◇◇◇

JENNY WALKED DOWN THE HALL to the room where the writing class was being held. She stopped at the door and peeked cautiously around the doorjamb. Just as she feared, the room was filled with *Englischers*. Not a single Amish person in the room.

She took a deep breath and started to walk into the classroom. Just as she did, someone collided with her from behind, knocking her bag and her notebook from her hand.

"Oh, excuse me," said a deep voice behind her.

Jenny turned. The perpetrator of the collision bent down to pick up her things. When he stood back up to hand them to her, Jenny saw that he was a tall, very handsome man with deep blue eyes.

"I'm so sorry," he said. "I saw you stop and I was going to step past you when you went again. I was in kind of a rush. Please forgive me."

"No harm done," Jenny said.

"Are you here for the class?"

"Yes, I am."

"It's interesting that you should come tonight."

An old irritation rose up in her. "And why is that?"

"I'm speaking for a few minutes tonight about the number of books that are being published about the Amish."

"Cookbooks, mostly, I assume?" Jenny said as she eyed the large satchel the man was carrying. *Why does he have to have blue eyes?*

"The Amish aren't just publishing cookbooks. I'm talking about novels and historical studies, devotionals and Bible studies. And several *Englischers* are writing about the Amish and getting their work published. It's becoming a huge market."

"So why are you speaking at our creative writing class?"

"Mrs. Blake thought I might encourage some fledgling writers to consider writing about the Amish community since it's such a large part of our local culture. Is that why you're here?"

"Well, it's not to learn how to make a grocery list." *Why is he getting me so agitated? And I'm not a fledgling.*

The man looked at her in surprise and then laughed out loud. "Here I thought the Amish were all gentle, kind people. You're the first one I've run into with a snappy comeback."

Jenny felt herself blush from head to toe. Her body went hot and then cold. "I'm sorry. Please forgive me," she said contritely. "I thought I had mastered the snippy side of my disposition. I guess I haven't."

"Okay, we didn't get started very well. How about if we try again? I'm Jeremy King, and I'm the owner of Kerusso Publishing." Jeremy extended his hand.

That's what Jonathan did. He started over after I bit his head off. Then he wanted to shake hands. And why does this man's name start with a "J"?

Jenny remembered the odd sensation she felt when Jonathan touched her, so she kept her hand at her side, and she didn't tell him her name.

"I'm not sure why I want to write, but I enjoy it, so I thought I would come and see if I could learn a few things to help me improve."

Jeremy put his hand back to his side and smiled. "Well, I hope this class will be of benefit to you." He turned abruptly and walked into the class. Jenny watched him and frowned.

That didn't go well. He seemed like a nice man, and I acted like a fool.

Jenny entered the classroom and found a seat in the back. She kept her head down and didn't look up until Mrs. Blake came into the room with another lady. They walked to the front of the room, and Mrs. Blake began to speak.

"Good evening, everyone. Welcome to our creative writing class. Our friend Evelyn Bergman will teach the first five sessions. Evelyn has taught for us before, and I know many of you have been blessed by her wonderful advice and instruction. I also see that we have several newcomers. And I see my longtime assistant, Jenny Hershberger, has joined us."

Jenny scrunched down in her seat. *Great! Thanks a lot, Mrs. Blake. Now he knows my name. Why don't you just give him my address too?*

"Jenny is a wonderful researcher and has helped me with many historical projects relating to the Amish in Wayne County. Some of her articles were published by Bob Schumann when he was still the editor at the *Daily Record*."

Jenny almost put her head down on the desk. Instead she smiled wanly and tried to ignore the pink glow that suffused her face. Mrs. Blake moved on to another subject.

"And speaking of the Amish, I'd like to start by introducing Jeremy King, owner of Kerusso Publishing. Kerusso publishes many books about the Amish and also many titles written by Amish authors. Since we have such a large Amish community in Wayne County, I thought it might be interesting to have Jeremy come and speak to us. There might even be a little inspiration here for some of you who are casting about for subjects to write about. Could you tell us a little about your company, Jeremy?"

The tall man stood and walked to the front of the room. In his hands he held several books.

"Good evening, everyone. Thank you, Mrs. Blake. Yes, I am the owner of Kerusso Publishing. I'm also the publisher, chief editor, main cook, and bottle washer."

The class tittered politely.

"I've been publishing Amish literature for about four years. At first we started with Amish cookbooks…" He held up a notebook-style publication titled *The Art of Amish Cooking* and smiled directly at Jenny.

"But we've expanded our titles, and now we have Bible studies, devotionals, historical nonfiction works, and even some novels. For some reason, the publishing industry has found a market for Amish fiction. Mildred Jordan has been writing novels since the 1950s, and there was an Amish novel published in 1908 called *The Masquerading of Margaret*. I think Amish fiction is a genre that will become very popular in the future. So if any of you are interested in writing novels and might have an idea for a story, send me a one-sheet."

A hand raised tentatively in the middle row. "What's a one-sheet?"

"Good question. A one-sheet is a simple one-page description of your idea for a story with your contact information at the bottom. If you send it to me and I like the idea, I'll ask you for some sample chapters. If I like what I see, I'll request a proposal for the whole book, which would include a description of the main characters, a synopsis of the story, and a chapter outline. Does that help?"

The questioner nodded. Several people made notes in their notebooks.

"How can we get your mailing address?" another class member asked.

Jeremy turned and wrote his name and address on a blackboard behind him. Several people wrote it down in their books. Jenny watched them and thought, *Most of these people don't even know how to write about our people, and they're taking down his address. Pretty silly!*

And then a familiar voice spoke into her spirit. *Don't you have a dream, Jenny?*

Jenny looked around as though someone had spoken to her out loud. She realized what it was.

"A novel? Is that what I'm supposed to write?"

"Why not?" asked the person next to her, who was writing down Jeremy's information. Jenny realized with a shock that she had spoken out loud. Without really knowing why, she took her pencil and scribbled down the information on the back of her notebook.

I won't use this. Why am I writing it down?

Jeremy was finishing his presentation, but Jenny's thoughts were whirling. And then Jeremy said something that grabbed her attention.

"And for those of you who might send me a story idea, I'm looking for Amish stories, and given that we live in the heart of quilting country, I'm also interested in quilting stories."

An idea came to Jenny. *My mama is the best quilter in Wayne County! I'll ask her to help me. Wait—what am I thinking? We Amish don't write novels.*

Jenny was so lost in her thoughts, she didn't even notice when Jeremy King said goodnight to the class, wished them luck, and walked out of the room. She only came back to herself when Mrs. Bergman came to the front of the class and began to speak.

"Mark Twain once said that writers should strike out every third word on principle. You have no idea what vigor that can add to your style. If we are to be writers who connect with our readers, simplicity is the key. One of the masters of simplicity was Ernest Hemingway, and you all know how well his books have done."

There was another chuckle from the class, and Jenny realized she didn't even have her notebook open to take notes. She had been staring at Jeremy's name.

Why does he have to have blue eyes?

An hour later Jenny walked out of the class. She had learned a lot, even in that short time, and Mrs. Bergman had proved to be an excellent teacher. Jenny was lost in thought as she stepped out into the hall. The deep voice startled her.

"Hello…Jenny."

Jenny looked up to see Jeremy King standing there. "Oh…hello, Mr. King. What are you doing here?"

"I felt like I offended you, and I wanted to apologize. We didn't exactly get off to a good start. And please, call me Jeremy."

Jenny dared to take a good look at the man in front of her. The fact that he was tall and handsome troubled her for some reason. But she made the best of it and held out her hand to him.

"I'm sorry too, Mr. King…Jeremy. I was rude. I'll accept your apology if you'll accept mine."

Jeremy took her hand, and Jenny noticed in a detached way that there was no tingle, just a pleasant warmth. Jeremy held her hand for a moment and then released it.

"There's a little coffee shop around the corner. Would you like to join me for a cup?"

Jenny looked at him again. She hadn't talked to a man other than her *daed* or Henry Lowenstein for many months. She realized with a start that she was actually longing for some male companionship, but she brought herself up short.

"I'm sorry, but I have to go home. My little girl is waiting for me."

"Oh," Jeremy said. "Are you married?" Now it was Jeremy's turn to be flustered.

"Yes, I am…"

Wait! You're not married. Jonathan is gone!

"Oh, I see," Jeremy said, a note of disappointment in his voice.

Jenny cleared her throat and managed to say the words she had so long avoided. "That is to say, I….was married. I'm a…widow."

Chapter Eleven

A Mother's Love

◇◇◇

Jenny stared at Jeremy King. The words she had just spoken reverberated in her mind like hailstones crashing on a tin barn roof.

I'm a widow. I'm a widow…

Jeremy looked at her with concern in his eyes. "I'm so sorry. Of course, I couldn't have known, but I am sorry."

"No, you couldn't have known," Jenny said. "My husband was killed when the boat he was on exploded off the New Jersey coast. He's been gone almost a year and…"

Suddenly the room began to spin, and Jenny felt faint. Strong hands took hold of her, and then she was sitting in a chair against the hallway wall with her face in her hands. Jeremy knelt beside her and put his hand on her arm. After a few minutes the paroxysm of grief passed, and Jenny lifted her head. She looked up at Jeremy as she sorted through her emotions.

"I'm sorry—I don't talk about it much. I must look silly to be so… sensitive."

"Not at all, Jenny. I'm sorry I upset you. Please forgive me."

Jenny reached down and pulled a handkerchief from her bag. She dabbed her eyes and then tried to smile.

"It seems like all we're doing tonight is forgiving each other. You didn't upset me, Jeremy. Jonathan's death has been extremely hard for me to come to grips with. We were the perfect couple—in all ways, blessed by *Gott*—so I wasn't prepared for my life to change so radically. After Jonathan's death, I moved back home with my parents, and I've been pretty much in seclusion for the past several months. Now I'm trying to get my life back together, but as I've demonstrated tonight, it's not so easy."

Jeremy took her arm and helped her to her feet.

"Look, I'm a great listener, and it seems like maybe you need that," he offered. "Are you sure you wouldn't like to have a cup of coffee and just talk?"

"What about my bus?"

"I'll give you a ride home. I'd be happy to. And you'll be home about the same time as if you took that clunky old bus that stops at every newsstand and apartment house on the way to…"

"Apple Creek. I live in Apple Creek. And yes, a cup of coffee actually sounds very good right now."

And that is how Jenny Hershberger, an Amish widow with a small child, found herself sharing a cup of coffee with Jeremy King, the handsome young owner of Kerusso Publishing, and telling him about Jonathan. As they talked, Jenny began to sense that somehow the Lord was at work in her life again. She hadn't felt that way for a long time.

The next day Jenny sat at the kitchen table with Jerusha. Brilliant rays of light streamed through the window with a shout, proclaiming the arrival of summer in Apple Creek. The kitchen door stood open, and the two women enjoyed a cup of coffee as the sun slowly warmed the coolness out of the morning air. A fresh breeze wafting through the back screen door probed the lace kitchen curtains with gentle fingers, and they responded with a slow, silken dance against the glass. Outside, the farm was bursting with life. The apple blossoms had dropped, and now Jenny could see the little green sets on the McIntosh tree outside the kitchen window starting their long journey toward harvest. Songbirds called gaily to each other in a symphony of chirps and trills, and for Jenny, it seemed that things were finally beginning to feel right in her life again.

Several of her notebooks were spread on the table, and Jerusha was reading through one of them. Jenny sat silently, hoping her mother would like what she had written. Jerusha was silent for a long time. Then she closed the book she was reading and set it down. Jenny looked at her. She was surprised to see tears in Jerusha's eyes.

"What, Mama?"

"I just read the poem about your papa's arms. It's…"

"What, Mama? It's what?"

"It's so beautiful. When I was reading it, I knew exactly what you meant. I have felt that same strength and tenderness in Reuben all the years we've been married."

Jenny's heart filled, and she smiled at her mama. "Thank you, Mama. That's so encouraging."

"Jenny, you have a wonderful gift. I remember many years ago I told you that no one in our community has such a grasp of the history of our people as you do. But along with that you have a wonderful way with prose and poetry. I see in your writing the beginnings of brilliant stories—stories that can tell the world how the Amish stay separated and put the Lord first before everything."

"Mama, do you really believe that?"

"I do. As surely as *du lieber Gott* has blessed me with a gift to quilt, He has gifted you with an ability to write."

"Mama, that's what I wanted to talk to you about. Last night a man spoke to our class. He owns a publishing company in Akron, and he came to tell us about how his company is interested in publishing books and articles—not only about the Amish, but written by Amish people. He gave the class an invitation."

"What kind of invitation, *dochter*?"

Jenny hesitated for a moment and then went on. "He said if we have an idea for a story, we should send him a…he called it a one-sheet. That's a one-page description of a story. And, Mama, this is what made me think that *der Gott, der unsere Schritte führt* was speaking to me. Jeremy—I mean, Mr. King—said he liked Amish stories and quilting stories."

Jenny looked at Jerusha and watched as a slow smile began to spread across her mama's face. Then Jenny began to spill out her idea in a rush.

"Mama, I was thinking I could tell the story of the quilt, Jenna's quilt, and about how you were lost in the storm and you found me and saved me, and how Papa and Uncle Bobby rescued us and how you kept me and made me your daughter."

Jenny paused and took a deep breath. "What do you think, Mama?"

"I think it is a wonderful idea, but I'm not sure what Papa would say. There are so many things in the world that try to tempt us away from our faith. Your papa is very protective of you, but he also knows that you are a grown-up woman and have a strong faith in the Lord and have been observant of the *Ordnung* all your life."

Jenny blushed. "Well, except when I cut off my hair and ran away."

"You were nineteen, Jenny. You had just fallen in love with Jonathan, and the most important thing in your life was to find out who your birth mother and father were. We—your papa and I—weren't listening to the Lord. Finally He had to show me how important it was for you to rebuild the foundation of your life. And when we helped you instead of standing in your way, He blessed you with a revelation of your Amish heritage, a wonderful husband, and a beautiful daughter. The Lord often works in strange ways, but He is always working all things together for good."

Jenny moved her chair closer to her mama and leaned against her. Jerusha put her arm around her daughter's shoulder.

"Do you think Papa will think it is all right for me to write a book?" Jenny asked.

"Your papa sees that your gift for writing is healing your heart. I see it also. The things you've written about Jonathan and your love for one another have released you to be present with us instead of lost in your grief. Your papa understands it, and I believe he will support you in this endeavor."

"Will you help me, Mama? I need you to tell me the story so I can get everything right."

"Yes, Jenny, I will help you."

Jenny put her arms around Jerusha and held her tight. "Mama, do you know how I know that *Gott* is real and He loves me?"

"How, Jenny?"

"He gave me you to be my *mudder*. I have felt His love for me through you all of my life."

Jerusha lifted her hand and stroked her daughter's brow with gentle fingers. Jenny pulled herself under Jerusha's arm and against her breast, where once again she felt the strong, steady beat of her mother's heart.

So Jenny and Jerusha began their journey. When they had a moment in their busy day, they sat together and Jerusha told Jenny the story. Often Jerusha took Rachel up on her lap, and the little girl sat quietly while Jerusha spoke. Jenny took notes, and then later, when everyone was asleep, she worked and reworked what she had written.

After a few weeks she could see that the story was good, so she went to Reuben and told him what she was doing.

Reuben looked at her for a long time. Jenny waited, not sure what he would say. Finally he spoke.

"Jenny, I think you have a wonderful gift for writing, and I believe it is *ein Geschenk vom Gott.* My only concern is this. You are a baptized member of the Amish church and have certain responsibilities to the church and to this community. I believe that you're strong enough in the faith to write this book to the glory of *Gott* and to keep yourself safe from worldly pursuits. However, I'm not the only one who has a say in this. We have a visiting *bisschop* over our section right now. He's here to help in the establishment of a new church in Dalton. He comes from Pennsylvania, and the Amish of Lancaster tend to be stricter in their interpretation of the *Ordnung.* As a *völliger diener* of our church, I am obligated to speak to the *bisschop* about your writing. We must trust the Lord in this. If the *bisschop* says you must not write the book, will you obey his ruling?"

Jenny sat silent for a few moments. Then she said, "Papa, I feel the Lord is leading me in this, but I asked you about this because I'm in your care and under your roof. If their answer is no, I will do as the elders of the church decide."

"Even if it's contrary to what you believe the Lord is showing you to do?"

Jenny stared in amazement at her *daed.* "I want to do what glorifies *Gott* and honors you. Would you have me do otherwise?"

Reuben took Jenny's hands in his. She felt the strength of his grip and the hard calluses that came from working all his life to care for his family.

"What brings *Gott* glory is to do as He asks. What brings me honor is to see my daughter using the gift that *Gott* has given her to bless others. If the elders are not in agreement, they will have to go a long way to show me why. Jenny, I will stand with you in this because I believe you're right. I believe *Gott* is healing you as you use this gift, and I believe that your writing could bring healing to others. It's a blessing not often given and much to be desired."

CHAPTER TWELVE

The Meeting

◇◇◇

Jerusha reached behind the quilting frame with her left hand and pushed the needle back to the surface of the quilt to complete her stitch. Wearily she pulled the needle through, quickly knotted the quilting thread, and broke it off. She had been working on this quilt for months, and as she leaned back in her chair, she knew it was the best she had ever made. Thousands of stitches had gone into the work, seventy every ten inches, and the work was indeed a masterpiece.

But somehow that knowledge couldn't soothe the ache in her heart. Tears quickly filled her eyes, and she reached up to wipe them away.

If only Jenna were here with me, I could bear this somehow.

The November sun shone weakly through a gray overcast of clouds, and the pale light from her window made the fabric in the quilt shimmer and glow. A fitful wind shook the bare branches of the maple trees, and the few remaining leaves whirled away into the light snow that drifted down from the gunmetal sky. Winter had come unannounced to Apple Creek, and Jerusha hadn't noticed. Her life had been

bound up in this quilt for so many months that everything
else in her life seemed like shadows.

Jenny stared down at the words on the page. She was pleased with
the way the book had started. She could feel the anguish in her mother's heart as Jerusha finished the quilt. It wasn't an unfamiliar story to
Jenny. Her *mudder* had told it to her many times in her childhood. But
writing it down seemed to make it real and permanent, and she felt a
sense of accomplishment. When she had read the first chapter to Jerusha, her mama had smiled and nodded.

"*Ja*, Jenny, you have captured it. It's what I was experiencing as I
made Jenna's quilt. I was so angry with *Gott* for taking Jenna from us
and so disappointed in your papa. All I wanted was to leave Apple
Creek and the Amish church forever. I wanted to pack my suitcase and
go and never look back."

Jerusha smiled at an inward recollection. "Do you know one of the
things I was going to do? I was going to buy a car. Me! I was actually
going to learn to drive and have my own car so I could go anywhere
I wanted without anybody telling me what to do. Can you imagine?
The good people of Ohio would have had to put up warning signs:
Watch out! Jerusha Springer *wird durch die Stadt heute fahren.* Jerusha is coming!"

The two women laughed. Working on the book together had
bonded them in a very special way, and their love and friendship were
deepening every day. Once while Jenny was feverishly writing down an
idea for the story line, her mama looked at her and smiled.

"When you were just a little girl, you asked me if *Gott* had given
you a gift that you could use to bless people. You were trying to learn
to quilt, and it was very difficult for you."

"Difficult! That's an understatement," Jenny snorted. "We cut up
the quilt I tried to make and used it for cleaning rags. No, Mama, quilting was not difficult for me—it was torture!"

Jerusha took Jenny in her arms and held her close. "Do you remember what I said to you?"

"I have never forgotten. You told me that my very life was a gift and a blessing to Papa and to you and to many others. And then you said that what happened with my life was up to *Gott*. You told me He had given me a quick mind and courage and determination and that He would begin to open doors for me to walk through and that when He did, I mustn't hesitate, but do exactly as He said. Then I would discover who I was and what my place would be in this world."

"And now here you are," Jerusha said. "*Gott* has opened many doors for you, and you are still young. I believe the greatest things He has for you are still in the future. And I believe that something very wonderful will come of all of this."

"Oh, Mama," Jenny whispered, "how you bless me. I love you so much!"

◇◇◇

When Jenny had written three chapters, she looked on the back of her notebook for Jeremy's address and posted a short note to him.

> Dear Mr. King,
>
> Thank you for your kindness the evening that we met. I was rather a mess, and you were right—I needed to sit and talk with someone, and you were a great listener. Thank you so much!
>
> I also took to heart what you said about sending you a one-sheet if I had an idea for a story. I do have an idea, and I have enclosed it. Let me know what you think.
>
> Blessings,
> Jenny Hershberger

A week later Jenny received a reply.

> Dear Jenny,
>
> It was so nice to get to know you, and I'm very glad I was able to be of some help to you. I had a wonderful time chatting with you and was encouraged to see that by the time I took you home, your spirits had lifted somewhat. I hope I played some small part in that.
>
> Now, as for your story idea, I think it's terrific! Do you have any sample chapters? If you do, please send them to me, and we'll see if God has something for us in this.
>
> Sincerely,
> Jeremy King

As soon as she read it, Jenny rushed in and showed the letter to Jerusha. Her mama read the note and then took Jenny's hand. "Jenny, I think we should pray."

"Yes, Mama, I do too."

Jerusha began. "Lord, it seems to us that You are opening a door to Jenny's future, and we want to be sure that we are hearing You speak and that everything Jenny does as she goes forward will bring glory to You and lift up the name of Jesus in this world."

"Amen," Jenny answered.

Jenny stood at the post office window with the large brown envelope in her hand. The clerk was busy putting stamps on a box of letters the previous customer had brought in, so Jenny had a moment to think.

What am I doing? Am I really serious about this? What if he hates the writing? Who said I could write…

"Can I help you?"

Jenny stepped up to the counter, her hands shaking. For a moment she almost turned and walked away. But then she felt a familiar prompting…

Mail it!

She slid the thick envelope over to the clerk. Inside were the first three chapters of her book. She had fretted about sending them in handwritten form and had mentioned it to her *daed*. Two days later Reuben brought her an old Underwood typewriter he found in a thrift store in Dalton. She sat up late for a week mastering the keyboard, and by dint of concentrated effort and with the help of some White-Out, she was able to produce a presentable copy. Now she was surprised to find her palms sweating as she handed her package over to the clerk. He took it from her and slid it onto a scale.

"Seventy-eight cents."

"What?"

The young clerk looked at her with a bored expression. "Seventy-eight cents is the postage, ma'am."

"Oh, yes, the postage."

Jenny fumbled in her bag and pulled out her coin purse. Carefully she counted out the money. The clerk raked it into his palm, dropped it into the open register, and then printed out a stamp from the postage machine on his desk. He wiped the stamp across a damp sponge in a little plastic holder, slapped it on the envelope, and flipped the package unceremoniously into a bin behind him.

"Will there be anything else?"

"No, thank you," she replied.

Jenny smiled sweetly at him, but inside her thoughts were in turmoil. *What about the trumpets and the angels and the voice from heaven? O Lord, please confirm this in my heart.*

She stood there for a moment, resisting the desire to ask for the envelope back. The clerk grew impatient.

"Will that be all, ma'am? We have other customers waiting…"

Jenny glanced behind her at the line of people who looked as bored as the clerk. She gave one more longing glance at the top of her envelope, which was peeking up out of the bin. Then she took a deep breath and walked away.

It's in your hands, Lord.

Jenny spent a very anxious two weeks. Just when she had reconciled herself to never hearing from Jeremy again, a letter came from Kerusso Publishing. She grabbed it out of the mailbox and hurried into the house. Jenny ran into the back room, where Jerusha was working on a new quilt, and held up the envelope.

"Mama! Look!"

Jerusha looked up with concern. "What is it, Jenny?"

"It's a letter from Mr. King. Oh, Mama, I just want to throw it in the fire. What if he hated what I wrote?"

"Jenny, *springen Sie zu Beschlüssen nicht.* Now sit down there, take a deep breath, and read it to me."

Jenny sat in the chair opposite her mother and tore open the letter. Inside on the Kerusso stationery was a handwritten note from Jeremy King.

> My dear Jenny,
>
> Please excuse my tardiness in responding to your letter. I have been up against some deadlines and have been remiss in answering my correspondence.
>
> I received your sample chapters, and I must say, I was very impressed by the quality of your writing. I think the story has the potential of being a terrific book. I would like to meet with you and make a proposal. I will be over from Akron meeting with one of my authors on Thursday, July 14. Can you meet me at the library in Wooster at two p.m? We could visit our coffee shop and share a cup while I go

over my idea with you. If you could call me and confirm
that time it would be helpful. My phone number is on this
letterhead.

Blessings, and looking forward to seeing you again,
Jeremy King

Jenny gasped and held the letter against her chest. "He likes the
story, Mama! Oh how exciting!"

Jerusha laid her quilt aside. "Let me read it, Jenny," she said.

Jenny handed the letter over as Jerusha picked up her reading glasses
from the small table beside her and perched them on her nose. She read
it silently and then looked up at Jenny. "You should confirm it right
away. You could ask Henry if you can use their phone."

"Oh, Mama. Do you think I should do this?"

"Jenny, I've learned many things in my life, but the main thing is
this. *Gott* is the director of our steps, and our times are in His hands. I
can see *Gott*'s hand all over this. If opportunity is knocking, you need
to answer the door."

A week later, Jenny sat with Jeremy King at a small coffee shop in
Wooster. He had the manuscript and was looking at some notes he
had made. Jenny sat waiting impatiently while he read through them.
Then he looked up at her.

"Okay, here's what I'm asking. Can you make this story into a
novel?"

"I hate to show my inexperience, but how many words are in a
novel?"

"Eighty to a hundred thousand." Jeremy smiled.

Jenny's jaw dropped. She stared at Jeremy and then remembered
Jerusha's words. "*When opportunity knocks…*"

"Yes, I can."

"And do you think you could come up with two more stories and make it into a series?"

"Yes, I can."

"Okay, then," Jeremy said. "Here's what I propose. If you can turn this idea into a book that will keep my attention all the way through, I would be willing to publish it, with a few caveats."

"Caveats?" Jenny shifted in her chair.

"Yes, and here they are. You show a lot of promise as a writer, but you're still rough around the edges. If you will let me work with you, give you suggestions, and edit the manuscript as we go, I would be willing to get involved in this project."

Jenny paused. It occurred to her that Jeremy's proposal involved spending time with him—a lot of time. For some reason the thought made her very nervous.

Part Two

THE LONG AND WINDING ROAD

When you are with the ones who love you, anyplace can seem like home. But without the ones you love, even home can be a prison.

"Home Is Where the Heart Is"
from the journals of Jenny Hershberger

Chapter Thirteen

An Open Door

◇◇◇

Jenny came into the house, hung up her coat, and walked into the bedroom. Then she pulled off her shoes and flopped down on the bed.

The book was progressing, but in the process of learning to write better, she found Jeremy to be a relentless taskmaster. Many times he had handed her back chapters with whole sections marked through with red ink. The notes were mostly the same.

"Show, don't tell, Jenny. Give me some internal dialogue if you have to, or break the narration up, but don't just ramble on about what's happening from your point of view. The reader needs to get inside the story, not stand outside and watch with you. Please rewrite."

Occasionally there would be an encouraging comment, such as "You turn a phrase really well, Jenny. That's your strong point."

But mostly it was a grinding, brutal, humiliating process that often found her the way she was tonight—lying flat on her back in her bed, staring at the ceiling with uncomprehending eyes and not one thought left in her head. But still, in the crush of it all, when Jenny stepped back and looked at the places where Jeremy had drawn a small star in the margin by a section that he particularly liked, she knew that underneath the incredibly hard work, she had discovered the thing that she really loved to do more than anything—writing.

So she kept at it. Her gift with words and phrases and her uncanny ability to get to the heart of things began to blossom under Jeremy's skilled tutelage. The book began to unfold like a flower in her hands. Many times she felt as though she were reading someone's personal letters to discover the story—and in a way she was. As she dug deeper into the story, she began to uncover things about her family she had never known.

One night she sat down with Reuben and asked if she could to talk to him about his part in World War II. At first Reuben was reluctant.

"Jenny, this is a part of my life that I'm not proud of. I was young and foolish and very rebellious, and the things I was involved in did not bring glory to Christ."

"I know, Papa. And if it makes you too uncomfortable, I won't press the matter. But I will say this. I think there's something in your story that will help others in our church."

Reuben looked puzzled. "How is that, *dochter*?"

"When you came back from the war, you believed joining the church and following the *Ordnung* as best you could would save you from the evil you had seen out in the world. But when Jenna died, you discovered that wasn't true. In that terrible time, you learned that only a real relationship with Jesus Christ can save you.

"If there was one thing Jonathan learned from you, that was it. And it guided his life. He loved the Amish church, he loved working the land…he loved everything about his new life. But he used to tell me that those things only gave direction to his life. It was his relationship with Jesus that made everything real and true. I believe that many of our people need to discover that for themselves, and by telling your story, you can help them."

Reuben sat silent. Then he reached up and wiped away a tear.

"Maybe you're right, Jenny. I did learn about having a real relationship with Christ, and the sad thing is I didn't learn it from the church, but from an old soldier on a mountaintop in Colorado. I will tell you my story. Maybe after I do, I'll be able to put some of my phantoms to rest."

For the next few weeks, whenever they could take the time, Reuben and Jenny sat together as Reuben told Jenny his story—how he grew up, how he met Jerusha, his life away from the church when he shared an apartment with Bobby Halverson, and how they both joined the Marines when World War II broke out. One night he told Jenny the story of his basic training.

"After we enlisted, we had a few days to get ready, and then we shipped out for basic training. The trip to South Carolina wasn't easy. I had an argument with your mama the day before we left, and I thought I would never see her again, so all the way to Parris Island I had a chip on my shoulder. I'm afraid I was a little cranky with your Uncle Bobby, and we almost got into a fistfight on the train."

Jenny put down her pencil in surprise. "You and Uncle Bobby?"

"Yes, Uncle Bobby and me. Back in those days he was a pretty no-nonsense kind of guy, and he certainly didn't want to put up with a sulky kid like me."

"How soon after the attack on Pearl Harbor did you join the Marines?"

Reuben paused for a moment and then went on. "We left for basic training on Monday, January 2, 1942. We went down to the train station with our suitcases and climbed aboard a troop train along with a bunch of other guys—just kids. They thought they were on a picnic. They didn't know that the moment they disembarked from the train, they would be stepping into an entirely different world."

"Was it that bad, Papa?"

"Well, we arrived at Parris Island in the morning. We climbed off the train and were just lounging around, laughing, smoking cig-arettes—you know, just a bunch of kids away from home for the first time. A couple of jeeps pulled up, and these really tough-looking Marines piled out. Within a few minutes we were running as fast as we could from place to place while being screamed at and made to feel like the know-nothing kids we were. They ran us to the chow hall and then down to sickbay. We rolled up our sleeves and walked down a row of Navy corpsmen and doctors who stuck needles in our arms, checked our eyesight, and drew blood."

Jenny scribbled furiously on her notepad.

"Then it was off to Administration for paperwork, dog tags, ID cards, allotments, service record books, and the all-important serial number. On the way between the meal and the dog tags, we were intro-duced to the base barbers, who buzzed us bald and sent us on our way. Quite a shock for a somewhat vain young man who thought his long dark hair made him look like a movie star."

Jenny snickered at the image.

Reuben looked at her. "What's funny about that?"

"Oh, Papa, it's just that I can't imagine what you must have looked like with your head shaved. And were you really that vain?"

"Yes, he was," came Jerusha's voice from the kitchen. "But rightly so, for he was the handsomest man I had ever seen."

Reuben smiled.

"What happened next, Papa?"

"We received our new clothes, our rifles, and our first PX issue of personal items. Then they put us into platoons of between forty-eight and sixty men, and just when we thought it couldn't get any worse, we met our drill instructor, Gunnery Sergeant Edgar F. Thompkins."

"Is that the man you told me about—the one who saved you in the battle?" Jenny asked.

"Yes, he is. Ed Thompkins and I didn't get along at first. He thought that because I came from an Amish family, I wouldn't fight when the going got tough. And I must admit I had my doubts. We were out on patrol one day, and a sniper killed one of our men. I was on point, so I was closest and had the clearest shot. When I got the guy in my sights, I couldn't pull the trigger. Ed crawled alongside me and shot him. The noise next to my ear made me jump, and I pulled my trigger at the same time, so it looked like I shot him too. But I didn't really, and Ed knew it. But he didn't give me away."

Reuben reached into his pocket and took out his wallet. He fished around in the back section and pulled out a piece of paper. When he turned it over, Jenny could see that it was a photograh, wrinkled and stained. A young Japanese soldier stood at attention in full dress uniform. Seated next to him was a beautiful Japanese woman with a small child in her lap. She was looking up at the man with love and admiration in her eyes. A tiny smile on her face broke the formality of the photo.

"I took this off the body of the sniper after we shot him. I've had it with me every day since then. It reminds me always that Jesus was right when He said killing is wrong. This young wife never saw her husband again, and the little boy grew up without a father. I carried a lot of guilt for many years—until I found out that Jesus would carry the guilt for me. But it still doesn't make what I did right."

Reuben looked down at the photo again. Jenny watched as a shadow passed over her papa's face. Jerusha came in from the kitchen and put her arm on her husband's shoulder.

"I think that's enough for tonight, Jenny. Your papa wants to help you, but I know that in all of us there are some wounds that never quite heal. He will talk to you again, but not tonight."

Reuben looked up gratefully and pulled a handkerchief from his shirt pocket. He blew his nose and then got up and walked into the kitchen. Jenny heard him clinking some cups around in the cupboard.

"Is there any coffee made, Jerusha?"

Jenny went into the kitchen and came up behind her *daed* and slipped her arms around his waist.

"Thank you, Papa. I know that was hard for you, and I won't ask you any more about it."

Reuben turned and took Jenny's face in his hands. Jenny could see the strong emotion working in his face.

"No, Jenny, I want you to know what happened. I've never told anyone about that last battle, and I need to put it to rest. You and your mother and I will sit down soon, and I'll tell you all about it. Just not tonight."

Jenny nodded. "Thank you for helping me, Papa. I think it will be a good story, and I'm praying that it may help others who went through some of the things our family did."

"Then you will need to write the story of you and Jonathan too, *dochter*."

"Maybe someday, Papa. But I don't think I'm quite ready to tell it yet. It's too soon."

"Well, I hope you don't keep your pain locked up as long as I have, Jenny."

Jenny picked up her pad and paper and went to her room to type up her notes. She sat at her desk and looked at what she had written. She thought about what it would be like to tell Jonathan's story. Then she put her head down on the desk and cried.

Chapter Fourteen

Uncovering

◇◇◇

Jenny and Jeremy sat at their table in the back of the small coffee shop around the corner from the Wooster library. Jenny's latest chapter was spread out in front of Jeremy, who was going over it with the dreaded red pen. Jenny sat and sipped her coffee and thought about the friendship that was developing between Jeremy and her. Over the weeks, as they worked on the book, they had created a neutral territory where they could spend time together without any complications. But the growing closeness of their relationship was troubling to Jenny. In a way she felt as if she were being an unfaithful wife. But then…

Someday I have to come to grips with the fact that I'm not a wife anymore.

She tried to look at the positive side of their relationship. Jeremy was handsome, engaging, and very solicitous of Jenny, yet when it came to writing, he was a consummate expert and uncompromising editor. So as far as she could see, their relationship was strictly a professional one. But he was a man and she was a woman…

Don't even go there, Jenny Hershberger!

She waited anxiously while he finished looking at the last pages.

"Well, how am I doing?" she asked when he looked up from his editing.

"You've got a good chapter here, but it needs more meat. I think the whole idea of an Amish man who goes to war is brilliant—a real enigma. But it needs more details. And I want the whole story, not just the beginning and the end."

"You don't understand, Jeremy. This is a very difficult area for my papa. He's an Amish man who still battles with a deep sense of shame for going against the tenets of his faith. He's also a human being who was dropped into the middle of one of the most horrific battles of World War II. You don't have to be Amish to have nightmares about an experience like that."

"I understand, Jenny, but we're talking about a book that needs to hold a reader's attention all the way through. I don't want people who buy this book writing me letters asking what really happened."

Jenny sat silent for a moment. Then, choosing her words carefully, she spoke. "It's not just about my *daed*, Jeremy; it's about me too."

"How so—or am I being too personal?"

"You are being personal, but for now I'll let it pass and tell you what I'm feeling. My papa said he would tell me the story of his experiences in the war, but I could tell by the way he said it that he doesn't really want to. And then I thought about what it would be like to try writing about Jonathan. I've written about his smile, his singing…I've even recorded my memories of being with him and the things he taught me. But to go through our whole story step-by-step and write it down… I don't know if I could do that—at least not now. The other night I thought about what it would be like to write that book, and it almost made me hysterical with grief. No, I couldn't tell that story."

"I understand. But how does that relate to your father?"

Jeremy looked frustrated, so Jenny tried to explain herself.

"If it is so painful for me to write about the terrible things that have happened to me, then it must be the same for him. And I don't know if that's something I want to ask of him."

Jeremy took a sip of his coffee. "Now can I tell you how I see it?"

Jenny felt an uncomfortable stirring in her heart. "All right, but be careful."

"Jenny, I believe that good writing helps people to access memories and emotions that may have been buried for years—some of them good, some of them bad. If someone reads what I've written and says, 'I remember feeling exactly that way' about something positive in their life, I'm doing my job. It's the same with the bad memories. Sometimes when something terrible happens to us, we take that memory and build a wall around it. But that doesn't make it go away. Instead, it festers in the dark and can poison our lives. As Christian writers, it's our job to help people bring those dark and terrible events into the light of Christ so we can see the truth about them and be set free. That's why I think it would be good for your father to tell his whole story."

"Jeremy, I understand what you're saying, but do you really know the Amish mind? We don't think like that. I thought you knew that. You know, you haven't really told me about your faith. You know I'm Amish, and so it's pretty plain where I stand, but what about you?"

Jeremy smiled at her question. "I'll tell you about that when we finish talking about this."

"But—"

Jeremy pressed on. "So for your father, it's my guess that if he can set this experience down on paper and get it out of the place he has held it for so many years, it will be extremely liberating. And I would say the same about you."

A great crushing weight began to press down on Jenny. "I don't think I want to go where you're taking this, Jeremy. I'm not ready."

"Look, Jenny, it's been a year and a half since your husband died. I think it's time you started to think about moving on with—"

Suddenly Jenny was standing, her chair knocked over by the abruptness of her movement. "What do you know about it, Jeremy? How can you tell me how I should feel?"

Jeremy sat in stunned amazement.

"It's none of your business what I do with my life. You're my editor, not my father—and you're not my husband! I'll get over Jonathan when I'm good and ready, and you don't have anything to say about it."

Jenny gathered up her papers, grabbed her bag, and stalked out of the shop, leaving a very disconcerted Jeremy King and several other customers staring after her.

Jenny burst into the house and went straight to her room. She had been seething inside all the way home from Wooster.

The nerve of him—who does he think he is to tell me when to stop mourning? Oh, Jonathan, why did you have to…to…to die?

When she got in her room she slammed the door and threw her bag down. She pulled off her *kappe* and undid her hair. It fell loosely about her shoulders. When she looked in the mirror, she felt as if she were staring at a mad woman.

"I don't want to do this!" she cried aloud. "I don't want to feel this! Jonathan, why did you leave me! God, why did you take him?"

Jenny collapsed on her bed, sobs wrenching her soul.

After a while there was a gentle knock on the door. "Jenny, may I come in?" Jerusha asked.

Jenny didn't want to see anyone, but by a supreme effort of will she swung her legs over the side of the bed and sat that way for a long time.

"Jenny? Are you all right?"

Jenny climbed to her feet and went to the door. She opened it to her mother and then returned to the bed without saying anything. Jerusha came and sat down by Jenny. She brushed the tangled curls away from her daughter's tear-stained face.

"What is it? What's happened?"

"It's just that…oh, Mama! I was working with Jeremy and he started saying things that…I guess they got too much inside me. I felt like I was being burned with a hot iron, right on an open wound. I yelled at him and left him sitting there in the coffee shop."

"Was he asking about Jonathan?"

"In a way. I mean, he didn't ask any personal questions, he just said that it was time for me to move on. It made me furious, and I don't know why."

Jerusha took her daughter's hand and softly stroked it. "I know, Jenny. I know the rage and the anger and the fear you're feeling. When Jenna died, I cursed *Gott* from the very depths of my soul. I couldn't understand how such a terrible thing could happen when I loved *Gott* so much, and when I loved Jenna so much."

"How did you deal with it, Mama?"

"Mostly *Gott* dealt with me. He knew I needed to grieve for my little girl, but He wanted me to know He wasn't the one who took her from me. After a while I saw that we live in a world marred by terrible things that happen to people every day, and I started to come to grips with my pain.

Jerusha got up and went to the window. She pulled the curtain aside and looked out.

"Disease and death are in the world because of sin, and we're all subject to their power. *Gott* dealt with it all by sending His Son to pay the price for that sin with His precious blood. We will be free from it someday, but never in this life. When we understand that, we can be more accepting when terrible things happen."

"When does the pain go away, Mama?"

Jerusha turned and looked into Jenny's eyes. "Never."

◇◇◇

Jeremy King looked at the short handwritten note on his desk. It was from Jenny. It had been a week since she exploded at him, and he sincerely regretted causing the incident. Now he eagerly read the words she had written.

Jeremy, my friend,

I'm so sorry for the way I reacted at our last meeting. I guess I've not yet dealt with some things in my heart. I know you were only trying to be helpful, and so I'm not angry with you. I have come to value our friendship in the months we've been working together and wouldn't do anything to harm that. If you want to go back to work on the book, I'm ready.

I talked to my papa, and he's willing to tell me the whole story about his experience in the war.

As far as my husband is concerned, I realized I'm still grieving, and so for now, it's a subject I'm not ready to discuss. If you will bear with me in that area, I think we can write a good book without too many more outbursts.

Jenny

Jeremy took a piece of plain paper and a pen and wrote a reply.

My dear Jenny,

Since our last meeting, I've been very remorseful about digging too deeply into your personal affairs. It's not up to me to decide how you go about your life. That's between you and the Lord, and I was extremely boorish in my behavior. I think the editor in me overrode my regard for you as a friend. If you can find it in your heart to forgive me, I would love to get back to work on the book! You can call me whenever you're ready with more chapters, and we will meet. My sincerest wish is that you find healing and happiness again in your life. I will be praying for you.

Jeremy

Jeremy folded the note and put it into an envelope. As he addressed it, he realized with a start that he was more than anxious to see Jenny again.

Chapter Fifteen

Opposition

◇◇◇

It was late September in Apple Creek. Jenny stood at the window and watched the red and yellow leaves of the Buckeye trees drifting down from branches that were rapidly being unclothed by the changing season. The afternoon sun was still warm, but behind it the teeth of winter prepared to bite the land. A year had passed since Jenny had come back to her old home, and her life seemed to be sorting itself out. The book was progressing, and her friendship with Jeremy seemed to be back on an even keel. And still her thoughts stirred as she gazed silently out the window.

Why do I seem out of balance? Everything is going smoothly, and yet my spirit is still uneasy.

She sighed and turned to find her daughter silently creeping up on her. When Rachel saw that she was discovered, she leapt up with both hands extended like claws.

"Boo!" Rachel shouted.

Jenny clutched at her heart with both hands and cried out in mock terror. "Oh, no! A bear! Save me, save me!"

She spun around to run but turned her foot and tripped. As she collapsed onto the sofa, Rachel pounced on her like a tiger.

"Raaawwwwerr! I'm going to eat you, so I'll be fat for hibernation time."

"Noooo, don't eat me, don't eat me," Jenny cried, laughing. "Take me home instead, and I'll clean your cave while you're sleeping and make you a big dinner of chicken and biscuits when you wake up in the spring!"

Rachel paused in her chomping motions.

"Chicken and biscuits? Okay, I won't eat you. But you'll have to keep the fire going too so the cave will stay warm all winter."

"All right, Mr. Bear," Jenny laughed again. "Whatever you say."

"But before I take you to my cave, I'm going to give you a big bear hug."

Jenny grabbed her little girl and hugged her. They lay on the couch, giggling together. Finally they got themselves under control and sat up. Rachel took Jenny's hand.

"Mama, can you tell me a story about Papa? Sometimes I have a hard time remembering things about him. I feel like I'm forgetting him, and I don't want to."

Jenny pulled Rachel close. A sharp, almost physical pain stabbed her heart, and she paused a moment before she spoke.

"When I first met your papa, he was what they called a hippie. He had just come to Ohio from San Francisco, and he dressed very strangely."

"What's a Safacisco, Mama?"

"San Francisco. It's a big city in California. That's a state right on the ocean, way west from here."

"Mama, we learned about the ocean in our school. I would like to see the ocean sometime."

Jenny thought about that. *I hope I'm not there when you see it, Rachel.*

She went on. "When I first met your papa, he almost ran me over in his van. When he got out to see if I was all right, he looked like he belonged in a circus. He had long hair and a leather jacket with fringes on it and striped pants with green boots. He looked very funny."

"Did you love him anyway?"

Jenny thought back to that day—the electric shock that had gone up her arm when he took her hand, the deep voice that had thrilled her heart, and then his eyes—oh, his wonderful deep-blue eyes.

"You know, Rachel, I think I did. Now that I look back on it, I think I loved your papa from the first moment I saw him."

"And did he love you back?"

Jenny paused again. *He said he loved me from that moment too. And I know he did. How does that happen?*

"Yes, Rachel, he loved me too."

"That's good, Mama. That's a good thing."

Jenny pulled Rachel even closer. "Yes, my darling, that was a very good thing."

"Thank you, Mama. I need to hear about Papa so I won't forget him. Will you always help me to remember?"

"Until my dying day, my precious one. Until my dying day."

That evening, Reuben came home late from the fields with a sour look on his face. Jenny could see storm clouds brewing in his eyes.

Jenny helped him take off his coat. "What is it, Papa?"

"Is there any coffee made?" he asked, ignoring her question.

"Yes, it's on the stove. I made it an hour ago, so it's fresh."

Reuben went into the kitchen while Jenny hung his coat and hat on the rack by the door. She heard him pour a cup of coffee, muttering under his breath. When she heard the chair scraping up to the table as he sat down, she went into the kitchen.

"Okay, Papa. What is it?"

He frowned and took a sip. Then he set his cup down and looked at her. "I had some callers today."

"Who, Papa?"

"The visiting *bisschop* and one of the elders."

"What about, Papa?"

"They came to talk to me about your book."

Jenny felt the unease stir back to life. *Maybe this is what I was sensing this afternoon.*

"My book? But what did they want to talk about?"

"They came to me because they heard you were writing a novel and they had deep concerns about it, especially the *bisschop*."

"What kind of concerns, Papa?"

"They don't think it's a good thing for an Amish woman to be an author, especially a fiction author. They say it's not edifying to the Amish community and will bring reproach on the name of Jesus."

A strange mixture of anger and pain stirred inside Jenny. "But it is the name of Jesus I want to glorify with my writing."

"I know that, but they do not. They want to read some of the book and meet with you about it. I'm not sure it will go well, Jenny. The visiting *bisschop* is from Lancaster. I think I told you before that they interpret the *Ordnung* much more strictly than we do."

Jenny twisted her apron between her fingers. "Why is he even out here then, Papa?"

"He has come to help oversee the founding of a new church in Dalton. Our *bisschop* knows him, and because he is so busy with the Apple Creek and Wooster churches, he asked *Bruder* Lapp to come assist him. While he's here, he has as much authority as our own *bisschop*."

"When do they want to meet?"

"They would like to come here next Sunday after church. I have agreed."

"Oh, Papa, what will they do?"

"It's an interesting situation. Our own *bisschop* is trying to stay out of it. I've explained to him about the book, and he seems more accepting of my side of the story. But *Bisschop* Lapp is insistent on looking into it, so Johann must go along with him. I'm sorry, Jenny, there's nothing I can do about it. I can't guess what they will do. I hope it doesn't become an awkward situation. *Bisschop* Lapp seems to be fairly stiff-necked."

Reuben clenched his fists and then spread his fingers out on the tabletop. "He reminds me of me about thirty years ago."

That Sunday afternoon, Jenny waited with trepidation in her heart for the elders to come. She sat through church that morning without really hearing a word that was said. She thought about all the work and effort and research that had gone into the book thus far. It was almost done.

Lord, it would be a pity not to publish the book. I'm sure You told me to write it.

After a while there came a knock on the door. All three of them stood up, but Reuben waved the two women back into their chairs. He went to the door and opened it. Jenny and Jerusha could hear Reuben greeting the men, and then they all came into the kitchen. *Bisschop* Samuel Lapp was a short, stout man with a red beard. When he took off his hat to greet the women, Jenny saw that he was bald. He had a beaked nose and small, gimlet eyes that seemed to take in the whole room at a glance. There were two men with him, *Bruder* James, an elder, and Johann Troyer, their own *bisschop*. Jerusha motioned for them to sit at the table.

"Welcome to our house," Jerusha said sweetly. "Can I fix you some tea or coffee?"

Bruder Johann smiled and started to answer in the affirmative, but *Bisschop* Lapp cut him off.

"Thank you for your hospitality, Mrs. Springer, but I want to get right to the matter at hand. May I see this book I've heard so much about?"

Jenny watched his face. He seemed to have a tic, for every once in a while his face gave a tiny twitch.

Jenny put on her most ingratiating smile. "Certainly, *Bisschop*. I'll be happy to show you what I've written. But at this point it's almost forty chapters long and still in draft form. Do you want to read it all in one sitting?"

"To tell you the truth, I don't want to read it at all," the *bisschop* said stiffly. "It's an unheard of thing for an Amish woman to be writing what the *Englisch* call pulp fiction. But if I must, I will look at a few sample chapters."

Then at last Johann spoke up. "*Bisschop* Lapp, I appreciate your concern, and I've come with you at your request, but let's put first things first. Jerusha has kindly offered us some coffee, and I for one would like a cup. As for calling the book pulp fiction...I have talked with Reuben about the book, and it is my understanding that it is a biographical work that tells the history of one of the families of our district and the ways that *Gott* has worked in their lives. So before we rush to judgment, *ja*, let's have some coffee."

Samuel Lapp shot Johann a grim look but acceded to his request. Jerusha went to make the coffee, and Jenny glanced at her *bisschop* gratefully.

"I'll fetch the book while Mama makes coffee. I will be right back."

Jenny stood in her room with the manuscript in her hand. Her heart thumped like a hammer in her chest.

I feel like this is my child. I have labored over it, wept over it, laughed, and rejoiced. And now I must give it to a man whom I fear has already judged it in his heart. Lord, before I do that, I must put this in Your hands, for it is Your book. You asked me to write it, and only You know if it is ever to be published.

She took the pages and went back out to the kitchen. The coffee was brewing, and the strong smell permeated the kitchen. *Bisschop* Lapp looked very uncomfortable as Johann and James chatted with Reuben. Jenny went out to the cooling shed and fetched some cream. Finally, when the coffee was poured and the men had a chance to relax, Jenny placed the book in front of them. Samuel Lapp reached for it, but Johann gave him a look that backed him off.

"Reuben, would you pick a few chapters that give us the general direction of the book?"

Reuben picked up the manuscript and carefully looked through it. He chose three chapters—the beginning, one from the middle, and the last chapter—and set them before Johann. The *bisschop* took one and gave one each to James and Samuel. The three men began to read. Jenny sat in silence with her eyes down. Once she glanced up at her papa, but his face was an unreadable mask. Jerusha saw the glance and smiled at Jenny. The men passed one another their chapters as they finished.

Finally they all had read all three chapters. *Bisschop* Johann was about to speak, but Lapp jumped in and went first.

"Just as I thought," he said. His voice was high-pitched and whiney. "This is not *gut.* Not *gut* at all."

Chapter Sixteen

A Shelter

◇◇◇

REUBEN SPOKE FIRST.

"And what is not *gut* about it?"

Samuel Lapp's face gave a little twitch, and he set the book down on the table.

"Well, for one thing, it contains romance. It's no better than one of those worldly novels in the drug stores. And the chapter about you killing Japanese soldiers with your bare hands goes against everything we hold to be true. And writing about a couple embracing, like you did in the last chapter, Mrs. Hershberger—why, it's shocking."

Jenny stared at the man. She felt anger rising up inside her, and she was about to reply to his remarks when she felt a gentle squeeze on her arm. She looked over, and Jerusha was giving her a tiny signal with her eyes. It told Jenny to stay out of it, so she clamped her jaw shut and sat silently, all the while burning with indignation. *Bruder* Samuel pulled out a handkerchief and mopped his brow. There was silence around the table. Finally *Bisschop* Johann spoke.

"I think perhaps you're reacting a little strongly, Samuel. I find the writing quite good and see nothing in what Jenny has said that is offensive or prurient. Perhaps the battle scene is shocking, but it is what happened, and I'm sure Reuben can enlighten us as to the purpose of the chapter."

He looked hopefully at Reuben. Reuben smiled back.

"I was hoping you would ask me, Johann. I gave you that chapter to read because it's the strongest chapter in the book, and it is my true story. It's also the root of the reason why my first daughter died and why this book is being written at all."

Jerusha put her hand on Reuben's arm. "Husband, this is all behind us. We don't need to go into it—"

Reuben shook his head. "No, Jerusha, I've carried this for thirty-five years, and I, for one, would like to clear up some things that have troubled me most of my adult life."

"Why do you say it was the cause of your daughter's death?" James asked.

"When I came back from the war, I was a ruined man, physically and spiritually," Reuben began. "I had killed men in hand-to-hand combat in the most violent and bloodthirsty ways. Sitting at this table, you cannot imagine the horror of that time. *Ich war ein gebrochener und bitterer Mann*, broken and bitter. I made up my mind to come home, join the church, and hide behind the *Ordnung* for the rest of my life. I was sure that as long as I kept the rules I would be right with *Gott*."

"And is that not the truth?" Samuel interjected. "Is it not the *Ordnung* that keeps us protected from the world and all its evil? Without it, we would be just another marginal religion that would have faded into obscurity long ago."

"There is truth in what you say, *Bruder* Samuel," Reuben replied, "but it's not the whole truth."

"I'm not sure I'm following you, Reuben," Johann interjected. "What do you mean it's not the whole truth?"

"The *Ordnung* does not save us," Reuben said quietly.

"What do you mean?" *Bisschop* Lapp asked. "The *Ordnung* is everything to us!"

"No," Reuben said quietly. "Jesus is everything to us. The *Ordnung* means nothing if we do not know Christ."

"This is bordering on the blasphemous!" Brother Samuel was aghast. "I don't want to sit here and…"

Johann placed a hand on Samuel's arm and spoke quietly. "Calm yourself, *Bisschop*. Remember, the Springer family has walked in the light for many years. They have been a great blessing to our district and to me personally. You must be careful before you start throwing words like 'blasphemous' around."

Bisschop Lapp's face was twitching, but as he looked around at the grim faces, he did his best to calm himself. "In Lancaster we would not tolerate such statements."

"You are not in Lancaster," Jerusha said quietly. "You are in Ohio. And my husband is right. Does not Paul say, 'For the law of the Spirit of life in Christ Jesus hath made me free from the law of sin and death'?"

"And now I would have a woman instruct me from the Bible? I know what the Bible says," the *bisschop* said.

Jenny had been listening carefully and watching the men. She looked at Reuben. He wore an expression she hadn't seen before, and it scared her. She looked back and forth between her papa and Samuel and realized that the look did not bode well for the whiney little man.

"You would insult my wife?" Reuben said quietly, but the look on his face was grim. It did not escape the *bisschop*'s notice.

Bisschop Lapp pointed at Reuben. "You see, he is threatening me."

"Brothers, brothers, where is the grace in all this?" Johann asked. "We are Amish! We do not fight among ourselves."

"I am a *bisschop*," Samuel said, trying to put authority behind his words. "I will not be corrected by a woman."

Reuben laughed. "Brother Samuel, I'm not threatening you.

Though if I wanted to hurt you, nobody at this table could stop me. I want to show you respect because you're a visitor to our community and an elder in your own church, but I find it very hard to do so. You remind me of Peter, who went from Jerusalem to Antioch and acted as if he were under the Law. Paul withstood him to his face, and I am doing the same. You can't impose the Law here simply for the sake of the Law. And I do not know of any part of the *Ordnung* that specifically states that Amish people cannot write a novel. If you can show me one, I might reconsider my position."

Bisschop Lapp leaned forward. "And just what is your position, Mr. Springer?"

Reuben looked at Jenny. "My daughter has been through a great sorrow in her life. When she turned to her writing, I saw a healing begin to take place. Now she has discovered that *Gott* has placed in her a gift for words. She is writing a story that can bring glory to Him and, I believe, help many of our people to come to a true understanding of their faith."

"And just what is this true understanding you speak of?"

"When Jenna, my first daughter, got sick, I believed exactly the way you do, Samuel. I believed that because I was so careful to keep the *Ordnung*, I had favor with *Gott*. Because of that, I wouldn't allow my wife to take Jenna to the *Englisch* hospital. Instead I called the healer. I have great respect for our healers, but in this case, it was not the right thing to do. Jenna had contracted bacterial meningitis, and the only thing that could have saved her was a massive dose of antibiotics. My friend from the war, Sheriff Bobby Halverson, finally ripped her out of my arms and rushed her to Wooster. He was too late. If I had taken her in two days earlier…"

Reuben's voice choked up, and he put his head down. Jerusha put her hand on Reuben's arm and leaned against his shoulder. The room was very quiet.

Finally Reuben looked up.

"You see, *Bruder* Samuel, I was so locked up in the *Ordnung* that I couldn't see beyond my own fear. And the price I paid was my daughter's life. In my anger and shame, I ran away. At a certain point I was going to take my own life, but an old soldier in Colorado shared the gospel of grace with me. He showed me in the Bible that all I have to do to be saved is to believe that Christ died for my sins, that He was buried just as the scriptures foretold, and that He rose from the grave and is alive today. Do I want to follow the *Ordnung*? Yes, I do. But why?

"My late son-in-law, Jonathan Hershberger, Jenny's husband, said it best. He was a convert to our faith and an outsider who willingly adopted our way of life. He had a very clear understanding of the Amish way. He once told me that he loved the *Ordnung* because it was like the stars a sailor follows across a dark sea at night. But he knew that the *Ordnung* did not save him. It was Christ who saved him."

"Did you say Jonathan Hershberger?"

"Yes, he was killed almost two years ago in a boating accident."

Samuel looked puzzled. "I heard about an outsider named Jonathan Hershberger who joined the church and lived in Paradise. He was married to *Bisschop* Borntraeger's granddaughter."

"Yes," Jenny said quietly, "that was my husband."

Samuel turned to Jenny with a look of surprise. "You are *Bisschop* Borntraeger's granddaughter? But how can you be if you are the Springers' daughter?"

"Mama found me in a great snowstorm many years ago. She saved me and kept me alive until Papa and my Uncle Bobby could rescue us. No one knew who I was, so Mama and Papa adopted me. Then when I was nineteen, I met Jonathan, and he and my papa helped me find out who my birth mother and father were. They were both dead, but my *grossdaadi*, *Bisschop* Borntraeger, was still alive. Jonathan studied with him for two years to learn our ways, and then we were married and lived with *Grossdaadi* until he passed."

Samuel took out his handkerchief and mopped his brow. "Perhaps I have been a bit hasty. Jonathan Hershberger and Lem Borntraeger gave very generously to their district for the support of the Amish community in Paradise. I heard about it even in Lancaster. Everyone said he was a very good man and one of the few *Englischers* who was able to truly assimilate into our community."

"It was because his family was originally Amish," Jenny said. "It was like he was born to be Amish. *Grossdaadi* often said that Jonathan took to our ways like a duck to water. When I was a research intern at the library in Wooster, I helped Jonathan discover his family roots. His family came from Switzerland with the first Amish who arrived in Pennsylvania. And interestingly, he was my mama's very distant cousin. That's one reason I want to write this book, *Bisschop* Samuel. I think it will help our people to come to a deeper understanding of their roots and the manner in which *du lieber Gott* has guided us and kept us in the midst of wicked and perverse generations."

"But the book is fiction—how can it be a historical work?"

"A biography can be written as a novel and still tell a true story. My publisher says that many people who are not Amish will read it because it is written like fiction."

"And who is your publisher, may I ask?"

"Jeremy King from Kerusso Publishing."

A grim look passed over Samuel Lapp's face. "Ah, the apostate, Jeremy King. Do you know that he once was Amish but left the faith many years ago and is under the *meidung* in Pennsylvania? So! Almost you convinced me to change my mind. But this is another matter entirely. King is under the *bann*. Therefore you cannot associate with him, especially in the matter of this book. If he was a man of honor, he would have told you that himself. And now, I think we are finished here. Brothers, shall we go?"

Bisschop Lapp and the others rose. Johann and James shook hands with Reuben while Lapp waited impatiently. Then Reuben escorted the three men to the door, leaving Jenny and Jerusha sitting at the table in stunned silence.

Chapter Seventeen

The Declaration

◇◇◇

The days that followed were gloomy ones in the Springer household. Jenny sat at her desk looking at her manuscript.

This is it? A year of effort put into this book, and now I can't publish it? It was as though her whole world had come crashing down.

I rebuilt my life around this book. I found joy and renewed strength to go on. Now what?

Bisschop Samuel's visit brought everything to a halt, and now Jenny was drifting aimlessly through her days. She prayed and sought the Lord, but in spite of her importuning, she was slipping back into the terrible depression that had filled the first days after Jonathan's accident. Then, a week after the meeting, she got a note from Jeremy.

> Dear Jenny,
>
> I have not heard from you in a week. What's happening with the book? I'm ready to do the edits so I can get it back to you for revisions. Can you please contact me and let me know what's up? I am eager to proceed.
>
> Jeremy

"What can I do, Mama?" she asked Jerusha. "He wants to finish the book, which is perfectly understandable, but I feel like he's been dishonest with me. I found out about his past in the most awkward way. It would have been much better if he and not *Bisschop* Lapp had told me he is under *meidung*."

"*Ja,* it was wrong of him. You must talk with him and tell him that, for now, the relationship must be put on hold."

Jenny was silent for a moment. "That's what troubles me, Mama. I don't want to put it on hold. I think…"

"What is it, *dochter*?"

When Jenny didn't respond, Jerusha asked, "Jenny, do you have feelings for this man?"

Jenny flushed beet red and then went cold again. She had sensed a certain desire to be with Jeremy, but it had never occurred to her she might be developing "feelings" for him. The thought stunned her.

"I…I don't know, Mama. I like Jeremy a lot. He's kind and considerate, and I'm grateful for his friendship. I guess it could be that I have feelings for him, but then there are things that speak against it."

"What would those be, Jenny?"

"First of all, I don't have the same kind of feelings I had when I met Jonathan. The first time Jonathan took my hand it was like being struck by lightning. And after I got to know him, I could only always think about him."

"And with Jeremy? What is that like?"

Jenny blushed again. "Mama, I don't want to burden you with… personal things."

Jerusha led Jenny to the kitchen table. "*Kumme, dochter, zetsen sie sich.*"

Jenny sat, wringing her hands. Jerusha placed her hands over Jenny's to still them.

"We may be Amish, but we're also women. We have feelings and desires, and it's all right to speak of them, just between us. Now…what about Jeremy?"

Jenny started out slowly. She trusted her mama, but still it was hard to share what was in her heart.

"It's not the same as with Jonathan. I like Jeremy, and I feel safe with him. He's very handsome and very pleasant. He likes me very much, maybe too much, and I can't help but respond to that."

"And what are the other things that speak against you being with Jeremy?"

"He's not Amish."

"But he *was* Amish, and if you two decided that *Gott* was putting you together, it would be a simple thing for him to repent of whatever he did to be shunned. We Amish are very forgiving."

"I've thought of that, Mama, but there's one more thing…actually, the biggest thing of all."

"Yes, Jenny?"

"I've never told anyone this before, but…I don't think I've ever really let go of my hope that Jonathan might still be alive."

Jenny saw the expression of surprise on Jerusha's face but went on anyway.

"I know Gerald told me that the explosion went right through the part of the boat where Jonathan was sitting with his father and that nobody could have survived. But, Mama, Gerald survived! And if he survived, maybe Jonathan did too."

Jenny put her face in her hands while Jerusha sat quietly. Then Jerusha spoke.

"Jenny, Jonathan has been gone for almost two years. He couldn't still be alive. You must reconcile yourself to that fact."

"Then why do I still feel so…so married, Mama? Why do I feel like he is always with me?"

Jerusha took her daughter's hand.

"You were given a very special gift when *Gott* gave you Jonathan. I remember telling you a time might come when you would meet a man whom you loved so deeply that you would gladly surrender everything of yourself into his care and protection."

"Yes, I remember when you told me that. And I especially remembered it when I knew that I had given my heart fully and forever to Jonathan. And that's the problem. I gave him my heart, and I can't seem to take it back. Even though he's gone, I can't break my promise to him. And that's my dilemma with Jeremy. I can't release my heart to another man. I don't think I ever can."

"Jenny, it will not be a sin if *Gott* brings another man for you to love. It won't be Jonathan. But if it happens, you can accept this man's love just as you accepted Jonathan's. *Gott* did not make man or woman to be alone."

"Then it must be that I'm just not ready yet. But when I'm with Jeremy, I miss the closeness I had with Jonathan. And I'm troubled by it. Perhaps it's a good thing if I don't see Jeremy anymore."

"Well then, if you really feel you're not ready, you must tell him. It's the only right thing to do."

Jenny sighed. "You are right, Mama. As always."

Jeremy looked at Jenny across the coffee-shop table. "You are forbidden to let me publish your book? Are you kidding? Are we back in the dark ages?"

"No, Jeremy, we're not in the dark ages. I'm Amish, and that's the way things are. You should have told me you are under the *bann*. It has made things very complicated for me. I really shouldn't even be here today, but I felt I needed to at least tell you what has happened."

"This is unbelievable. The Lancaster church has followed me here to Ohio and is imposing that ridiculous shunning on me again?"

"Jeremy, please tell me why you were shunned. I must know. Maybe it's not as serious as they made it seem, and you can go to them and repent. *Bisschop* Lapp wouldn't be able to keep you out of the church."

"Lapp? Do you mean Samuel Lapp?"

"Yes, he came here to help our *bisschop* start a new church in Dalton."

"So Samuel Lapp is behind this. I should have known. He's the only one who would know about me out here. He's the one who had me shunned—and unfairly so."

"Is that why you won't repent?"

"I won't repent of something I didn't do."

"Jeremy, you are speaking in riddles. You must tell me what happened."

Jeremy looked down at his hands and flexed them. Then he looked back at Jenny. "Samuel Lapp and I were in love with the same girl. She favored me. When we passed *rumspringa* and I was baptized, Sarah and I talked openly about beginning an official courtship. Lapp couldn't stand it. He got two of his toadies to swear with him that I was visiting…well, women of the evening."

"And were you?"

"Jenny, how can you ask that? Of course not. But Lapp got the men to swear before the elders. I think he had something on them and pressured them into it. The elders put me under the *bann* until I confessed and repented. I tried to defend myself, but the false witnesses would not recant. I wouldn't repent of something I didn't do. So they excommunicated me.

"After Lapp had me put out, he went to Sarah's father and asked to court her. His large landholdings and his position as the *bisschop*'s son swayed the man, and he consented. They were married, and that was that. I had no reason to return to the church, so I left Pennsylvania and came to Ohio and started Kerusso Publishing. And now that I've been out of the church for several years and had some success, I see no reason to return. I still love Christ, and I've found a way to glorify Him and help people come to a better understanding of Christianity and particularly the Amish church."

"A better understanding?"

"Yes, Jenny. For some reason the world thinks the Amish are a perfect people who live faultless lives away from the world. They've romanticized the whole Amish lifestyle. But I know from personal experience that the Amish have as many troubles as people out in the world. Many of them aren't even saved. They're religious, but they don't really know Christ. I want that for them, and I believe your book can help them. Your mother and father both had to find a saving relationship with Christ in order to endure the terrible ordeal of Jenna's death and everything that happened afterward. It's a wonderful story and needs to be told."

Jenny listened to the impassioned words pour out of Jeremy. She saw his heart for the first time and was drawn by what he was saying. Then to Jenny's surprise, Jeremy reached across the table and took her hand. She tried to pull her hand away for a moment, but he held it in a grip of steel and looked straight into her eyes.

"Jenny, there's something else. I've struggled with this for several months, and I don't know any other way to say it. I'm in love with you. I think you're the most beautiful woman I've ever seen. You're smart, full of life, and a brilliant writer. I know you're still sold on the Amish way of life, but I can't help that. I love you, Jenny, and I want to marry you."

A crushing weight gripped Jenny's heart. It was the moment she had dreaded and yet longed for. She felt a great struggle raging inside her. She missed the closeness of a married relationship. And yet….no, it could never be. *I am still Amish and he is not. He will not go back. If we were to be together, I would have to leave my church.*

She pulled her hand away and said, "Jeremy, I could almost surrender to you. Almost. But I can't go against who I am—I'm Amish. Beyond that, I'm not ready to fall in love again. I still love Jonathan. Even though he's been gone for two years, my heart is still his. It would not be right for me to give myself to you. You would always be playing second fiddle to Jonathan's memory. No, Jeremy, I can't marry you."

Jenny got up to leave.

"But then what about the book, Jenny?"

"I don't know, Jeremy. I will have to pray about that."

Then she turned and walked away.

Chapter Eighteen

The Quilt

◇◇◇

"WHAT IS HAPPENING TO ME, Mama?" Jenny cried. *Meine Leben wird alles verwechselt!* What is *Gott* doing?"

Jenny flopped down on the sofa in the front room of the Springer home. Jerusha stood in the kitchen doorway, a bemused expression on her face. "I take it the meeting with Jeremy was upsetting?"

"Upsetting? It was more than upsetting. I felt like I was in the middle of a hay baler—getting scooped up and tossed around and wrapped up and spit out. It was terrible."

Jerusha sighed.

"Mama, Jeremy asked me to marry him!"

"So you were right about his feelings for you."

"Yes, Mama. And he was so persuasive, it would have been so easy to just surrender and turn my life over to him. He's smart and successful, he could make a home for Rachel and me, and he would be a good husband."

"Did you find out why he is under the *meidung?*"

"Yes. According to Jeremy, the *bisschop* isn't the paragon of virtue he pretends to be."

"What?"

"If what Jeremy told me is true—and I do believe him—before Samuel Lapp was *bisschop,* he forced Jeremy out of the Lancaster church so he could marry the girl Jeremy was in love with. He lied about Jeremy and got some others to back him up. Jeremy is reconciled to what happened, but he won't repent of something he says he didn't do."

"If what you say is true, *ist es ein schreckliches Ding.*"

"Yes, it is terrible. I thought the Amish were different, but it seems we are not."

"You can't judge a whole church by one man's actions, Jenny."

"I know, but he's a *bisschop*! He should be an example. I didn't like him from the first moment he spoke, and I remember Papa had to control his anger at our meeting. For a moment, when he insulted you, I thought Papa was going to hit him."

"Yes, and *Bisschop* Lapp would not have fared too well. I have seen what Reuben can do to a man when he is protecting me."

Jenny looked at her mama in surprise. "You saw Papa hit someone?"

"It was a long time ago, Jenny. It was just after we met at my *grossmudder's* funeral. I was walking through the woods to the village, and two men accosted me. Just as they were about to pull me into the woods, Reuben appeared out of nowhere. Those men didn't stand a chance. Before I could even say a word, Reuben stretched them out on the ground."

"Papa did?"

"Yes, but I should not have said anything. You will think badly of him. He was very young and not in the church at the time. In fact, it was just before he went to be a soldier."

"I don't think badly of him, Mama. In fact, I think it's very romantic."

Jerusha smiled and blushed at the memory. "Yes, it was. I have never admitted that to anyone before, so please keep my secret. But go on about your meeting with Jeremy."

"There's not much more to say. The book is not going to be published, I hurt Jeremy's feelings by turning him down, and I've earned the enmity of a *bisschop* of our church. What else could go wrong? Mama, everything is all mixed up, and I don't know what to do."

Jerusha looked at Jenny thoughtfully for a moment. "*Kommen Sie mit mir,*" she said. Then she turned and walked back to her sewing room with Jenny following her.

Jerusha knelt down at the old cedar chest and opened it. She pulled out some pieces of fabric and batting and laid them aside until she got to the bottom. She took out a package wrapped in brown paper and tied with string, setting it to one side. Then she put everything back into the chest and closed it.

"Is that the quilt?" Jenny asked.

"*Ja*, it is," Jerusha replied. "The story of the Springer family seems to be sewn into this quilt, and I wanted us to look at it again. Maybe we can find some perspective in the midst all of this *wahnsinn.*"

Jerusha unwrapped the package reverently. Inside was the magnificent Rose of Sharon quilt. She unfolded it and laid it out on the floor. The beautiful red silk rose glowed in the morning light streaming in through the window. The lovely royal blue background was set off perfectly by the cream-colored backing. The double layer of batting inside was thick and warm.

"Mama, it's so beautiful. It's the nicest quilt you ever made."

"*Ja*, it is, but I had a great deal of help with this quilt. Even when I was making it, *du lieber Gott* was leading me. I thought I was making it for Jenna, but it was for you."

"I wish I would have known Jenna. I always wanted a sister."

"I don't know why *Gott* didn't give us more children. I think it's because He wanted us to concentrate on you. And He was so gracious to tell us the story of your life through the quilt. I wish I had been more attentive to His prompting when you were young. I almost missed what He was trying to show me about you. The whole time you were growing up, the quilt was right in front of my eyes. *Du lieber Gott* kept trying to use it to show me about your life, but it was like I was deaf and dumb. You were so much a part of us from the first day I found you that I didn't even think about the possibility that you came to us wounded and in need of healing."

"But you finally saw when I was in danger?"

"*Ja.* It was so important for you to find your birth mother, but Reuben and I didn't understand. We just thought you had gotten a crazy idea into your head and were being very stubborn about it."

"Well, it's not like I wasn't stubborn in those days."

"*Ja*, you were, Jenny. And I'm grateful that you were. If you hadn't been so stubborn, you would have given up your search, and your life would be very different."

"And the Lord showed you about my life by using the quilt as a picture you could understand?"

"*Ja*, and that's why I've gotten it out today. Something about this quilt is so special. It's not like any other I have made. The materials I used are definitely not the Amish way. We would never use such worldly fabric. But I was going to leave the church, so when I found the red and blue silk, my pride and stubbornness overcame what wisdom I might have had, and I used it in the quilt. If I had actually gotten to display it at the Dalton fair that year, it would have caused *viel klatsch* among the women of our village."

Jenny took the quilt in her hands and turned it over, inspecting each part. "And then you ruined it when you rescued me. But see! You have repaired it so wonderfully that I can't even see where the damage was."

Jerusha pointed to a small, almost invisible stain near the border between the blue and the cream. "Here there was a very large stain."

She turned up a corner and pointed to a barely visible serpentine stitch. "And here I had to replace the batting I tore out to start the fire that saved us, and then I had to restitch this whole corner."

Jenny looked closely, but only when Jerusha actually put her finger on the repaired place did she see it.

"This was where I started to repair—inside, in the secret place of the quilt. I remember exactly what He said to me. 'My substance was not hid from thee, when I was made in secret, and curiously wrought in the lowest parts of the earth.'

"The Lord knew that in the inner part of you, a wound had to be healed. That was why it was so important for you to find Mama Rachel. Without knowing your Amish roots, you would never have come to know the Lord as you have. And Jonathan would never have given his life to the Lord. And there's one more thing. When I was repairing the quilt, I found that I could think of Jenna without pain. As I remembered her, there was only joy. So *Gott* was healing me too."

Jenny thought for a moment and then asked, "So you're saying that *Gott* knew I came from an Amish family, and that was why He put me with you? So that I would understand who I really was when I finally discovered the truth?"

"*Ja*, Jenny. And then He blessed you by bringing you back to *Grossdaadi* Borntraeger and giving you the farm."

"The quilt is wonderful, but where are we going with all this, Mama? I'm still confused."

"Jenny, I'm thinking that if *Gott* showed us a picture of your life in this quilt, the story didn't stop when you found Jonathan and your *grossdaadi*. Somehow I feel your story is not yet finished."

"And that's why my story is about the Rose of Sharon quilt?"

"I think so. I don't know whether the book will ever be published, but I'm sure you must finish it. Look here."

Jerusha pointed at the red rose in the center of the quilt. It was perfectly sewn, with not a pucker or a wrinkle anywhere.

"One hundred and twenty silk rose petals are sewed together to make the rose. This was the hardest part. Each one had to be sewn in such a way that it's impossible to see where one stops and another starts. I think our lives are the same way. Each moment in our life is sewn to the next one in such a way that we feel only the days and years going by. But *Gott* sees each moment and each connection as complete and separate events."

"You know," Jenny replied, "I haven't looked at it that way in a long time, but I understood it once. Wait a moment."

Jenny hurried down the hall to her room. She picked up the box that held her letters to Jonathan and searched for the one she wanted. When she found it, she went back to the sewing room. Jerusha was sitting in her chair, and Jenny curled up at her feet.

"This is part of a letter I wrote to Jonathan before we began courting. Let me read it to you."

I want to thank you, my dearest, for helping me to locate my *grossdaadi*. Finding him has put a seal on my life. The questions are all answered, the journey is over, and all the fear is gone. Now I finally know the truth. I am Amish, I have always been Amish, and I always will be. And now I will marry an Amish man, and my life will flow on in the unending ways of our people.

It's like the quilt my mama made for Jenna, the one she wrapped me in to save me so many years ago. Every piece of the quilt fits together in a perfect pattern, and none of it is haphazard or unplanned. Every color means something, and the whole quilt tells a story.

So it is with my life. God has always been with me, and He has always been with you. All the pieces of our lives were planned before we were born, and God has fitted them together perfectly, every stitch in place and every piece in perfect relationship with the one next to it.

And now I wait for the day when we can begin courting and the story of our lives will be complete and whole. I love you, Jonathan, and I always will. I wait now with peace and great joy in my heart for the day when we will be married.

"*Ja*, and the story does not stop with Jonathan's death, my *dochter*," Jerusha said. "It goes on until you die. You don't know which pieces you will discover tomorrow, but they are there, already determined by *die Vorkenntnisse des Gottes*. He has already planned them. Now let me show you one more thing as a reminder."

Jerusha moved the quilt until the rose was under her hand. "Look! Do you see it?"

Jenny looked but couldn't see what her mama was pointing at. And then she remembered and looked closer. There it was! In the center of the rose, a small key-shaped piece of red silk was so finely stitched that it was almost invisible.

"*Ja*, Jenny, a key. The Lord had me add it to the quilt so that we would always remember—"

"That He is the key to our lives, and without Him we cannot hope to comprehend what is happening to us and why?"

"*Ja*, Jenny, and if you put your life into His hands, He will guide your path, and you will understand everything."

"I had forgotten all about the key." Jenny looked more closely at it.

"It's the strangest thing. Mama, did you know that Rachel has a key-shaped birthmark right above her heart? She's had it since the day she was born, and it's almost the same color as the rose. That makes me think I was wrong in what I wrote to Jonathan. Maybe *Gott* is still speaking to us through the quilt. Perhaps the journey is not over after all. In fact, we may be coming to a new beginning. That's a hopeful thought."

Chapter Nineteen

The Journals of Jenny Hershberger

◇◇◇

FOR JENNY, THE FOLLOWING DAYS were filled with much soul-searching and contemplation. The questions came rushing at her heart like hailstones in a driving wind. What was *Gott* doing? What about Jeremy? What about the book? And the other books that lay unwritten in the recesses of her heart—what about them? How did the quilt fit into everything that was happening? Was *Gott* using it the way He had with her mama? What was He trying to show her?

At the end of a week, she realized that she had never felt such an intense need to write, and it became clear to her that she was to tell the stories of her family. As she looked back at all that had happened to her and everything she had learned, she began to sense that this was the task that had always been ordained for her. So as the first snow began to fall and Apple Creek fell into the slumber of winter, Jenny Hershberger began the work that would become a lifelong endeavor.

December 6, 1980

Slowly and softly the flakes drift past my window. The cold December wind is bitter, and the trees groan with the weight of the freshly fallen snow, their naked branches lifted like the arms of starving men. At times, the pale moon peers through the stream of clouds as though through cracks in the night. The storm rumbles across the unmoving heavens, and weary travelers look to these broken fragments of moonlight to light the way home. As I watch the night sky, I remember how Jonathan described the *Ordnung* of our faith. He said it is like the stars that guide sailors at night on a dark sea.

Gott has set me on a journey, and I am sailing a dark sea. I will need the boundaries of my faith to keep me on course, but I must be sure that I listen for His voice and let His Word be a light unto my path. I see now that my whole life has resolved to this one pinpoint of time. A door has opened, and if I step through, I think I will find a strange, wonderful way set before me. And as I set sail, let all that I do or say bring glory to Him.

Jenny took up her unfinished book and began to go through it, making revisions and changes. She tried to remember what Jeremy had taught her about editing, but it was a grueling process. Even though she wanted to spend all her time writing, she had her part to play in the family. She had Rachel to care for and everyday tasks to do. After a few weeks, though, she settled into a routine. Reuben got up every day at four to care for the stock and do the chores. Jenny got up with him and made coffee, and together they went out to tend the farm. Jenny loved these cold winter mornings with Reuben. They didn't say much but worked quietly, tending the cows and feeding the chickens.

When the sun peeked over the eastern hills, Jenny went into the house. Jerusha had Rachel up for school, and the three of them fixed breakfast. When it was ready, Rachel fetched her *grossdaadi*, and they ate their morning meal together. Once Rachel was off to school, Jenny went to her room for two hours of writing.

Often Jerusha stopped by Jenny's door to listen to the clacking of the typewriter keys and lift a prayer for her *dochter*. Sometimes there would be long periods of silence. Once she heard Jenny exclaim, "*Du Schlecht'r!*" followed by the sounds of a sheet of paper being torn roughly from the typewriter and wadded into a ball.

Jerusha called through the door to her daughter. "Jenny Hershberger! You should not use bad words!"

There was a moment of silence, and then Jenny answered. "Yes, Mama. I'll be more careful."

Jerusha smiled and went on about her day. After two hours, Jenny came out of her room, and the two women spent the day cleaning, baking, preparing meals, or washing clothes. When Rachel came home, Jenny sat with her to go over what she had learned in school.

As the weeks and months passed, Jenny found a deep and quiet rhythm settling into her life. Time was no longer measured in minutes and hours but in days and sunsets and the cycles of the fields and the farm. She was connected to the land and the land was forever. She began to see deeply into the ways of her people, and there was comfort and safety in her connection to the Plain way. Her family was like a living history of the Amish. In it she saw the past and the future— recorded in the unending cycle of work and rest. She drew strength from her mama and papa, and they encouraged her to unveil the gift God had placed within her.

◇◇◇

"Whew!" Jenny said, letting out a sigh. "I'm almost finished with my revisions. Only six chapters to go. It's been *sehr schwierig*, but I've learned so much."

"What will you do now that the book is almost finished?" Jerusha asked from her seat on the couch. "You are still under the *bisschop*'s instruction not to publish it."

"I don't know. I'm not sure if it will ever be published. Right now I might simply be creating a legacy for Rachel and her children and for our people. I'm filling my journals with stories of our family, and as I write them, I've started to uncover the deep reality of my own faith. There is great peace in being part of a way of life that has flowed unchanged for centuries."

Jenny rose and stood in front of the fireplace. Her face became animated as she began to share her dreams with her mother.

"I've been praying a lot about what to do next, and I think I'm ready to write Jonathan's story. If I can just put it down on paper, I'm sure I'll find solace and comfort in it. You know, Mama, writing is almost like talking to someone about your problems. I know I share with you, but when I'm putting it down on paper, I seem to clear my mind of the things troubling me."

"Your papa and I have seen the healing come since you began your journals. That's why we encourage you to go on. You have written more besides the book?"

"Yes, Mama. Sometimes when the words don't come so easy, I just stop and write what's in my heart. I also have notebooks filled with different things I discovered when I was working at the library. And I have the study I did about our family when I was still in *schule*. They're like a treasure box full of rare and precious things, and as I read them again and again, always they inspire me. I feel as if I have the whole history of our family inside me—all the way back to Switzerland and even earlier. It's like I've already written it, and the story is just waiting for me to set the words free."

Jerusha looked at her daughter and smiled. Jenny had changed so much in the past few years. She was her own woman, strong and beautiful, and Jerusha knew that the fires of her trials had refined her as pure gold.

◇◇◇

Dr. Schaeffer came into the room with Bobby and a nurse.

"Bobby!" Jerusha said. "I know you had something to do with finding me. Thank you."

"If it wasn't for Bobby, you wouldn't be alive today," Reuben said.

Bobby took Jerusha's hand. "I'm grateful to God that I was able to help," he said.

Jerusha and Reuben looked at each other and smiled.

Dr. Schaeffer came to the bedside, peered over his glasses, and said, "Well, one of our patients is doing better, I see."

"One of our patients?" Jerusha asked.

"Well, there's this one too. She came in with you."

Dr. Schaeffer pointed to a smaller bed pulled up next to Jerusha's. A little girl lay in the bed. Her eyes were open and she lay looking at Jerusha solemnly.

"You found me," she said to Jerusha. "I was lost, and you found me."

Jerusha stared at the little girl. For a moment she thought it was Jenna. But it couldn't be Jenna. Jenna was gone. And then she remembered everything—the storm, the wrecked car, the cabin. She remembered God's healing touch and holding this little girl through the long nights.

The child started to try to get out of bed, to move to Jerusha's bed, but Dr. Schaeffer moved forward. "I don't think—"

Bobby tapped him on the shoulder. "I think I just heard a nurse calling you, Doctor. They need you in the ICU."

The doctor looked at Bobby and then at Reuben and then to Jerusha and the little girl.

"Yes, I believe you're right. I'll be on my way." He turned and left.

Reuben walked around to the little girl and picked her

up. He placed her in the bed beside Jerusha. Jerusha took the little one into her arms.

"What's your name, darling?" she asked softly.

"My name is Jenny."

Reuben and Jerusha looked at each other in amazement, and then tears began to flow down Jerusha's cheeks. She pulled Jenny close against her breast.

"*Thank You, O my Lord! Thank You.*"

Reuben knelt beside the bed and took them both into his strong arms. And though the wind blew and the storm raged outside, inside their hearts it was spring in Apple Creek.

Jenny stopped typing. She was finished with the final revision. The story of Jerusha and Reuben, of Jenna and Jenny was complete. As she read the words, Jenny knew a chapter of her life was closing. A strange foreboding came over her, as though something had left her life that she would never find again.

CHAPTER TWENTY

Jeremy

◇◇◇

JENNY STOOD ON THE STEP leading up to the Wooster library, reading a letter from Jeremy.

> Dear Jenny,
>
> I need to talk to you about the book. I have a proposal I would like to go over with you. Please meet me at the Wooster library on Thursday of this week at three p.m. I promise I will only talk business.
>
> Your friend,
> Jeremy

Jenny started up the stairs and then turned around and went back down. She stopped and turned. Indecision rooted her to the spot.

What am I doing here? Jeremy is under the bann. *But I want to see him. I miss him!*

She took a deep breath, ordered her feet to move, climbed the stairs, and went through the front door.

Jeremy King stood in the lobby, smiling. "That was a real battle for you, wasn't it?"

"What?"

"I've been standing by the door watching you trying to decide whether you should come in. Does Samuel Lapp really hold that much power?"

Jenny blushed. "Actually it's not about *Bisschop* Lapp, if you must know."

"What was it then?"

Jeremy's smile was getting under Jenny's skin.

"And I don't like you laughing at me," she said. *I never should have come here. This is just going to mean trouble.*

"Jenny, you're a strange little thing. I'm not laughing at you. Now, let's just go over to the coffee shop and get a cup of coffee. I promise to be on my best behavior."

"All right, Jeremy, but I can't stay long."

They walked in silence to the café around the corner. It was crowded, and they took a table in the back.

Jenny got right to the point. "So, what do you want to talk about?"

Jeremy frowned. "Okay, have it your way—no small talk." He took a breath. "Here's my proposal. You already know I think your book is terrific. I think it could be a best seller. Interest in fiction about the Amish is growing, and I know the book could do well. If it troubles you to be an Amish woman writing fiction, you could publish it under a different name—what they call a pen name."

"I know what a pen name is, Jeremy."

Jeremy looked straight into her eyes. His gaze was so piercing that she had to look down at the table.

"Look, Jenny, let's just get something clear," he said. "I only want the best for you. I have no ulterior motives. You've made it clear where we stand romantically, and I'm fine with that. But can't we at least be friends? I would never do anything to hurt you, so you don't have to be defensive or short with me. Please."

Jeremy's directness was like a slap in the face, and Jenny relented.

"You're right, Jeremy. I shouldn't be short with you. You've only always been kind and helpful to me. You *are* my friend. I'll be nice. It's just my way sometimes when I am trying to sort things out."

"What are you sorting out?"

Jenny looked up into his eyes again. "Well, if we're going to be direct, then I'll tell you. I'm sorting out my feelings about you. I told you I wouldn't marry you, but I'm still conflicted by your proposal. You're a wonderful man, and you would be the answer to most women's dreams. You're kind, considerate, articulate, and generous. You've made a place for yourself in the world, and you could offer a woman happiness and security. But for me, there is more to it."

"Jenny—"

"You asked, so let me finish while I'm able, all right?"

Jeremy nodded.

"I've been writing a lot since we last spoke. I've been doing a lot of research and digging deeply into my Amish roots. In the process it's as though I've come to the bedrock of my faith. And I discovered something about being Amish I never realized before."

Jenny took a deep breath.

"Jeremy, it's a good thing that we do. The Amish people may not be perfect, but the premise behind the Amish way is a good one. You've left the Amish faith and have chosen not to return. That for me is the most important thing. I love my faith. I can't leave the church, even if I'm drawn to you, and…the truth is, Jeremy, I *am* drawn to you."

"You…you could care for me, Jenny?" Jeremy's eyes opened wide. "But what about Jonathan?"

"That's the other thing. I had a wonderful life with Jonathan. Even though I do care for you, I wouldn't be honest if I told you that my feelings for you are the same as they were for my husband. He was my first love. I thought we would grow old together. When he died, I had no way to come to grips with the loss. He went out to sea on a boat, the boat exploded, and that was that. No body laid out in the front room, no funeral, no grave. It's like he just vanished without a word and left me here with no answers."

"I understand that, Jenny," Jeremy said. "And if you accept my proposal, I could live with that. Thank you for being honest with me. Now let me ask you something."

"What?"

"Suppose I told you that I might be able to go back to the church?"

"But you said you would never repent of something you didn't do."

"I wouldn't have to repent if I could prove my innocence."

"Jeremy, what are you saying?"

He opened his briefcase and pulled out an envelope. "This came to my office a few days ago. It's from one of the men who falsely accused me in Lancaster. He's had a change of heart and wants to confess his part in Samuel Lapp's treachery. He's willing to testify before the elders."

"Jeremy! That's wonderful! I…"

And then the reality of what Jeremy was saying hit Jenny. *If he were back in the church, I would have no reason not to marry him!*

Suddenly Jenny's emotions were in turmoil. "When will you be able to work this out?" she asked.

Jeremy put the letter away and took Jenny's hands. "If everything goes well I should be able to meet with the elders next week."

"Next week?" Suddenly the choice being set before her was almost too much for Jenny to bear. She wanted to run away, far away. She wanted to hide and put all this away from her mind.

"I don't know what to say, Jeremy."

"What needs to be said? If all goes well, you and I would be free to begin courting in a month."

"But what about your publishing business?"

"I wouldn't have to give up publishing. Amish people run all kinds of businesses—manufacturing, retail stores, builders…there are even Amish accountants. Being a publisher wouldn't keep me from being Amish. I would just concentrate on the Amish community. And your book could be our star."

"Star?"

"Yes, Jenny. I believe in you, and I believe in this book. So that takes me back to my first suggestion. We could publish it under another name—even a man's name if you like—and you could remain just plain Jenny. You could keep doing what you love, I could do the same, and we could get your books out where they could do some good."

"I don't know what you mean by 'do some good,' Jeremy."

"Look, Jenny. I've been doing some research of my own. There haven't been many Amish fiction books published, but the ones that are out there have done quite well. I wondered about that, and I have my opinion about why that's so. I think people outside the church are interested in the Amish way because we offer something the world doesn't have—peace. We're not caught up in the hustle and bustle of the world. We live a plain and simple life, we're tied to the land, and we have an identity that goes back for centuries. Most people today move around so much they have no roots. They no longer live where they grew up, miles divide families, and the sense of community is gone. If they could read about a life that brings them back to the simple things, I think it would become a huge market, and we would be positioned to go with it."

"Go with it?" Jenny asked.

"Yes, Jenny, we could be part of something that could make us very wealthy."

Jenny looked at Jeremy across the table. Her emotions began to calm, and suddenly she saw things very clearly.

"I never thought about having a big success, Jeremy. And now that you put it so clearly, I'm not sure this is what I want for my books.

I'm Jenny Hershberger. I'm an Amish woman. I love the Plain way. Wouldn't that kind of success just take away our peace? Wouldn't we become like those who are out there in the world?"

"And isn't that a very old-fashioned way to look at it?" Jeremy patted her hand. "Jesus said we would be in the world even though we're not of the world. I think we could work it out. Just trust me in this, Jenny. Let me do this for you."

Jenny felt like he was patronizing her. *Am I willing to sacrifice everything I love just to have a man in my life? Do I really want fame and fortune? What about Rachel? Can we raise her in the Amish way if we have so much money?*

Jeremy kept pressing his point. "What do you say, Jenny? If I can get reinstated in the church, are you willing to consider what I'm asking—about the book and our relationship?"

Jenny looked at him for a long moment, collecting herself. Then finally she spoke.

"This is very sudden, Jeremy. I had reconciled myself to the fact that you and I could never be together. And I had given up on the book ever being published. Now you tell me that you can probably go back to the church and you still want to publish the book. I need to pray about all of this, and I need to talk to someone."

"Your parents?"

"No, I need to talk to Jonathan."

Jeremy and Jenny hadn't noticed the man sitting at the table in a far corner of the room. He had been watching them intently. Now he finished his coffee, put some money on the table, and walked out of the shop. He walked down the street to the row of telephone booths in front of the library. He stepped inside, put in a quarter, and dialed a number. After a few rings, someone answered on the other end of the line.

"Yes?"

"Can you get in touch with *Bisschop* Lapp?"

"Yes...who is this?"

"Matthew Bender. I'm a friend of the *bisschop*. I saw the Hershberger woman in Wooster today, and I followed her. She is with Jeremy King."

"Jenny Hershberger?"

"Yes. They met at the coffee shop, and they were holding hands."

"Thank you. I'll make sure he gets the message. "

CHAPTER TWENTY-ONE

Trouble

◇◇◇

"I NEED SOME TIME ALONE, Jeremy. And there's still the matter of your *bann*. Until that's settled I need to be careful. We shouldn't be seen together. I don't want to complicate things any further."

Jeremy understood. Jenny left the shop and went to the bus stop. She felt trapped, and she knew why. A choice she had never wanted to make had been thrust upon her.

Why couldn't he just leave it alone? If he's allowed back in the church, I can't use his bann as an excuse. I will have to deal with my feelings, and I don't want to.

The troubling thoughts turned over and over in Jenny's mind all during the bus ride home. When she got off the bus in Apple Creek, she had barely walked a block toward home when a car pulled up next to her.

The windows were darkened, so she couldn't see who was inside. Then to her surprise the back door opened and Samuel Lapp got out.

"*Bisschop* Lapp—what are you doing here?"

The stout little man ignored her question and instead said, "I thought I forbade you to see the apostate, Jeremy King. But I see you are continuing your relationship with him."

"How do you know that?"

"I have my ways. And now it will give me great pleasure to put you under a *bann* also. You have violated a direct order of the church."

"Why are you making trouble for us? We've done nothing to you."

"You have flouted the church's decision to shun Jeremy King. In addition, you have continued to pursue the notion of writing fiction books. The whole idea of an Amish woman writing dime-store novels is an affront to the faith and a reproach to our church. I suspect this defiance of yours comes from your upbringing. Your father strikes me as a very temperamental man. I think maybe he did not truly repent of his violent ways when he came back to the church. I'm sure we can find a way to deal with that."

Jenny couldn't help what came out of her mouth next. "You, *Bisschop*, are the one who needs to be disciplined. You are an evil man. Jeremy King is not the apostate—you are. You had him thrown out of the church so you could marry the girl he loved and who loved him. He knows the truth, and he can prove it. He's going to expose you."

Lapp's face paled. "What do you mean?" he demanded.

Jenny knew she had said more than she should, but she couldn't stop herself now. "One of your false witnesses is going to recant. You will be the one who is thrown out. You will lose everything."

Lapp grabbed Jenny's arm. His steel grip caused her to wince in pain.

"What are you talking about?"

"Get your hands off me!" Jenny cried. Before she could stop herself, she slapped his face.

Lapp's face contorted and he raged, "How dare you slap me!"

He drew back his fist and hit Jenny, knocking her to the ground.

"*Bisschop* Lapp! What are you doing?" Two men climbed out of the car and rushed over to Lapp as he stood over Jenny, shaking with rage. The two men grabbed him and pulled him back.

"Samuel, are you mad? You are a *bisschop*. Do you know what you have done? She will tell the elders."

Jenny climbed slowly to her feet. A trickle of blood ran from the corner of her mouth, but she wasn't afraid.

"You're a contemptible human being, Samuel Lapp. *Sie sind ein Lügner und ein Hund*. Your friends are right—I will go to the elders." Jenny turned to walk away.

"Wait, Mrs. Hershberger!" the *bisschop* called after her. "You must know I didn't mean to do that. I don't know what got into me."

Jenny turned. "I think you know very well what got into you. You are no more than a wolf in sheep's clothing. And we have just seen the wolf in full display."

Lapp's fear turned again to rage. "Do you think your word will stand against mine?" he hissed. "These witnesses will swear that you attacked me. I can ruin you! You had better not say anything, or it will go hard for you."

Jenny turned and walked away. She could hear Lapp calling after her, but she looked straight ahead. Only when she turned into the lane leading to her papa's house did she finally burst into tears.

Jenny sat at the kitchen table with Jerusha. Her mouth was swollen, and there was a large bruise on the side of her face. Jerusha reached over with the cold wet cloth and gently wiped Jenny's mouth. Jenny grimaced at the pain.

"I cannot believe that an Amish man hit you, much less a *bisschop! Es ist außer dem Verständnis*...beyond comprehension!"

Just then they heard the door open, and Reuben came into the house. He walked into the kitchen, and when he saw the look on Jerusha's face, he said, "What's happened?"

Before Jesusha could answer, he saw the bruise on Jenny's face. "What...?" he asked

"I was hit."

Reuben's eyes went cold. "Who did this?"

Jenny looked at Jerusha. Jerusha nodded. "Papa, it was Samuel Lapp."

"What! The *bisschop*? What would make him do such a thing?"

"I told him that Jeremy was going to expose him as a liar before the Lancaster elders. He grabbed my arm, and I was so angry I slapped his face. That's when he knocked me down."

Reuben's voice grew very quiet. "He hit you in the face?"

"Yes, Papa."

Jenny saw a look on her papa's face that she had only seen once before—when Samuel Lapp insulted Jerusha. But now there was something else in his eyes, and it frightened her. It was death.

"Where is he now?" Reuben asked.

"I don't know, Papa. He was riding in a big black car with two other Amish men and their driver. They stopped me out on the street. I left them there after it happened."

Reuben didn't say anything, but he got up and walked out of the house. In a few minutes he was back from Henry's.

"Henry will drive us to *Bisschop* Johann's house. We must deal with this matter right away."

"But, Papa, he said he would have his two friends lie and say I attacked him. He said he would ruin me."

"Jenny, you will come with me to see Johann. We will see who is the liar."

"I'm coming too, Reuben," Jerusha said.

"What about Rachel?"

"We will be home before she returns from *schule*."

Just then Henry's car pulled in the driveway.

"Papa, I don't want to make trouble for you," Jenny said.

Reuben put his hands on Jenny's shoulders and looked into her eyes. "*Dochter*, we must stand for what is right. If Lapp gets away with this, he will continue in his evil ways when he leaves. Who knows how many have been hurt or compromised by his unchristian behavior. No, he must be exposed."

When they arrived at Johann's house, several buggies with horses were tied up outside. Reuben went to the door and knocked while the two women stood behind him. *Bisschop* Troyer came to the door and ushered them in. When they walked into the living room, *Bisschop* Lapp was in an animated conversation with several men. Jenny recognized the two men who had been with Lapp in the car. As soon as Reuben walked into the room, Lapp crowded behind his two henchmen.

"See here, he brings his daughter to accuse me when it is her who should be accused!"

The little man was agitated, and the tic in his face was pronounced. Reuben tried to push through the men to confront him, but Johann stood in his way. "Reuben, you must not resort to violence."

The look on Reuben's face was grim. "I don't want to hurt him. I only want to have the truth told. This man assaulted my daughter. He must answer for it. There will be grace enough later, after he confesses. Jenny, tell Johann what happened."

Jenny stepped forward and faced Lapp. "I was on my way home. Samuel Lapp drove up in a car and got out to accuse me of violating a church order by seeing Jeremy King. I said some things that made him angry. When he grabbed my arm and hurt me, I slapped his face. Then he hit me and knocked me down."

"She's lying," Lapp hissed. "I only wanted to talk to her about Jeremy King, and she assaulted me with no provocation. These two men will bear me witness."

"Tell Johann what you said to Samuel Lapp that made him so angry," Reuben interjected.

Jenny looked at Reuben, who nodded at her. "I…I told him that I knew he had falsely accused Jeremy King so that Jeremy would be placed under the *bann*. He did it so he could marry the girl Jeremy loved. I told him that one of his false witnesses had contacted Jeremy and was willing to recant. *Bisschop* Lapp became furious."

"That is a lie!" Lapp pointed to the two men with him. "These are the two men who testified in that case, and they were there today. They will back me up."

He turned to the men. "Tell them."

One of the men stepped forward. "*Ja,* what the *bisschop* says about this woman is true. She assaulted him for no reason."

Lapp looked at the second man, who stood with his hat in his hands, nervously shifting his weight from one foot to the other.

"Tell them," he said.

The man looked around him with desperate eyes. He clearly wanted to leave. Reuben stepped toward him and spoke.

"Do you have something to say in this matter?"

The man looked at Reuben and then at Samuel Lapp. Lapp's face had a dark look that did not bode well for the man, but the look on Reuben's face was even more frightening. Finally he gave up the struggle and spoke.

"I cannot support the *bisschop* on this anymore. I am the one who contacted Jeremy King. I told Jeremy that I testified falsely against him because *Bisschop* Lapp holds a note on my land and threatened to call it in if I did not do as he wished. Jeremy King is innocent. As far as Mrs. Hershberger is concerned, *Bisschop* Lapp told me he was going to take care of the Springer family because they were too worldly. He instigated the confrontation with Mrs. Hershberger. Samuel Lapp is the one who is lying."

Lapp's face grew red. "I will have your farm for this," he hissed.

"Do what you will. I just want the truth to be told."

The men in the room looked at each other with astonishment. They couldn't believe that a *bisschop* could resort to such deceitful ways. Johann Troyer looked at Samuel Lapp.

"Never in all my days in the church have I heard such a story. To think that an Amish *bisschop* might be party to such underhanded ways is beyond my comprehension. Unfortunately, we have two witnesses with conflicting testimony, so we will need to call a formal meeting of the elders and look further into these allegations. As for Jenny…"

"As for Jenny!" Lapp shouted. "As for Jenny! As for this woman who accuses me and yet all the while she is writing this filth—war and violence and embracing and kissing! It's disgusting! Married to an *Englischer* who pretended to adopt our ways!"

Jenny started to say something, but before she could, her *daed* moved past her. Reuben took the little man by the lapels of his black jacket and lifted him so he was standing on his toes. Reuben looked into his eyes, and every man in the room felt the intensity of his words.

"If you say one more word, I promise you will regret it."

The men in the room moved to lay hold of Reuben before he could do violence. They pulled him away from Lapp, who then pointed at Reuben and said, "Look at you! You're ready to kill me. You are a violent man who does not belong in the Amish church. And you permit your daughter to write sacrilegious books and associate with men who are shunned."

Lapp looked around at the Apple Creek men. "You may have the upper hand here, but I'm the one with influence in Pennsylvania. I'm leaving now, but I'm not finished with you."

He turned to Johann. "My driver has not returned, so I need your buggy. I will leave it where I am staying, pick up my things, and go back to Pennsylvania."

"*Ja,* you may take my buggy," Johann said. "I will come for it this evening. But there is the matter of your violence against Jenny Hershberger. That act alone calls for immediate discipline. I adjure you to remain until we have made a final decision."

"If you want to restrain me forcefully, you can do so," Lapp said. "Otherwise, I am leaving now and returning to Lancaster."

He moved through the group of men. No one raised a hand against him. At the door he motioned to his one remaining follower, who went outside to get Johann's buggy. Lapp turned to speak. "You have not heard the last of me, Reuben Springer."

Chapter Twenty-Two

Tragedy

◇◇◇

After Samuel Lapp left, the men in the room looked at each other in amazement. None of them had ever seen anything like what they had just witnessed.

"I am sorry to have been part of that," Reuben said at last. "Perhaps Lapp was right. Perhaps I haven't fully dealt with the violence in my heart."

Johann stepped over to Reuben and put his hand on his shoulder. "*Nein, Bruder* Reuben. You showed remarkable restraint. It was the *bisschop* who revealed his true colors today. And he is right. If he leaves for Pennsylvania, we can do nothing. I will write a letter to the church there, but I'm not sure it will do much good."

Another man spoke to Reuben. "We all deal with anger and rage at some time, Reuben. We would be liars to say we didn't. You were angry with Lapp, but you did not sin. We know you to be a good and kind man. Don't think badly of yourself for wanting to defend your daughter."

The other men nodded.

Reuben thanked them and took Jerusha and Jenny outside, where

Henry was waiting for them. They climbed into the car and headed back toward the village. As they drove down the street toward the train tracks, they saw some people running along the sidewalk. Ahead, the lights at the crossing were flashing red, but something was wrong with the crossbar. As Henry pulled up, they saw *Bisschop* Troyer's buggy laying on its side. The harness had tangled around the horse's legs, and the animal had fallen and was thrashing in the street. The crossbar had come down right on top of the buggy, knocking it over and breaking the bar. In the distance they could hear the whistle of the approaching train.

Reuben sprang into action. "Henry—help me! Jerusha—you and Jenny wait here."

Reuben jumped from the car and ran to the buggy. The top was crushed, and Lapp was trapped in the back. Lapp appeared to be stunned. His driver had managed to crawl away from the wreckage before he collapsed, and he was now lying motionless a few feet away.

"Henry, have you got an axe or a hatchet? I've got to cut this away."

"I've got one in the trunk, Reuben!"

Henry hurried back to the car while Reuben struggled to pull Samuel Lapp free of the wreckage. He had him halfway out when Lapp's eyes opened and he saw that he was in Reuben's powerful grip.

"Don't kill me, Springer!" he cried, as he tried to wrench himself free. His frantic movements broke him loose from the buggy, and he rolled into the street. He rose unsteadily to his feet and shouted to the people that were gathered around.

"He's trying to kill me!"

Lapp grabbed Reuben's arms and tried to hold him.

"Let go of me, you fool! We've got to get the horse free!" Reuben cried.

Reuben shoved Lapp so hard that he sprawled on his back. A look of rage and fear came over Lapp's face. Reuben turned his attention to the horse.

"Henry! The hatchet! Now!"

They heard the whistle of the approaching train—much closer this time.

Behind Reuben, Samuel Lapp looked around. A support from the buggy's top was lying in the street. He snatched it up and swung it hard down on Reuben's back. Stunned, Reuben fell forward onto the horse. The frantic animal beneath him lashed out with its feet and knocked Reuben unconscious. Henry, his head in the trunk as he tried to find the hatchet, didn't see what was happening.

"Reuben!" Jerusha screamed.

Before Jenny could stop her, Jerusha jumped from the car and ran to Reuben's side. She tried to pull him away from the tracks, but he was tangled in the harness, and she couldn't lift him. The engineer had applied the train's brakes, but it was obvious to onlookers that it wouldn't be able to stop in time, and the few who had approached to help now backed away in horror as the train bore down. Jenny jumped from the car and ran toward her parents.

"Mama!" Jenny shrieked.

Jenny sat in the waiting room at Wooster Community Hospital with Henry Lowenstein, both in a state of shock. After the accident, paramedics had arrived and pulled Reuben and Jerusha from the mangled wreckage and loaded them into an ambulance.

Jenny and Henry had followed the ambulance to the hospital and watched helplessly as Reuben and Jerusha were rushed into the ICU. Now they were waiting for a report from the doctors.

Just then the swinging doors of the ER flew open, and Sheriff Bobby Halverson rushed in. Jenny stood up, and Bobby took her into his arms.

"Jenny, what in the world happened?"

"It's Mama and Papa...they've been hurt badly...oh, Uncle Bobby, what if they die?"

"Pray, Jenny! Pray that they don't."

Two hours later, a doctor came out of the ICU and took off his mask. He approached Jenny and said, "I'm Doctor Beck. Are you the Springers' daughter?"

"Yes, I'm Jenny Hershberger. How are they, Doctor?"

"I'm afraid they're not doing well. Mr. Springer is unresponsive, and Mrs. Springer is in and out of consciousness. She has called for you, but you need to wait. We're moving them into a shared room in the ICU, where we can monitor them closely. Both your parents have severe internal injuries and broken bones, and I'm afraid the outlook isn't good. As soon as we get them moved you may come in."

"Can Uncle Bobby come in with me?"

"Is this a police matter, Sheriff?"

Bobby took off his cap and scratched his head. "I'm not sure yet, Doctor Beck. I haven't really had a chance to interview anyone. When I went out to the wreck, some of Reuben's friends were there, and they told me that Reuben and Jerusha were hurt, so I came right over. My men are doing the fieldwork right now, so I should know more when I get back to my office. If the Springers are conscious, I would like a few words with them."

"All right, Sheriff. Just let me know if you need anything from me. Mrs. Hershberger, I will come get you when you can come in."

"Thank you, Doctor."

The doctor turned and went back through the door. Jenny stared after him as an awful darkness enveloped her. She felt faint and put out her hand. Bobby and Henry took hold of her and helped her to a chair.

"Sit here, Jenny," Henry said. "Is there anything I can do for you?"

"Yes, Henry. Could you pick Rachel up at school and take her to Amanda Bechler's house? Explain to Amanda what's happened. Ask Amanda if Rachel can stay there until I come for her."

"Sure, Jenny. I'll go right now. I need to be doing something. This waiting is too much for me."

"Thank you, Henry. You've always been there for my family, and we love you for it."

Henry blinked and wiped his eyes with the back of his sleeve. "I'll tell my folks too, and we'll be praying. I'm so sorry, Jenny. This is just awful."

Henry turned and walked out of the room. Bobby and Jenny sat together without speaking. In about half an hour, a nurse came out.

"Mrs. Hershberger?"

"Yes, I'm Jenny Hershberger."

"You can come in now, Mrs. Hershberger. Your mother has been asking for you. You can come too, Sheriff."

They went through the swinging doors and down a long, linoleum-tiled hallway. When they came to the nurses' station, they were directed down the hall to room 104. The door was open and Jenny went in, afraid of what she might see. Reuben and Jerusha were lying in separate beds, but they had been pushed close together. Jenny walked over and looked down at her parents. Reuben had a large bruise on his face, and his head was wrapped with a bandage. His face was calm and his eyes closed. Jerusha had a cut above her eye that had been stitched closed. Her face was peaceful and lovely as though nothing else were wrong with her. Jerusha's right hand and Reuben's left were clasped together as they lay side by side.

Jenny and Bobby stood beside Jerusha's bed. In a little while Jerusha's eyes opened. She looked up at Jenny and Bobby.

"Hello, my darling girl."

Jenny bent over and kissed her mama's cheek. "Oh, Mama, you've just got to get well. I need you and Papa so much."

Jerusha lifted her hand and brushed a tear away from Jenny's cheek. "You must not be anxious, Jenny. *Du leiber Gott* is working all things together for *gut*. Our times are in His hands."

Jerusha looked over toward Reuben. The bruise marred his strong face, and his breathing was shallow. He had tubes in his arms, and bandages covered his head.

"How is your papa?" Jerusha asked.

"The doctor said he has a concussion and he is hurt inside, like you."

Jerusha tried to raise up to look closer, but she could not. The pain from her injuries was too much, and she fell back in the bed. Bobby walked around to Reuben's side and looked down at his old comrade in arms.

"What a long, strange journey this has been, gyrene. You can pull through, old friend. It's not any worse than the Battle of the Ridge, and you made it through that one."

Bobby laid his hand on Reuben's and swallowed hard.

"You've always been a good friend to him, Bobby. And to me," Jerusha said. "You were here the last time I was in the hospital."

Jerusha managed a weak smile.

"That was a long time ago, Jerusha—a different time."

Bobby came back around to Jerusha.

"I just want you to know that except for my mom and dad, you and Reuben and Jenny are the only family I have. You mean a lot to me."

"Why, Bobby, *sie haben ein weiches Herz schließlich.* You old softie," whispered Jerusha.

Just then the nurse came in. "They should probably rest now," she said.

Jenny looked at her parents. "May I please stay with them? I want to be here if anything…if anything happens."

"Yes, I'll have a chair brought in," the nurse said.

Bobby gave Jenny a hug. "I've got to go back to my office. Please call me if you need anything. I'll come by after work and look in on them."

"Thank you. Oh…and, Uncle Bobby, you need to find Samuel

Lapp. He's the man who hit Papa and knocked him down. Then the horse kicked him. I watched it from the car. Papa couldn't get up, and that's why he and Mama got hurt."

"He hit Reuben?"

"Yes. When Papa was trying to clear the harness so the horse could get free, Samuel Lapp snuck up behind him and struck him with a piece of wood. Then he ran away."

A grim look came over Bobby's face. He put his hand on Jenny's shoulder. "Don't worry, Jenny. I'll get this all sorted out."

Bobby turned and walked out of the room.

And then Jenny was alone with her mama and papa in the darkened hospital room. The ICU machines sat impassively on carts behind Reuben and Jerusha, their red lights glowing like strange eyes in the dim light. The only sound was the tiny beep as the monitors kept time with the beating of their hearts.

CHAPTER TWENTY-THREE

The Truth

◇◇◇

BOBBY HALVERSON SAT AT HIS desk at the Wayne County Sheriff's office. Johann Troyer sat across from him.

"Where is this Samuel Lapp now, Bishop Troyer?"

"He's at my house, Sheriff. He showed up at my door in a terrible state. He was semi-coherent and ranting about how Reuben tried to kill him. We hadn't heard yet about the accident, so we took him in."

"Well, I'm going to need to speak with him. Is he in any shape to talk?"

"He had a gash on the top of his head and some cuts and bruises, but *ja*, I think he's come to his senses. What about Amos Stutzman? Have you spoken to him?"

"Who is that?"

"He's the man who was driving *Bisschop* Lapp back to where he is staying. He must have seen what happened."

Bobby clicked down the intercom switch. His secretary answered.

"Yes, Sheriff?"

"Jill, I want you to call the hospital and find out if anyone else was brought in with the Springers. Specifically an Amish man named Amos Stutzman. I need that info right away."

"Sure, Bobby. I'll call right now."

"How are the Springers doing, Sheriff?" Johann asked.

"Not good, Bishop. They both have severe internal injuries, and Jenny told me Reuben was kicked by the horse as he was trying to free it from the harness. I need to find out what in the world happened out there."

The intercom buzzed, and Bobby pushed the button.

"Yes, Jill."

"The hospital does have an Amos Stutzman. He was semiconscious when they brought him in, but he's awake now. They're holding him for observation, but you can talk to him if you need to."

"Thanks, Jill."

Bobby looked back at Johann. "Now, what's this about Lapp saying Reuben was trying to kill him?"

"We had a meeting at my house this afternoon. Reuben and Jenny brought an accusation against *Bisschop* Lapp."

"What kind of accusation?"

"Jenny accused Lapp of striking her with his fist. She did have a swollen face. We tried to resolve it, but Lapp was adamant that Jenny attacked him and he was just defending himself. One of Lapp's men bore witness to the testimony, but the other refuted it. We couldn't force *Bisschop* Lapp to stay, so he left. Reuben was very angry with Lapp, and Lapp was frightened. Reuben controlled himself, but such a look he gave Samuel."

Bobby smiled. "I've seen that look before myself. I can tell you that once you see it, you don't want to push Reuben any further."

"There were other, more serious allegations brought by Jenny and one of Lapp's men that are internal church matters. But I can tell you that *Bisschop* Samuel Lapp is not what he appears to be. However, that matter is out of my hands. It's for the church in Lancaster to decide."

"Well, whatever happens, I'm going to bring this guy in for questioning. There's the matter of the assault on Jenny and now Reuben. I'm going over to the hospital to talk to Stutzman, and I'm sending someone over to pick Lapp up for questioning."

"*Ja,* Sheriff. I'll tell him to wait for you."

"Thanks for your help, Bishop."

Bobby got on the intercom. "Jill, would you send Bull in?"

"Yes, Sheriff."

In a few minutes, Bull Halkovich, Bobby's chief deputy, walked into the office. "What's up, Bobby?"

"Bull, I want you to go over to Bishop Troyer's house and pick up a man named Samuel Lapp. I don't want the guy to leave town before we get there. When you get him, bring him over to the hospital. I'll be there with a man named Amos Stutzman. There are some serious allegations being made, and I need to get to the bottom of this."

"Sure, Bobby. Consider it handled."

◇◇◇

Amos Stutzman looked nervous. He looked at Bobby and then looked away.

"I'm going to ask you again, Mr. Stutzman. What happened at the train crossing? I need to sort this out. Two very dear friends of mine are lying in this hospital badly hurt. There are serious allegations being made against your friend, Samuel Lapp—that he's responsible for what happened to Reuben and Jerusha. They are not in good shape and if they…if they die, I will have to detain you and Bishop Lapp on manslaughter charges until I get it sorted out. So why don't you just give me your version of the story now and avoid any complications. *Verstehen sie?*"

Amos Stutzman wiped his forehand with his sleeve. "*Ja,* Sheriff, I don't know how I got involved in this in the first place. First of all,

Bisschop Lapp is not my friend. I work for him on his farm. I testified falsely for him this afternoon, and that's why he was even on the road. If I had gone against him, *Bisschop* Troyer would have instigated immediate discipline."

"What happened at the train tracks?"

"We were approaching the tracks, and the red signal lights began flashing. I wanted to stop, but Samuel was afraid that Reuben Springer would come after him. He yelled at me to cross the tracks before the crossbar came down."

"Then what?" Bobby asked.

"We were crossing the tracks and something frightened the horse. Maybe it was the bells and the motion of the crossing arm—I don't know. But the animal stopped dead and reared up. He wouldn't move. The arm came right down on top of the buggy, and the horse bolted. The arm hit me and crushed the roof. The horse was terrified and pulled the buggy over on its side. I fell out and hit my head. I think I managed to crawl away, but Samuel was still trapped in the buggy, and the train was coming."

"Jenny Hershberger says that Lapp hit Reuben with a board and knocked him down into the wrecked buggy. Is that true?"

"I don't know, Sheriff. I don't remember anything more until I was being put in the ambulance." Stutzman looked down at his hands. "Are the Springers going to live?"

"I don't know, Mr. Stutzman. For Samuel Lapp's sake, I certainly hope so."

A nurse walked in and signaled Bobby. He walked out in the hall with her.

"Officer Halkovich is here with an Amish gentleman. They're in the waiting area."

Bobby walked briskly down the hall. He couldn't quite comprehend what was happening.

Fighting among the Amish! I've never heard of such a thing. Leave it to Reuben to be in the middle of it!

When he walked into the waiting room, Bull was standing with a very short, very nervous-looking bald-headed man. Bobby noticed right away that his face had a tic and that right now it was very pronounced.

"Mr. Lapp?" Bobby asked.

"I am *Bisschop* Lapp, and I resent your officer hauling me down here like—"

Bobby stepped up close to Samuel Lapp and looked him in the eye. The little man's outburst faded to nothing as he looked into Bobby's eyes.

"Mr. Lapp, I think you've seen this look once before today, and it should tell you something. Do not mess with me. My best friend and his wife are lying in this hospital near death, and my witnesses tell me that you had a hand in them being here. So I would keep your little outbursts to yourself. Understood?"

Lapp hesitated and then nodded.

"Now that we are clear on that, let's get down to brass tacks. My witness says you smashed a pole or a board on Reuben's back while he was trying to help the horse, and knocked him down into the train's path. Is that true?"

"Who is your witness?"

"Jenny Hershberger."

"Oh, *ja*! Jenny Hershberger. The woman who consorts with reprobates and writes trash—"

That was as far as Lapp got. Bobby stepped up and took him by the lapels of his coat.

"Lapp, you are making me very angry. So I'm telling you one time and one time only. Reuben may not have done violence to you today, but there's no Amish bishop around to keep me from slapping you into next week. And Bull here happens to be a friend of Jenny's too, so I imagine that any action I performed on you would go unreported. Am I right, Bull?"

"Just as long as you give me a shot at him when you're finished, Bobby."

Lapp wanted to say something, but the determined look on Bobby's face made him think better of it.

"Now, I've known Jenny Hershberger since she was a little girl," Bobby said. "She may be headstrong, but I have never, ever known her to lie. I trust her word implicitly. You, however—I wouldn't trust you as far as I could throw you. So open up, or bishop or no bishop, you're going to be spending some time in the Wooster County Jail."

"All right, Sheriff. Since you put it that way, I will cooperate. When the accident happened at the train crossing, I was trapped in the wreckage. The impact knocked me out for a few minutes. When I came to, Springer was bending over me and pulling on me. I wasn't thinking right, and I thought he was there to hurt me. I got frightened and tried to protect myself. He shoved me down, and I thought he was going to beat me, so I grabbed a piece of the buggy and...and I hit him."

"That's not what I heard, Mister Lapp. I heard that you came up behind Reuben while he was trying to get the horse up, and you cracked him a good one across the back of the head. And given the way you've talked about Jenny, and the look in your eye while you're telling your story, I say you're lying."

"How dare you say such a thing—"

"Because you *are* lying," said a voice behind them.

They turned to look. It was Amos Stutzman.

"I can't do this any more, Samuel," he said. "You've been a liar since you were a boy. I used to back you up because you were the *bisschop*'s son, and there were certain rewards for faithful followers. Even when your lies drove Jeremy King from the church, I backed you up. After all, what did it hurt except a man's reputation. But this, Samuel! You have been part of injuring a man and his wife, and they might die. I want no more of it."

"You'll keep quiet if you know what's good for you," the *bisschop* said.

"Or what? You'll kick me out of the church? After I say my part, you won't have the authority to kick anyone anywhere."

Amos turned to Bobby. "I wasn't telling the truth when you questioned me, Sheriff. I was awake when Reuben came. He was trying to help, but Samuel is such a coward. He knew he was guilty of hitting Jenny Hershberger without provocation. He grabbed her and was hurting her. She slapped him, and he knocked her down. A grown man hitting a woman…shame! And then at the train tracks, when Reuben tried to help him, Lapp went crazy. He grabbed Reuben, but Reuben pushed him away so he could save the horse."

"Don't believe him, Sheriff! He's lying to save his own skin!"

"Shut up, Lapp," Bobby said. "When I want something from you, I'll tell you. Go on, Mr. Stutzman."

"When Reuben pushed Samuel away, he knocked Samuel down. Then Reuben turned to help the horse. Samuel snuck up behind him. I saw his eyes. They were burning with rage. He grabbed the piece of wood, struck Reuben, and knocked him down on top of the horse. The horse kicked Reuben and knocked him out cold. Mrs. Springer came running and tried to pull her husband away. Samuel saw the train and ran away—such a coward!"

Amos turned to Samuel Lapp. "You've always been a bully and a coward. I curse the day I ever met you. You caused these people to be hurt, and I hope you pay the price for it. As for me, Sheriff, you can do what you want with me. I'm just glad to be clean and free from this hypocrite."

"Thank you, Mr. Stutzman," Bobby said. Then he turned to Lapp.

"Bishop Samuel Lapp, I'm arresting you for assault with intent to cause grave bodily injury. If my friend dies, you will be facing much worse. Bull, get him out of my sight."

CHAPTER TWENTY-FOUR

One Heart—Two Lives

◇◇◇

THE ROOM WAS DARK EXCEPT for the glow from a small lamp on a stand in the corner. The soft beeping of the heart monitors was the only sound. Jenny dozed in a chair by her mother's bed. Jerusha stirred and groaned, and the soft sound brought Jenny back to wakefulness. She had been dreaming about her childhood—images and flashes of riding on her Papa's shoulders, standing in the kitchen watching her mama make a streusel cake, flying up high in the swing her papa had made in the big willow tree by the creek. The dream had been filled with joy and peace, with nothing of the trauma of her earliest childhood, before she came to live with Jerusha and Reuben.

Now she rubbed her eyes and looked at her parents. They lay still, resting. Jerusha held Reuben's hand in hers. They had been that way since the doctors moved them to this room.

Earlier in the evening, Reuben's breathing had become labored, and the doctor put him on oxygen. The tubing in his nose and the large bruise obscured his face, but he was still beautiful to Jenny. She longed to feel his arms around her, to see the smile behind his eyes one more time. Then Jerusha stirred again.

"Jenny?"

Her mama's voice was weak, almost a whisper.

"I'm here, Mama, how do you feel?"

"Better, I think."

"Do you have any pain, Mama?"

"Some, but its bearable. How is Reuben?"

"He has never awakened. They put some tubes in his nose earlier, and his breathing is easier. Oh, Mama, I'm so afraid."

Jerusha lifted her hand and placed it in Jenny's. Jenny could feel her mother's heart beating through her fingertips.

"Jenny, I want to tell you something."

"What, Mama?"

"I want to tell you how much I love you and how proud I am of you. You have been the most wonderful daughter a woman could ever have."

"Even when I went my own way and brought trouble to our home, Mama?"

Jerusha smiled. To Jenny, it was like sunlight breaking through the trees on a soft summer morning.

"Your papa and I loved all your ways, Jenny. You brought such joy to us. And when you came to the trials in your life, it only made your papa and me better people as we learned to trust our *Gott* to bring you through."

"Mama, do you know something?"

"What, *dochter?*"

"When I was searching for Mama Rachel, it was never because I wanted her to be my mama. It was just that I felt incomplete not knowing who I was. You were always my mama. And I remember one day when we were in New York and Uncle Bobby told me that Joe—the bad man who hurt Mama Rachel—that he was not my father. I knew then that Papa was *mein Vater* and that he always had been *mein Vater*, and that I could never have another."

Jenny felt Jerusha give her hand a squeeze.

"Jenny, I've loved you as though you were from my own body, as though you had grown inside me and I had given you birth. It was always as if I had two daughters that were my own flesh and blood—Jenna and Jenny. And *du leiber Gott* did that. You were *ein Geschenk vom Gott* to Reuben and me."

Jerusha closed her eyes.

"Rest, Mama. I'm here with you."

It was early in the morning. A faint light came through the window. Jenny stirred in her chair, and then she felt a light touch on her shoulder. She opened her eyes. Bobby Halverson stood beside her.

"Uncle Bobby, I'm so glad you're here."

Bobby gave Jenny a gentle squeeze. "How are they, Jenny?"

"I don't know. Mama and I talked a little last night, but Papa hasn't stirred."

Just as they were speaking, Reuben gave a slight groan. Bobby and Jenny went around to his side.

"Papa? Papa, can you hear me?"

Reuben's eyes slowly opened. He saw Bobby and Jenny standing there beside the bed.

"Hello, my friend," he said, lifting his hand.

Bobby took Reuben's strong hand in his. Jenny saw a look pass between them, a look that only men who have shared the most terrible trials and the greatest friendship can know. Then Reuben released Bobby's hand and took Jenny's. Jenny looked into Reuben's wonderful eyes, the deep sea-blue eyes. The old smile was there behind them, the smile that had been a light to Jenny all her days. He looked over at

Jerusha as though to assure himself that she was still with him. Then he pulled Jenny close.

"Jenny, my precious girl."

Jenny felt Reuben's breathing begin to slow—one breath, another and then…nothing. "Papa! Papa!" Jenny called, "No!"

Alerted by her cry, a nurse hurried into the room and checked Reuben's pulse.

"I'm so sorry, Mrs. Hershberger…he's gone."

Jenny's eyes lifted to the monitor above Reuben's bed. The steady beep and the little blip on the screen continued unabated.

"But nurse, his monitor…"

The nurse looked up with surprise. "But he's gone…I…"

And then she looked and saw that Reuben's hand was still clasped in Jerusha's. "It's your mother's heart, beating through him, Mrs. Hershberger. It's like they have one heartbeat."

Yes! Of course they do. Two lives, one heart. My mama and papa…

Jenny looked at Bobby. A tear ran down each of his cheeks. Slowly he came to attention and saluted his fallen comrade. He held the salute for a long time. Then he took Jenny into his arms, and the two of them cried together.

A few minutes later, Jerusha spoke.

"Yes, husband, I'm coming."

Her eyes opened, and she looked at Jenny and Bobby, who stood by her bedside.

"Take care of my girl, Bobby. She will need you."

Jenny slipped to her knees by Jerusha's side. "Mama, please…don't go."

The sweet hand that had comforted Jenny as long as she could remember reached out and softly stroked Jenny's cheek.

"I won't say do not grieve, Jenny. I know you will. But I must go. Reuben is waiting for me, and Jenna too. And we will wait for you. Always remember that I love you."

Jenny looked at Jerusha.

"Mama, please…"

Jerusha smiled at Jenny and then closed her eyes. Jenny could hear the monitor beeping, marking the beat of Jerusha's heart, and Jenny remembered how safe she felt in every storm when her mama held her close. Her mama's heart.

She heard the monitor beep once, twice, and then it stopped.

Jerusha was gone.

A nurse came rushing in, looked at the monitor and called the doctor. They gathered around Jerusha. Finally Doctor Beck turned to Jenny and Bobby.

"I'm sorry, Mrs. Hershberger," he said, the words coming at her from a long way away and echoing strangely as though she were in a long, dark tunnel.

◇◇◇

Bobby arranged for an ambulance to take the bodies back to Apple Creek. *Bruder* Johann brought three men, and together they stripped the Springers' front room of all furnishings. Then they placed two sets of sawhorses in the front room and set coffins on them. Johann's wife and several women came to help Jenny. They washed the bodies and prepared them for burial. Jenny brought out Jerusha's simple wedding dress for her to be buried in. As she lay on the bed, she looked beautiful and at peace. Then they were placed in the two coffins, side by side. The coffins were simple, handmade by Johann himself, out of pine. They had no handles or veneer and no padding inside.

For the three days before the funeral, a steady stream of people passed through the room to view the bodies. The Amish people of Apple Creek, Dalton, and Wooster passed silently. They didn't show any emotion or grieve openly, but as Jenny watched from the kitchen, she could tell by the looks on their faces that the whole community was in shock. When *Bruder* Johann and his wife came, they stood silently by the coffins for several minutes. Jenny sat with Rachel at the kitchen table. Johann came in, and she could see strong emotion working in his face. He placed his hand on Jenny's shoulder.

"Your papa and mama will be missed by more people than you will ever know," Johann said. "They were a blessing to all who knew them."

Jenny reached up and patted Johann's hand. "Thank you, *Bisschop*."

In those three days, she did not see Bobby Halverson. She knew him to be a man who did not express his emotions very well, so she understood his reluctance to come. There were so many thoughts and images swirling in her mind. She found it almost incomprehensible that both her parents were gone. On the second day, the postman brought a special delivery letter to her. It was from Jeremy King. She opened it with trembling hands.

> My Dearest Jenny,
>
> I have heard from Sheriff Halverson about the passing of your parents. I am deeply saddened for you. I know how close you were to them. If there is anything I can do for you, please contact me. You have my phone number. I will be praying for you and Rachel.
>
> Your friend,
> Jeremy

At one point, when Jenny was overcome by grief, she went out alone to the orchard and stood among the trees that her *Grossdaadi* Hershberger and her *daed* had planted. It was late spring, and the apple blossoms filled the air with a sweet perfume. All around Jenny, the farm burst forth with new life. In the fields, the winter wheat was turning to gold. It stirred and flowed like the sea as the spring breeze passed over it.

Like the sea—the sea that took Jonathan. How is it that death can come in the midst of such life? O Lord, I do not understand Your ways.

And then a quiet voice spoke in her spirit.

My ways are not your ways, Jenny. They are beyond your understanding. But know this: My grace is sufficient for you.

The words were not a comfort, but they strengthened Jenny. She walked on. Here was the field where she had dislocated her ankle and her papa came and found her; here was the barn that she had hidden in on long summer days, dreaming of the future and wondering what it held for her; and here was the path to the creek where she had fished for crawdads and come home muddy and happy to her mama's waiting arms.

Unable to remedy the disconsolate feeling in her heart by wandering among these precious places, she returned to the house and went to her room. Mrs. Troyer had taken Rachel for the afternoon when they left, and now Jenny was alone. She sat at the desk and ran her hands over it. This was the desk that Reuben had made, so simple and yet so gracious—every piece fitted perfectly and the surface sanded to such a fine grain that it was almost soft to the touch. She took out her book and began to write.

> Jerusha stood on a high cliff. Clouds billowed all around her, but she was not cold. She heard the sound of footsteps and she turned. Someone was walking up the hill toward her through the mist. For a moment she was afraid—and then she saw him. It was Reuben!
>
> He came slowly up the hill until he stood beside her. He took her hands in his, and she looked into his eyes— the wonderful sea-blue eyes that drew her into him, the eyes that she loved. She could see the smile behind them, and she felt the fierceness and the gentleness of his love for her. The strange feeling came over her that always happened when she was with him, as if she were falling off a high hill. But now they were on the hill together and she was not falling. He smiled at her.
>
> "I love you, Jerusha. I always have, and I always will."

Then Jerusha heard a voice. It was a child's voice, calling to her with joy.

"Mama! I'm waiting. Come up, come up!"

She knew that precious voice. It was Jenna! She looked at Reuben and saw the light in his eyes and the joy on his face. Together they stepped to the edge of the precipice. She looked at him again. "Don't be afraid, my dearest," he said, and then they stepped off into the air. She was not falling. Instead she began to rise with her beloved, up, and up, and up into the light.

"The Day My Mama Died"
from the journals of Jenny Hershberger

Chapter Twenty-Five

The Third Day

◇◇◇

On the third day after the passing of Reuben and Jerusha, the Amish community of Wayne County, Ohio, came together to bury the Springers of Apple Creek. Jenny got up before dawn and opened the windows and doors to the cool morning breeze. Rachel was asleep, and no one else was with them. Jenny went into the front room to look upon her beloved mama and papa one more time as they lay in their coffins, together in death as they had been in life.

As the light began to soften the horizon, the day seemd to pause with a cool stillness that heralded a beautiful sunrise. A songbird ventured forth with his lovely trilling. Then suddenly, a small breeze began to rustle the curtains on the front windows, and the room was filled with the wonderful scent from the lilac bush by the front porch, sweet and heavy—her mama's favorite. It was as though Jerusha had come to say goodbye. Jenny almost felt her presence, and she could hear Jerusha's words to her.

"I cannot say do not grieve, Jenny. I know you will. But I must go. Reuben is waiting for me, and Jenna too. And we will wait for you. Always remember that I love you."

"And I you, Mama."

Jenny leaned over and kissed Jerusha's pale cheek. She went to her papa and lifted his hand and held it against her face. It was cold, but she did not mind.

"Goodbye, Papa. I will see you again."

Then the breeze swept the smell of lilacs from the room, and the first shaft of sunlight broke over the hills to the east, and Jenny was alone.

An hour later, *Bisschop* Troyer came with the elders of the church and their wives for a brief service. Then Johann and three of the elders closed the coffins and carried them out to the waiting buggy that would transport them to the cemetery. Jenny and Rachel were dressed in black, as were all the Amish that day. When Jenny walked outside, she was amazed to see the long line of black buggies in the lane in front of the house. She could not count them, but she thought there must have been more than a hundred. *Bisschop* Troyer spoke quietly to Jenny.

"There is room in our buggy for you and Rachel if you would ride with us."

"Thank you, Johann, that's very kind of you."

She and Rachel climbed into the buggy, and they began the slow seventeen-mile drive to the graveyard, where Jerusha and Reuben would be buried next to Jerusha's *grossmudder*, Hannah. Rachel leaned against Jenny.

"Why does everyone we love die, Mama?"

Jenny put her arm around Rachel. "I can't answer that, dear one. I don't know the reason."

"Are you mad at *Gott*?"

"No, my *dochter*. There's no reason to be angry with Him. We read in the Bible that long ago Adam disobeyed *Gott* and that's why people die. But we also read that Jesus died on the cross so we could live forever. Your papa and *grossdaadi und grossmudder* have gone to a place where they will never die again. And one day we will go too. No, Rachel, it is not *du lieber Gott's* fault people die. There is no reason to be angry with Him."

"All right, Mama. But can I still be sad?"

"We will be sad for a long time, dearest. But we still have each other, and we will have to love each other so much in the days to come that it will help to fill the empty places. *Ja*?"

"*Ja*, Mama."

Soon the steady sound of the horse's hooves lulled Rachel to sleep, and Jenny sat silently for the rest of the ride.

When they came to the cemetery, Jenny saw something strange. A group of men were standing by the side of the road in a military formation. They all wore hats, and as she looked closer, she saw that the men were veterans of the armed forces. And then she saw Bobby Halverson in the front rank. He and the other men stood at attention. As the hearse came by, a sharp command rang out.

"Preeesennnt arms!"

The hand of each man rose in a slow salute, showing the soldier's greatest mark of respect. The men stood at attention, holding the salute. *Bisschop* Troyer, who was next in line behind the hearse, stopped his buggy. He looked at Bobby and the rest of the vets, and then he motioned to Bobby to come into the procession ahead of him. Bobby nodded to his guidon. Another sharp command rang out.

"Orrrderrr arms!"

The hands came down.

"Slow march! Forwaaarrd, march!"

The group moved out onto the road.

"To the right flank…march!"

The column slowly turned to the right and fell into line behind the hearse. The men's arms were checked at their sides. The procession passed through the gates and into the cemetery. After Bobby and his men passed, the *bisschop* chucked his horse and started up. And so an Amish man and Congressional Medal of Honor winner Reuben Springer went to his final rest, his beloved wife at his side, as the honor guard marched with a slow, measured step behind the hearse and the long line of Amish buggies followed along.

After the two-hour service, Jenny and Bobby stood at the grave. It was a beautiful spring day. The two coffins lay together in one large grave. Two simple headstones stood ready, etched with her parents' names, the dates of their births, and the date of their deaths. The long line of mourners had passed silently by, and each had dropped a clod of dirt on the coffins. Jenny wondered at the multitude of people who had come.

So many…so many loved you!

Now she stood with Bobby and held a clod of dirt in her hand. She did not want to drop it—it seemed like such a final thing. She didn't want to close the door on this part of her life, but she knew she must. Slowly her clenched hand released, and the handful of dirt dropped silently into the grave. Bobby followed her, tossed in his handful of dirt, and then turned to Jenny.

"Your father was my best friend from the first time I met him in Wooster before the war. I never thought I would outlive him."

Jenny smiled at Bobby. "Papa never let us know much about what he was feeling, but I do know this, Bobby Halverson. He loved you deeply, he prayed for you always, and he was blessed by your life as it touched his. And because you were his brother, I have something for you."

Jenny reached into the pocket of her apron. She grasped the cloth strap, pulled the object out, and handed it to Bobby. It was Reuben's Medal of Honor.

Bobby reached out and took it.

"Shouldn't you keep this for Rachel and the rest of your family to remember what he did?"

"For the Amish, it's not something that's important to us—not as important as it is to you, since you were there. I was going to bury it with him, but instead I wish you to have it. It's something my papa would have wanted."

Bobby turned the medal over slowly in his hands.

"Reuben won this by taking life. But at the same time he also preserved life—mine in particular and the lives of hundreds of men who would have been killed outright or been hunted down or starved in the jungle if the Japanese had overrun our position. I think that was something he came to understand in the last few years, and I believe he was able to release the guilt he felt."

"I think you're right, Uncle Bobby. In the last few months I know he found peace."

She reached into her pocket again. "This is something Papa showed me when he was telling me about the war. He carried it with him all his life."

It was the family portrait Reuben had shared with Jenny—the Japanese man standing stiffly at attention, looking straight at the camera, dressed in formal military attire, his lovely young wife sitting next to him and holding their son on her lap.

Bobby took the faded paper from Jenny's hand and said, "This is a sniper that Reuben killed one day when we were on patrol. He took this picture from the man's dead body. He showed it to me once. He said he carried it to remind him that taking human life is wrong. He mourned the fact that a man he killed would never return to his wife and son. He also used it to remind himself how much of a blessing Jerusha and his daughters were to him."

"My papa was a good man, wasn't he, Uncle Bobby?"

"He was the finest man I ever met. He truly understood what *semper fidelis* meant."

"*Semper fidelis?*"

"Yes, Jenny. It's the Marine Corps motto. It means 'always faithful.'"

"Always faithful. Yes, that was my papa."

"And your mother was like a sister to me. She and Reuben…" Bobby paused, unable to go on.

"Will you come in to the reception when you take me home, Uncle Bobby?"

"Probably not, Jenny. I've had a full day already, and I have a lot to think about. I'll come see you in a few days."

Jenny looked around. It was a beautiful day. The sun shone down on them, and the sweet smell of the Ohio fields filled the air. Soft clouds drifted by in an azure sky. Birds sang in the trees around the cemetery, and everywhere the grass was green and verdant.

Jenny sighed. "I was expecting a gray day today—I guess because I felt gray inside. But I think my mama would want us to remember them this way—with God's beauty alive all around us."

She took Bobby's hand and said, "Well, I will expect you to come soon and spend time with us, Uncle Bobby. Remember what my mama said to you."

Bobby exhaled as he squeezed Jenny's hand. "Okay, Jenny. I'll come."

They looked down at the grave one more time, each one with memories of these two beloved people alive in their hearts. She didn't really know why, but Jenny lifted her hand and waved.

"Goodbye, Mama. Goodbye, Papa. The Lord be with you."

Bobby and Jenny turned and walked from the grave.

Jenny was alone in the empty house. Rachel was asleep, and all the visitors were gone. The dishes had been cleaned up and the food put away. Now she sat with a beautiful quilt spread across her lap. A cool evening breeze swept in through the open windows, and Jenny pulled the quilt around her shoulders.

It was a beautiful piece. Iridescent royal blue silk made a dark backdrop to the beautiful deep red rose-shaped pattern in the center of the quilt. The rose had hundreds of parts, all cut into the flowing shapes of petals instead of the traditional square or diamond-shaped patterns of Amish quilts. The setting sun cast its fading light on the rose, and it glowed with a fragile luminescence. Deep red…like the blood of Christ.

The quilting pattern was the most complicated her mother had ever done. It was all set on a cream-colored backing and filled with a double layer of batting. Jerusha had carefully basted the layers together on her hands and knees, starting from the center and working out to the edges. Delicate tracks of quilting stitches made their trails through the surface of the quilt, and to Jenny it was a true memorial to her mama's life. A quilt for Jenna…a quilt for Jenny…a quilt for Jerusha.

"My Mama's Quilt"
from the journals of Jenny Hershberger

Chapter Twenty-Six

The Dream Slips Away

◇◇◇

IN THE DAYS THAT FOLLOWED her parents' funeral, Jenny disengaged from life in Apple Creek. The loss of her husband and her parents within two years was a weight that seemed to grow heavier with each passing day. She tried to involve herself in the running of the farm, but the joy had gone out of the daily routines. *Bisschop* Troyer and the men of her church stepped in to help, and soon things were fairly normal as far as taking care of the livestock and caring for the fields, but for Jenny it seemed that she was detached from all of it and standing a great distance away—a stranger watching other strangers do things she cared nothing for.

Jenny tried inviting some of the women over to the house. Elizabeth Troyer had become an especially great help to her, and Jenny wanted to cultivate her friendship, but the afternoons she spent with the Amish ladies seemed pale compared to the deep connection she had shared with Jerusha. After she put Rachel to bed each evening, Jenny often sat at the kitchen table until late in the night, listless and at loose ends with herself. She tried writing, but the fountain of words that once bubbled from her spirit seemed to have dried up. She would set her pen to paper and an hour later stare down at a page full of doodles or a few words strung together like birds sitting on a telephone wire.

The only bright spots in her life were Rachel and Bobby. Bobby kept his word and visited as much as he could. They sat quietly on the porch after having something to eat, not saying much—each one lost in memories—and then after awhile Bobby would bid her good night and leave. Still, it was comforting to have him there. And Rachel! Rachel was such a resilient soul, and though she grieved for *Grossdaadi* and *Grossmudder*, she seemed to have an innate understanding of the realities of life and death that somehow escaped Jenny. Where Jenny found it hard to accept what had happened, sometimes expecting Jerusha to come home from the market or her *daed* to walk in the back door, his clothes dirty from working in the fields, Rachel came to grips with the tragedy sooner. At least it appeared that way. Then one day when they were walking by the creek, Rachel asked a question that caused Jenny to think perhaps Rachel was grieving more than she let on.

"Is death forever, Mama?"

Jenny was taken aback by the unexpected query and hesitated for a moment before answering.

"It is forever, as far as being gone from this life, Rachel. But for those who know Jesus as their Savior, death is only a doorway into the next life."

"What is the next life like, Mama? Do we turn into angels?"

"No, darling. We stay as people, but we have bodies that never grow old."

Rachel hesitated for a moment and then asked the question that had been troubling her. "Is death a bad thing that comes and gets you and makes you die?"

"Who told you that, Rachel?"

"My friend at *schule* said that death is a ghost that comes in the night. So sometimes I'm afraid to go to sleep."

Jenny paused. She realized she had become so absorbed in her own grief that she hadn't considered Rachel's grief. Rachel's silence after the funeral made Jenny assume that her *dochter* was dealing with the tragedy. But the little girl's questions showed Jenny that Rachel was seriously thinking about the subject of death.

"What else did your friend tell you, Rachel?"

"She said that you have to be careful when someone dies so that you don't catch it and die too. Did *Grossdaadi und Grossmudder* catch it from Papa?"

"No, Rachel. What happened to my papa and mama had nothing to do with your papa. They didn't catch dying from him."

Jenny led Rachel to a place under the willow tree that grew close by the creek. The small brook burbled its way through the farm on its way down to its junction with Apple Creek not far from where they were sitting. Soft grass lined the banks, and the smell of wildflowers filled the air. Jenny sat for a few minutes, thinking about what to say to her daughter. Then she took Rachel's hand.

"Are you worried about anything, Rachel?"

Rachel stared at her mama for a long moment, and then she burst into tears. "I…I don't want you to die too, Mama! Everybody has died, and I'm scared!"

Jenny pulled Rachel close to her side and put her arm around her. She waited until her sobs quieted. Then she took Rachel's face in her hands and kissed away the tears.

"I know this has been a very hard time for you, Rachel. We lost Papa, and now we lost *Grossdaadi und Grossmudder*. It's been *ein sehr hartes Ding*, a very hard thing. But we have to put our faith in God and—"

Rachel pulled away and crossed her arms. "How do I know there is a God, Mama! I can't see Him or hear Him. And why would He let everyone I love die? I just don't understand. Why should I believe in Him?"

Jenny sat for a long moment. And then she realized that she didn't understand either. She took Rachel's hand and drew the little girl back to her side.

"I don't have the answer to that, Rachel. What I do know is that believing in something is different from having faith in something. Belief is when you think something that someone else told you is right, but faith is knowing that something is true without having proof. Does that make sense?"

"Kind of, Mama."

"Well, for instance, your friend told you that death is a ghost, and you believed her because she told you. You didn't really know that death is a ghost, right?"

"Well…no I didn't, but she seemed so sure."

"Yes, but she was just saying something that wasn't true at all. Death is not a ghost that comes in the night. But still you believed her. Now let me ask you this—what season is going to come after summer?"

"Fall."

"And after the fall?"

"Winter."

"How do you know that?"

Rachel thought for a moment. "I don't know, I just know it."

"So you know that winter will come this year even though right now it is summer, and you don't know how you know that it will."

"Yes, I know that winter will come because it always has."

"But there is no way you can prove that to me, so you must have faith that it will come, see? And the only proof you will have will be when it really comes."

"So…faith is knowing something is true without being able to prove it?"

"Yes, dearest. Only when winter is here will you have the evidence that your faith that winter would come is real. And that is how *Gott* is. We know He is real because He is real. I can't prove it to you by showing Him to you, but the evidence that He is real is all around us."

"Where, Mama? Where is the evidence?"

Jenny reached down and picked a wildflower. It was a beautiful lavender color, and each petal was perfect in form. A delicious fragrance came from it as Jenny held it under Rachel's nose.

"Look at this flower. It is so beautiful. The color is wonderful, and what about the smell?"

"It smells *gut,* Mama."

"Yes, it's perfect. Now I want you to make me one just like it."

"I can't make a flower! That would be too hard."

"So if you took some dirt and some paint and some grass and piled them up and stirred them, it wouldn't make a flower?"

"No, Mama. It would just be a mess."

"But someone made it, Rachel. It's so perfect and beautiful. There is a plan and a design in this flower. It couldn't just make itself, could it?"

Rachel's eyes widened. "Did *Gott* make it?"

"Yes, Rachel. *Gott* made it. And He also made you—beautiful on the outside and full of questions on the inside."

"Is it bad to ask questions, Mama?"

"No, dearest. Questions are good. And as you get older and keep asking questions—as you live life and experience these things for yourself—the answers will make more sense to you."

"Will they, Mama?"

"Yes, Rachel. And though I don't understand everything, I do know this—*Gott* knows exactly how long each one of us will live because He made us and He has a plan for each of us. No one knows how long that might be, but we do know that while we're alive we must love each other as much as we possibly can and trust that *Gott* only wants the best for us."

Rachel snuggled up close and Jenny held her tight. "All right, Mama, I believe you…I mean, I have faith that *Gott* is real."

Jenny looked down at her daughter.

I wish it were as easy for me!

That night Jenny took out the book—the story of Jenna's quilt. She read through it slowly. Here was the quilt being made, now the story of the big storm and the car crash that killed the bad man. And here were Uncle Bobby and Papa fighting in the war. When she read the part about Jerusha holding her through the long, cold night and saving her, Jenny cried. She cried because she remembered the beating of her mother's heart. That had been her earliest memory—her mother's heart beating strong and sure, keeping her safe and warm in the midst of every storm. And now that heart was stilled.

When I was writing this, I was so sure Gott *told me to do it.*

Every word in the book had flowed so easily, and as Jerusha told her the story, she and Jenny grew so close. It seemed that only *Gott* could do such a wonderful thing. When the book was finished, it was as though she had painted a picture of her family's life, a picture that had just been waiting for her to set it down on paper and fill in all the little details. The historian in her had filed away all of the bits and pieces, the stories and the memories, and the work had fulfilled her as nothing else in her life except her marriage to Jonathan.

But now none of it made sense. She had the book, but she didn't have her parents. She had the memories, but she didn't have her husband. A great wheel had turned in her life, and everything had changed. She was lost in a strange land where nothing was familiar anymore.

There was nothing to hang on to, and nothing seemed real. Even this house seemed unfamiliar and in some ways frightening. Rachel's questions about death had challenged her own fears, and now the home where love once lived stood like an abandoned castle, full of ghosts and empty hallways.

Without her mama's love to guide her and encourage her, the writing now seemed empty and meaningless. The words on the page seemed to mock her. The joy that her mama and papa found, the restoration and healing—what did it all mean if they were gone? Jenny put her head down on her desk. She was tired...so tired.

Gott, *why did You let me do all this if You were just going to let them die?*

And then she heard the quiet voice, the one that was the substance of things hoped for, the evidence of things not yet seen.

I didn't do it for them, Jenny. I did it for you. And I did it for those who need healing and restoration in their own lives. But that time is not yet. Give the book back to Me.

Jenny lifted her head and spoke out loud. "Give it back?"

Yes, Jenny. Put it on the altar as a sweet savor of incense to Me. I have the keys that will open the doors that cannot be shut. And I will open those doors in My time. Give Me the book.

And so Jenny put the book back into its envelope and tied it with a red string. She went to the cedar chest where Jerusha kept the quilt and put the book inside. When she closed the lid, it was as though time stood still for just that moment. And then that season was over.

CHAPTER TWENTY-SEVEN

The Decision

◇◇◇

When you are with the ones who love you, anyplace can seem like home. But without the ones you love, even home can be a prison.

Jenny read the words again. She remembered writing them one morning when she was thinking about moving from Paradise back to Apple Creek. They had just floated into her mind, and she had pulled out her little pad and jotted them down. Now as she read them again, they seemed to be terribly prophetic. The Springer house in Apple Creek had become just that—a prison. Without the presence of her mama and papa, the rooms were quiet and still. This morning, after she sent Rachel out to play, she pulled out her journals and began to leaf through them. She came upon the scrap of paper, stuck between two pages. As she read it, the reality of what had happened began to push its way into her thoughts.

Home? Where is my home? The ones I love are gone, and I feel as though I have flown off into space, never to feel solid ground again.

She slipped the paper back between the pages and then sighed and got up from her desk. She walked down the hall into her parents' room and sat on the bed, taking in each article in the room as though some essence of Jerusha and Reuben remained that she could touch or hear or smell.

This is the bed where they slept, my papa keeping watch over Mama even in his dreams. And here is the dresser my papa made for Mama. She sat here every morning and brushed her wonderful blonde hair and then pinned it up into a bun and hid it under her kappe. Papa loved her hair. When she took it down at night, I could see in his eyes how he loved her. My papa's eyes...Jonathan's eyes were like Papa's, deep and blue and...

She stood up quickly and walked out of the bedroom. It was dangerous to dwell on the things that had happened. There were so many emotions locked inside her. The smallest thing would make them spring unbidden into her heart—a word or a picture or the way the sunset shone through the kitchen window on a summer evening—and with them would come the awful reality that reminded her of those she had lost.

They are not lost—I am lost. Everything has been stripped away, and I don't know who I am anymore. All the landmarks are gone, and I'm wandering in the mist, dark trees reaching for me with twisted branches...

"I want to scream!" Jenny cried out.

A familiar voice interrupted the moment. "Jenny? Are you all right?"

"Jeremy?" But it couldn't be.

She went out of the kitchen into the living room. The front door was open, and Jeremy King stood behind the screen with a worried expression on his face. Jenny looked at him in surprise.

"Jeremy! What are you doing here?"

"May I come in first?"

Jenny blushed at the thought that Jeremy had heard her ranting in the kitchen. She opened the screen. It was so good to see someone, anyone. Jeremy stepped inside.

"I heard you cry out. Are you all right?"

Jenny could feel her cheeks burning. She looked at him, and then to her surprise she was in his arms, weeping. He stood surprised for a moment, and then his arms closed around her, and he held her tightly. She looked up at his face and she could see the love in his eyes. She lifted her face and he bent down to kiss her.

Reality stepped in. Jenny turned her face into his chest.

"No, don't, Jeremy. I'm sorry, that's not what I intended. *Ich werde so verwechselt...* I'm so mixed up. It's just so good to see a friendly face."

Jeremy held her for a moment more and then turned her toward the couch, where they sat down together. He reached into his pocket and pulled out a handkerchief and handed it to her. Then Jeremy laughed.

"Almost you surrendered to me, Jenny Hershberger...almost. But I understand. I don't want you to come to me just because you're lonely. And you are lonely, aren't you?"

"I have Rachel...and Bobby comes to see me."

"But the silence is getting to you, isn't it? I heard you cry out just as I came to the door. When my mother died, I felt the same way. To lose both your parents at once must be incredibly hard. I'm not sure I could bear it."

"That's why I was yelling in the kitchen, Jeremy. I think I'm starting to get a little *verrückt*. Sometimes the pain and the loss feel so much bigger than my body, I can't hold them inside. I think I'm going to explode into tiny pieces and float away on the wind."

Jeremy took her hand. "Look, Jenny, I know this is a hard time for you, and I know I shouldn't try to press my case just now. But things have changed, and I need to talk to you before I go."

"Go?"

"Yes, I'm moving the company back to Lancaster."

"But what about—"

"The *meidung* I was under? It's been lifted."

"But how?"

"When Samuel Lapp was arrested here, it sent shock waves through the Lancaster district. And then when Sheriff Halverson charged Lapp with involuntary manslaughter after your papa died, his whole little empire came apart. The two men who testified against me recanted and asked for forgiveness. And then many people in the community who had been used or abused by Lapp started coming forward. It seems he ran a very tight ship and had a lot of control over people."

"What will happen to him?"

"After the sheriff deals with him here, he will be brought back to Lancaster. It seems the authorities want to speak to him about some illegal land deals. Samuel Lapp is in a lot of trouble."

"The *bann* is lifted?"

"Yes. The elders of the church in Lancaster contacted me, and I made a trip home to see them. They asked me to forgive them for being taken in by Lapp and said they would restore me to the church."

Jenny felt the old turmoil starting in her again. *If he rejoins the church, I won't have an excuse not to reconsider his proposal...*

"What are you going to do?"

Jeremy let go of her hand and stood up. "I'm going back to Lancaster County, but I'm not going back to the church."

"Not going back?"

"No, Jenny. I'm too involved in Kerusso. I've found my niche in life, and I'm going to stay in it. It's a real ministry for me. I'm moving it back to Lancaster now that the stigma has gone off my life. That's where the action is as far as finding Amish writers and people who are writing about the Amish. But go back to the church? No."

Jenny didn't want to ask the next question but she did anyway. "Then what about…what about…?

"What about *us*?"

Jeremy knelt down on the floor in front of Jenny. "That's why I've come today, Jenny." He took her hand again. "I want you to marry me and come to Lancaster. I love you with all my heart, and I have since the day we met at the library."

"But if you're not in the church, what will I do, Jeremy?"

"You'll write books for Kerusso Publishing."

She looked at him in amazement.

"Jenny Hershberger, you're a good writer. You reach into places that most people don't even know exist, and you bring back the wisdom and the revelations about life that you find there. Good writing makes people access their memories and emotions. You do that so well—it's like it's instinctive."

"It's a gift…"

As Jenny spoke the words, she remembered something Jerusha had shared when she was telling Jenny the story of Jenna's quilt.

"When I was just learning to quilt, and it was becoming obvious that I had a natural talent for quilting, my grossmudder *said to me, 'You have been given a way to give back to the Lord, as He has given to you. It is a special gift not everyone is given. But to whom much is given, much is required. You must always give back to God from the gift He has given you. And there are dangers along the way. If you become a good quilter, it is quite possible for you to become arrogant and think that somehow you are more special than others.'*

"Always remember that, Jenny, for peril can be hidden in the most beautiful places."

"It's a gift from God, Jeremy, and I must be very careful how I use it. And as for leaving the church…I don't know, Jeremy."

"Your parents are gone, Jonathan is gone...what is there to hold you?"

Jenny paused and then said, "When I was a girl, I had one burning desire—to know who my real parents were. I imagined them to be rich, and they were—or at least my father was. I imagined so many things about them and what I might have become if things had been different. And then one day my journey led me to the front porch of Abel Borntraeger, my *grossdaadi*. And that was the day I discovered who I really am. I am Amish. My mother was Amish, and her mother before her. My family went back into history, wrapped in the safety and solidity of the Amish way, and it will extend into the future, unchanging and certain."

"But, Jenny, what has the church done for you that has any lasting reality?"

"It's not the church, Jeremy, it's the way in which we live and the closeness I feel to *Gott* because I am Amish. And it seemed that *Gott* was so determined that I be Amish that He gave me to the people who became my real father and mother, Reuben and Jerusha Springer. And so I am Amish. I can't change that. It's who I am in the deepest part of my being, my memories, and my history. To step away from that would be *ein sehr hartes Ding*—too hard, I think."

"I'm your friend. I know that if everything were right, you could learn to love me. I would be a good husband to you and a good father to Rachel."

"I know, but—"

"Let me finish. I'm asking one thing. I'm asking you to pray about my offer and ask God what He wants you to do. And as for leaving the church, you wouldn't really leave. You would be right in the middle of everything Amish. I want you to tell the world about the Amish. I want the *Englisch* to see that in spite of the fact that we are Amish, we are just like other Christians—Episcopalians, Methodists...all of them. We struggle in our relationship with God, we have crises in our faith, and we get angry at the church and the people in it. I think that's a realistic approach and one that would take the veil off and show people that everything isn't perfect for us—that the Amish aren't exempt from the arrows of the devil just because they're Amish. And you could tell that story."

Almost, I could go with him, Lord. Almost, I could love him. He is a gentle, true man. But...but he is not Jonathan.

Jenny smiled to herself.

"What?" Jeremy asked.

"I will do as you ask, Jeremy. I will pray about it. But I can't promise what the Lord will say."

And then the still, quiet voice.

The book is Mine and you are Mine. I have the key, and I open the doors that cannot be shut.

Jenny looked at Jeremy once more. She heard what the Lord was saying, but her heart ached to love and be loved. Not in heaven, but in this world—now.

CHAPTER TWENTY-EIGHT

Another Homecoming

◇◇◇

JENNY DID PRAY. AFTER JEREMY left she prayed, prayed some more, and wrestled with God. She made her case before Him about her loneliness, her desire for intimacy, her need to be in a family once more. She pleaded, she begged, she wept…but except for the one thing she had heard—which had not been an answer, but a statement—the heavens were like brass.

One day, two days, a week went by, and still she didn't know. Her heart was torn by her feelings for Jeremy, her concern for Rachel growing up without a father, and her fear of finding herself alone at the end of her life—Rachel married and gone, her books unpublished, and her life withering away like the cursed fig tree.

One evening she was reading to Rachel. When they were finished, she set the book aside and asked Rachel the question.

"Rachel, what would you think if Mama got married again?"

"Who would you marry? Is Papa coming back from heaven?"

"No, Rachel. I would marry someone else."

"Who, Mama?"

"Jeremy King has asked me to marry him."

Rachel tilted her head to one side and considered that for a moment. "I like Jeremy King. He's a nice man."

"I like Jeremy too, Rachel."

"Do you like him the way you liked Papa?"

"Not in the same way, Rachel. Your papa was a special man, and there will never be anyone like him for me again."

"Then why would you marry Jeremy?"

Jenny hated it when Rachel went right to the heart of the matter.

"I didn't say I didn't love him, Rachel. What I said was I didn't love him the way I loved Papa. Jeremy is a wonderful man. He would be a good husband and a wonderful father. And…oh, Rachel, your Mama is lonely to be with someone who really loves her."

"That's not a reason to marry someone, Mama. And besides, I really love you. Isn't that enough?"

Jenny looked at her daughter. Wise beyond her years. "Has someone been telling you the answers, Rachel?"

"*Gott* has."

The answer was so direct that Jenny could only stare at Rachel.

"*Gott* has been telling you?"

"Yes, Mama. I've been praying for you."

"Why hasn't He told me?"

"Because you are trying to tell Him the answers instead of just listening."

So Jenny went back to prayer, but this time she did not beg—she listened.

And then one night soon after that, Jenny woke up out of a sound sleep. She had been dreaming about the night her mama died. She was there in the ICU. The lights were dim, and the heart monitor was beeping softly. She stood with Bobby Halverson by her papa's bedside and looked into Reuben's wonderful, sea-blue eyes. The old smile was there behind them, the smile that had been a light to Jenny all her days. He looked over at Jerusha as though to assure himself that she was still with him. Then he pulled Jenny close.

"Jenny, my beloved girl, my precious girl."

Jenny felt Reuben's breathing begin to slow—one breath, another and then…nothing. She cried out, and the nurse hurried into the room. She came to the bedside and checked Reuben's pulse. He was gone, but the steady beep continued unabated.

And then she looked and saw that Reuben's hand was still clasped in Jerusha's.

"It's your mother's heart, beating through him, Mrs. Hershberger. It's like they have one heartbeat."

Yes! Of course they do. Two lives, one heart. My mama and my papa.

Then from years ago, Jerusha's words came to her.

"I will tell you that there may come a time in your life when you meet a man whom you will love so deeply that you will gladly surrender everything of yourself into his care and protection."

Her mama had surrendered everything to her papa. They had loved each other completely. And when they died, it was as though one heart was beating in both their bodies.

"You showed me that, Lord!" Jenny cried out. "You showed me that Mama and Papa had a special kind of love. The kind that only comes once."

Yes, dochter, *a special love. And I gave that kind of love to you too.*

"When you gave me Jonathan."

Yes, Jenny, I gave you what you always needed, and what you will never need again.

"Because it was enough…because loving Jonathan was enough for me, because it was real love. Love born of You, Lord, and not from my own needs."

Jenny knelt beside her bed and spoke to her *Gott.*

"Thank You, Lord, for the gift of Jonathan. Thank You that our love was born in Your heart and was pure and complete. Thank You, Lord, for my papa, who showed Jonathan and me how a real man loves his wife. And thank You, Lord, for my precious mama, who showed me that one love is more than enough for any woman if it is true love. Thank You, Lord, for showing me on the night they died that they were two lives with one heart. And now I know that is how it was with Jonathan and me. We were two lives with one heart."

And you still are, My dochter, *you still are.*

After that night, Jenny felt the turmoil and the emptiness slipping away. There were many questions still to be settled, but now she had a surety in her heart that the Lord would give her the answer. And He did in a most unusual way.

One night Bobby Halverson had come by after work. The three of them shared a meal of fried chicken and mashed potatoes with corn and beans on the side. When dinner was over Bobby had pushed back his chair and groaned.

"Jenny, you sure learned how to cook from your mama."

Jenny smiled and said, "Jonathan used to say that my cooking had become at least edible over the years we were together."

"It's more than edible, Jenny. It's downright good eatin'. What do you think, Rachel?"

"My mama makes the best fried chicken ever!"

"Even better than *Grosmudder?*"

"*Ja,* Uncle Bobby, even better."

Bobby put his hands on his full stomach and smiled. "Well, Jonathan must have been pulling your leg, Jenny."

They both fell silent for a moment.

"I miss Jonathan," Bobby said. "He was a wonderful young man."

"Yes, he was, Uncle Bobby. The years I spent with him in Paradise were the happiest of my life."

"Jenny, do you think you'll ever marry again?"

"Funny you should ask, Uncle Bobby. A man I like very much has asked me, but—"

"But he's not Jonathan, is he?"

Bobby smiled and Jenny laughed.

"Why is it that everyone says that to me, even the Lord?"

"Because it's true, Mama," Rachel chipped in.

"Well, I have turned him down again. I sent him a letter yesterday. He is a very good man, but—"

"But he is not Jonathan," Bobby and Rachel said together.

They all laughed. It felt good.

Finally Bobby asked, "Jenny, if Paradise was the place you were the happiest, why don't you go home?"

"Home, Uncle Bobby? But this is my home."

"Is it really, Jenny? Reuben and Jerusha are gone, and this house is just a house now. If you're going to live out your years, why don't you go back to Paradise? Seems to me that's really your home. Doesn't the Bible say something about that?"

"Therefore shall a man leave his father and his mother, and shall cleave unto his wife," Jenny replied.

"Seems that would go for a woman too."

"Uncle Bobby, are you trying to get rid of me?"

"No, Jenny. I just see you drifting here. You don't know what to do with yourself. You used to read me things you had written, but you haven't done that in a while—not since..." Bobby paused. "Jenny, I think you should sell the place and go back home to the place you and Jonathan made together. Just a thought."

Jenny sat silent for a moment and then said, "If I go back to Paradise, would you come live with us?"

"*Me?*" Bobby said with surprise in his voice.

"Yes, you. You're the only real family I have left, and from what you say, I'm the only family you have. Your mom and dad are gone, and you've been sheriff a long time. Isn't it about time for you to retire? I have more than a hundred acres of land, and there's a small house on the property that *Grossdaadi* Borntraeger's helpers used to live in. It would be perfect for you."

"Well, I have been thinking about retiring. It's been almost twenty-five years, and it is wearing me out. But what would I do there?"

"First of all, you would be with two people who love you, and we would take care of you. And second, you could help on the farm or go hunting or just sit around if you felt like it."

Bobby had a bemused expression on his face. "It's a very interesting proposition. Let me think on it. It would be strange leaving Apple Creek, but I suppose I could get used to it. Especially if we had chicken like this about three times a week. What do you say about me coming, Rachel?"

"Yay!" Rachel shouted. "I say yes!"

"Okay, Jenny," Uncle Bobby said. "I'll give it some thought. I can't promise anything, but I'll definitely consider it. And what about you?"

"You know, I think you may be right about Paradise. It was the one place that I really felt was my own home—a home I made for Jonathan and me. Maybe I should go back. I think I would see it in a different way if I did."

"You let me know what you're going to do, and I'll help you any way I can. Now, how about we go sit on the couch and have some rhubarb pie?"

Rachel clapped her hands. "Yay again!"

◇◇◇

In the days that followed, Jenny realized that the Lord had been speaking to her through Bobby. The thought of going home to Paradise grew on her until she knew moving back was what she should do. So she went to Johann Troyer and talked to him about it.

"We will be sorry to see you go. But it's not as though the Springers and the Hershbergers will be gone from Apple Creek. Your family is deeply rooted here."

"I've spoken to Papa's brother, Amos, who lives in Galion, *Bisschop* Troyer. He has always loved our place and would give me a very fair price for it. Mama's brother died long ago, but my mama's cousin has been farming *Grossdaadi* Hershberger's farm for many years. So that land would stay in the Hershberger family."

"*Ja, das ist gut,*" Johann said. "You are a Borntraeger by blood. To go back where you made your home on the Borntraeger farm in Paradise *würde ein sehr gutes Ding sein*, a good thing indeed. I will help you however I can."

The next month was a blur. Jenny packed up the things that were important and sent them ahead—her mother's dishes, some of her clothing, and Jerusha's collection of quilts. She shipped a few pieces of furniture off to Paradise, including her desk and her mama's porch swing, and the rest she left for Amos. She kept the Rose of Sharon quilt with her. Her Uncle Amos came, and they went through Reuben's tools. Amos kept many of them, and what he didn't want, Jenny gave to Henry Lowenstein, who was delighted to take them.

"When I was a kid, your dad used to teach me how to use these," he said. "I'd hang out in his shop, and we would talk about all kinds of things. He's the one who told me about Jesus, and it's the greatest gift he ever gave me. I'll think of him every time I use these tools."

"Henry, it's not that far to Paradise. Won't you come and visit us?"

Henry brightened at the idea. "Why, sure, Jenny. I'd love to. I could make it there in about six hours. That would be great. And by the way, don't ask anybody else to drive you there because I'm going to. I've been driving the Springers and the Hershbergers for too many years to quit now."

Bobby helped her sort out a lot of the other things, and soon the day came when they closed the house on Richenbaugh Lane for the last time. Jenny stood on the lawn with Bobby and Rachel and said good-bye to the old place. Then she turned to Bobby.

"Have you thought any more about my offer?"

"I've been thinking it over, Jenny. I can't come yet because I need to finish out my last term before I retire. But I might come visit in the spring and see how I like it."

She took his arm as they walked to Henry's car. "Yes, Uncle Bobby, that would be wonderful. I'll look for you when the daffodils start to bloom."

Part Three

THE TREES OF EDEN

◇◇◇◇◇◇◇◇◇◇◇◇◇

When I left Paradise in 1978, it was a time of great bitterness in my soul. The days were dark, my heart was empty, and my future stretched away before me like some great desert—a place of burning sands and bitter winds. Thorns came up in my palaces, and nettles and brambles, and my life became the habitation of dragons.

But today I look homeward, and though my heart is weary with the adversities of the last years and I bear their scars like great scourgings, in my heart a joy begins to rise as I remember the words from Isaiah 51 and Ezekiel 36.

> I will make your wilderness like Eden, and your desert like the garden of the Lord; joy and gladness shall be found therein, thanksgiving, and the voice of melody.
>
> And they shall say, this land that was desolate is become like a garden.
>
> And I will dwell among the trees of Eden, and I will be glad.

"The Trees of Eden"
from the journals of Jenny Hershberger

Chapter Twenty-Nine

The Fountain

◇◇◇

And so, Jenny and Rachel returned to Paradise. The sale of her parents' farm in Apple Creek had taken some emotional toll, but Jenny knew it was for the best. There would be no looking back.

The day they arrived, the old farmhouse almost seemed to welcome them back. Rachel ran straight to her room and jumped onto her bed.

"I'm home, room!" she cried.

Jenny went into her room and closed the door. She looked around, and then she knelt down by the bed.

"I've come home, Jonathan. I'm home to stay. I will thank God every day that He gave us this place to make it into a home. Everything I shared with you is here. Rachel was born here, and we had true love here, so this is where I'll stay, content, until the glorious day I see you again."

Then she got up and went about the business of coming home.

That first winter back in Paradise passed quickly, and then it was spring, and the daffodils were in bloom. Jenny stood on the porch one morning beating a carpet when she saw an old Ford pickup coming up the drive. A familiar face smiled at her through the open window. Bobby Halverson had retired as sheriff of Wayne County and had come to visit as he promised. They sat up late the next few nights talking things over, and in the end, Bobby agreed to come and live with them. Lem fixed up the old bungalow that sat on the rise just beyond the barn. Bobby brought his things, and then he was there and that was that. At first the local Amish wondered at an *Englischer* living on an Amish farm, but when *Bisschop* Troyer came to visit and told of the love the Ohio Amish had for the man, they accepted Bobby unequivocally.

Jenny made the spare bedroom upstairs into an office and set up her desk there. Lem and Bobby took out the old tall window with the sliding sash and put in a wide picture window so Jenny could look out onto the rolling fields of her place while she wrote. And write she did!

The wellspring of inspiration that had dried up in Apple Creek began to flow again—first a trickle, then a stream, and then a torrent. She wrote poems, short stories, and articles. She delighted in the Amish life, and her articles were full of insight and humor about the highs and lows, the perfections and foibles of her faith. She wrote often about Apple Creek, about her mama and papa, keeping their memory alive with wonderful stories about growing up among the Ohio Amish. The stories made her think about the book—it lay in its place at the bottom of the cedar chest—but she never got it out. As far as she was concerned, that was a closed chapter.

At a certain point Bobby read one of her Apple Creek stories and encouraged her to submit it to the local newspaper. The editor loved it, and soon Jenny was writing a weekly column. After a year, the local paper was purchased by a bigger publication in Lancaster, and Jenny's column went with it. Soon she was getting a flood of mail, asking her questions about the Amish, their ways and culture and faith. She printed her answers in her column, and readers began calling her "Dear Jenny."

◇◇◇

Five years passed, years of peace and calm and productivity. Rachel grew from a sprout to a precocious teenager, and Bobby and Jenny aged gracefully. And then one day Jenny had a visitor. And with the visitor came change and turmoil and the hand of the Lord moving in her life again. The visitor was Jeremy King.

Jenny was out in the back garden pulling up some onions and spreading them on the ground to dry. It was late August, and the afternoons in Paradise were heavy and languid. The last days of summer heat did their best to keep the impending fall at bay, but instead they made the fields heavy with the coming harvest, and the fall came anyway. Jenny's garden was overflowing with beans, carrots, and turnips—all the staples that she would put up for the winter. As she bent over the row of onions, she head a voice call her name.

"Jenny, Jenny Hershberger!"

"I'm out back…come around the house."

Jenny stood with her hands on her hips, the rebellious curls still doing their best to escape from the bun under her *kappe*. Jeremy King walked around the corner and stopped. If anything, the years had made Jenny even more beautiful, and there was life in her eyes and joy in her greeting.

"Jeremy! What a surprise—and a delight. How are you, my friend?"

Jenny put out her hand, and Jeremy took it.

"You're as pretty as a picture, Jenny. And you look happy. It does my heart good to see you in such fine spirits."

Jenny laughed. "I was a wreck when I was staying with my folks in Apple Creek, wasn't I? You must have thought me a basket case."

Jeremy laughed too. "Maybe. But the most delightful basket case I've ever met."

"So, what brings you to Paradise?" Jenny asked.

"I want to chat with you about an idea."

"Come inside. I'll make some coffee and we'll chat."

They went in the back door, and Jeremy looked around. "Where's Rachel?"

"Rachel's fourteen and in her last year of *schule*. But she's an excellent student, and she wants to know why she can't keep going. I'm going to have to wrestle with her and some other people over this, I'm afraid."

"Times are changing, Jenny. The old ways are disappearing."

"That's the problem, Jeremy. If the old ways disappear for the Amish, there will be no Amish."

"Still convinced that the Amish way is the best way, Jenny?"

"It's who I am, Jeremy. Without my faith and my culture, who would I be then?"

"I left, Jenny, and I'm still who I am."

"To each his own, Jeremy. It's not something I can explain. Now, what did you come about?"

Jeremy laughed. "Why don't you just get out a hammer and hit me between the eyes with it, Jenny Hershberger? I guess I better get to the point before you do. You're still the most direct person I've ever met."

Jenny put the coffee on, and they sat down.

"I've been reading your column in the local paper in Lancaster. It's wonderful, you know. You're funny, wise, insightful, and sometimes even prophetic. And your readership is growing every day. The paper must be happy to have you."

"It is going well with the column and the articles, Jeremy. Years ago you said that the interest in all things Amish was the coming trend. Well, it's happening just like you said. And it's not just from people who live around here. I get letters from all over the country. People send someone one of my articles, and then I get a letter from California or Montana, and so on. The newspaper is thinking about syndicating the column, and then I don't know how I'll handle all the mail."

"That's what I want to talk to you about. How would you like to do a book based on your articles? In fact it could be just that—your articles with questions and answers and an index with information on how to find out more about the Amish. I'm sure it would be extremely popular, and it would just be a setup for more books. What do you say, Jenny?"

Jenny thought about it for a moment. "You know, Jeremy, I think that would be a good idea. I've always wanted my writing to glorify God and help people to understand the Amish more. How would we do it?"

"We'll have to get permission from the paper to reprint the articles. I might have to pay them a small royalty or a flat fee, but I know the publisher, and we can work that part out. Besides, a book will just increase their circulation. All I need is to write up a contract and have you go over it, and if it's fair, you can sign it and I'll do the rest."

"That sounds fine, Jeremy. I'll wait for your contract. Now, how about some coffee?"

Jenny talked it over with Bobby and Rachel that night at dinner. Bobby listened while she laid out the proposal and then nodded in agreement.

"Do you think by putting my articles in a book I'll be going beyond the limits of what the *Ordnung* says, Uncle Bobby?"

"Jenny, you've already been writing articles for the paper for three years. You either write them by hand or on your old manual typewriter. You're not making personal appearance tours; you're just helping people to better understand the Amish. I know that I sure do after I read your articles. Funny how you can live among a people for years and never really know what makes them tick."

Rachel was a little more reticent. "Are you sure you want to get into something that is going to bring you a lot of attention from the world, Mama?"

"As always, my darling girl, your questions go straight to the heart of the matter. I prayed about it this afternoon, and I have no check in my spirit. For some reason, I believe the Lord is going to do something wonderful."

Later that week, the contract from Jeremy came. Lem sent Jenny to a local attorney who advised the Amish on legal matters. The attorney read through the contract and gave his approval.

"It's a standard publishing contract. In fact, it's very generously weighted in your favor. The fellow who wrote it up must like you."

Jenny thought about that.

I wonder if Jeremy is still carrying a torch for me. I hope not. I certainly don't want to stir all that up again.

The book came out in the spring of 1986. Within a few months it was wending its way up some regional best seller lists. The manager of the Christian bookstore in Lancaster displayed it and reported steady sales. The Amish and their separated lifestyle definitely piqued the interest of readers. Jenny started getting more letters from people here and there around the country who wanted to know about the Amish, and she was in awe at the positive response to her book.

Then one night, when things seemed to be going well with the book, there was a knock on Jenny's door. When she opened it, there were three elders from the local congregation on her doorstep. Jenny could not read the expressions on their faces, but a little warning leapt up in her heart.

The lead elder spoke up. "Jenny, we need to talk to you about your writing. It seems to be stirring up some amount of…interest among the members of the local district, and we wanted to discuss the matter with you."

Jenny nodded and invited them in. The three men filed past her into the house. Jenny had a sense of déjà vu—she had been through this before. And she didn't feel very good about the prospect of going through it again.

Chapter thirty

Songs from the Heart

◇◇◇

Richard Sandbridge heard the buzzer on his intercom, but he didn't answer it. Instead he continued to strum his guitar. The song idea had been eluding him for days, and he was determined to capture it this time around. The intercom buzzed again. With a sigh, Richard put down his guitar and pressed the intercom button.

"Yes, Deborah, what is it?"

"Sam Westerbrook from Cross & Crowne is on the phone. He wants to talk to you about getting in the studio again. Says his guys are ready for another big hit."

"Okay, Deb, I'll take it. Thanks."

Richard switched to line one. "Richard Sandbridge."

"Yeah, Richard, this is Sam Westerbrook. How are you?"

"If I was any more blessed, I'd be twins," Richard said.

"What?"

"Don't worry, Sam. It's a joke."

"Uh…okay, whatever. Say, Richard, do you have any new songs for us? The guys are pretty tired of playing "Crown of Thorns" for the thousandth time. Don't get me wrong, it's a wonderful song and the kids really dig it, but I'd like to have something new and fresh out there. Got anything for us?"

Richard started looking for some dates on his desk calendar as he held the phone between his shoulder and his ear.

"What about the guys in the group? I thought they wanted to write their own songs."

Sam grunted on the other end of the line. "Yeah, well, it's one thing to say and another to do. The new girl singer we got has a few interesting things going on, but nothing like your songs, Ricky."

"Sam, don't call me Ricky, okay?"

"Yeah, whatever, *Richaaard*."

"Thanks, Sam. Appreciate it."

"Well?"

"Well, what?"

"Do you have some songs for us so can we get back in the studio?"

"Okay, Sam. I've got one."

"Yeah! Now that's what I'm talkin' about. Can I bring Gary over this afternoon?"

"Sure, but why don't you bring the girl, too…what's her name?"

"Nadine. Nadine Carbone. Why should I bring her?"

"Look, Sam. Here's the deal. If I write all the songs for you guys, I make all the money. Your guys get performance royalties and gig money. That's it. The big money is in publishing. If I'm providing the songs, you, as manager, are seeing bubkes, nothing, nada. Someone in the group needs to start writing the songs, or you stay a high-level cover band for the rest of your life. You get my drift?"

There was a momentary silence at the other end of the line.

"How much did you make off 'Crown of Thorns,' Richard?"

"I'm not going to tell you the exact number, Sam, but it's in six figures. You go ahead and figure out what twenty percent of that is."

There was a whistle on the other end of the line. "Okay, Mister Sandbridge, I get your drift. I'm bringing the girl too."

"Around four, Sam."

"You got it."

Richard Sandbridge hung up the phone. He sighed and looked around. Several gold and platinum records hung on the walls of his upscale penthouse office. Each record on the wall represented lots of money and prestige. His songs had been recorded by big-name artists—country, rock, R&B—and now by a big-name Christian rock group.

Christian rock! Now there's an oxymoron.

When Richard became a Christian, he was already a highly successful songwriter. Three gold records were on his wall, and his two biggest hits, *Tonight* and *Anna*, had gone multi-platinum, recorded by the R&B group Soul Circle in 1981. Now, a decade later, he had three more platinum hits, the latest with the crossover Christian group Cross & Crowne. Billy Cross and Gary Crowne had played on the combination of their names to find a modicum of success in the Christian market. But it wasn't until Richard gave them *Turn to Me* and *Crown of Thorns* that they achieved their greatest success.

Richard picked up his guitar again, smiled to himself, and thought, *I guess I'll see if I can write another big hit before they get here.*

At four o'clock, Sam, Gary, and the new girl walked into Richard's office. He had just finished putting the final touches on the elusive new song. Gary Crowne looked around Richard's office the way he did every time he came by, obviously in awe of the symbols of Richard's success. The girl singer looked like she was all flash and no content. She had the band-girl look and a prominent tattoo on her shoulder.

"Hi, Richard."

"Hey, Gary. How's it going?"

"Great, Richard, just great—thanks to you. This is our new singer, Nadine Carbone."

She reached out her hand. "It's a pleasure to meet you Mr. Sandbridge. I'm a big fan."

"You can call me Richard if I can call you Nadine."

"Okay, Richard. But my friends call me Deeny."

She smiled, and Richard caught just a hint from her eyes that there might be something in there besides a vacuum.

Gary nodded at his manager. "Sam says you might have something for us to record. Can't wait to hear it."

"Yeah, I just finished something you guys might like. But I thought you were going to start writing some of your own stuff."

"I've been trying, but I haven't really come up with anything."

The girl piped up. "I have a couple of songs, Mr. Sandbridge…I mean, Richard. I'd like to show them to you."

Richard heard something in her voice that got his attention—ambition, a flash of intelligence.

Sam and Gary both scowled.

"Let's hear something."

"Sure," Deeny said. "Do you have a keyboard?"

Richard pointed to a corner where his mini-studio and a nice little Yamaha electric piano were set up.

"Help yourself."

Deeny sat down at the keyboard and started to play. She was nervous and flubbed the first chord. She stopped, looked up, smiled, and started again. This time she started smoothly.

> Your love is wonderful
> So pure and clean
> Flowing down from Calvary
> To a sinner like me

And Your blood is wonderful
So pure and clean
Flowing down from Calvary
To a sinner like me
And now I am free

Thank You, Jesus, thank You, Jesus
For all You are to me
You're my life, my hope
You're my one desire
Thank You, Lord, for dying for me

Deeny's voice was clear and sweet, and once she got into the song, it was apparent to everyone that she was singing from her heart. Richard's first impression of her went out the window as he listened to the song. When she finished there was a quiet moment. Then Sam jumped in.

"Yeah, great voice, kid, but it's a little too religious for me. Got anything like *You Light Up My Life*? You know, something that people could put in their boyfriend's name in place of Jesus?"

Deeny scowled. "Right! Like "You Light Up My Life, Elmer"?"

"I think Deeny's got a great song," Richard said. "I don't know if it would be the single from the album, but any real Christian would end up listening to it over and over. And by the way, Sam, you guys are signed to a Christian record company, remember? If you want to do secular music, maybe you should go hit up Warner Brothers."

"Whoa, Richard," Sam said. "We're very happy right where we are! I mean, we're all Christians and we all love the Lord, right? I'm just looking for the breakthrough song that's going to put us on top, that's all. Just lookin' out for my guys."

Deeny stared at him, and he got the message. "Uh, my gal too. So Richard, you said you had a new song?"

Just then the intercom buzzed. Richard flipped the switch. "Yes, Deborah?"

"Jeremy King on line one."

"Okay, thanks."

Richard turned to the group. "I have to take this call. Give me five minutes and I'll be right back."

Richard left his office and went to the conference room across the hall. The red light on the phone was flashing, and he picked it up.

"Hey, Jeremy. Thanks for getting back to me."

"Sure, Mr. Sandbridge."

"It's Richard. Listen, we've been watching Kerusso Publishing, and you folks are really starting to make a mark in the Christian publishing arena. I'd like to get together with you and talk about some ideas we've been throwing around over here at Charis Records."

"Well, I'm flattered that you've heard about us, Richard. I'd love to chat. When do you want to meet?"

"How about next Monday? Can you drive over to New York on Sunday? We'll put you up, and then we could spend Monday together."

"Sure, that sounds good. Can you tell me what it's about?"

"We'll talk about that when you get here. I've got to get back to a meeting. In the meantime, I'm going to give you back to Deborah. Give her a timeline that would work for you, and she'll book the hotel room. See you on Monday."

"Sure…Richard. See you then."

Richard hung up the phone with a smile of satisfaction on his face. If everything worked out, the Jeremy King deal could be a blockbuster.

Jeremy leaned back in his chair. The call from Richard Sandbridge had him wondering what was up. Charis Records was a big deal in Christian circles. They had three number one hits on the Christian charts, and one was starting to see action on secular radio stations in the Midwest. Richard Sandbridge was an enigma to everyone. He had literally come out of nowhere with his hit song *Tonight* in 1981. The song was huge, and Sandbridge had followed it with another monster hit. Along the way he had proven his skills as a musician and had produced a few independent hits for some major labels. Then had come his highly publicized conversion to Christianity and his move to Charis Records. As head of artists and repertoire, he had discovered Cross & Crowne, and the rest was history.

Jeremy walked out to the front office. The move back to Lancaster from Akron five years earlier had taken a toll on his business, but for the past three years sales had headed back up. The offices were a bit run-down, but he was publishing new books almost every month and was satisfied that he had made the right move, especially since interest in everything Amish was growing.

His secretary looked up when he walked out.

"Judy, can you call Charis Records back and coordinate with Deborah there on a hotel? I need to drive to New York on Sunday, and Charis is putting me up."

"Sure, Jeremy. What's up?"

Jeremy shook his head. "I don't know, but whatever it is, it's big. Charis Records is leading the way in Christian music. It will definitely be an interesting trip."

When Richard walked back into his office, a heated discussion was going on. It seemed to be Sam and Gary against Deeny.

"I'm a Christian," Deeny was saying. "I got saved out of a life that was killing me. Now I just want to glorify God and sing His praise. I'm not really interested in going back into secular music. I spent too many nights in bars and dance halls, hanging out with the wrong people. I don't want to go back."

"We're not saying we should go secular, Deeny," Gary said. "Maybe just lighten up on the real heavy religious stuff. I mean, after all, we don't want to offend anybody."

Deeny stiffened. "The gospel *is* an offense. It makes people confront their sin, and most of them don't want to do that, so they find the whole thing offensive. But if we're Christians, we have a responsibility to tell them the truth. No apologies, no surrender."

Sam shook his head. "I don't know, Deeny. Maybe you're just a little too radical for Cross & Crowne."

"I'd rethink that, Sam," Richard said. "Deeny will add a great sound to Gary and Billy's voices. Take it from me as your producer, if you want to go all the way, this young lady could be the missing piece."

Gary and Sam looked skeptical but quieted down. Sam spoke up. "So…the new song?"

Richard picked up his twelve string. "Right. I've been working on it for two weeks and just got the bridge today."

As Richard began to sing, he could see Deeny's eyes light up with admiration. Gary and Sam looked at him as if he were some kind of saint. Richard wondered what he was doing in a Christian business that did everything it could to keep its eyes on men and not on Jesus.

CHAPTER THIRTY-ONE

Big Business

◇◇◇

RICHARD SANDBRIDGE WALKED INTO THE Waldorf Astoria Hotel in uptown Manhattan. The place was definitely five-star all the way. Richard liked the older-style hotels—something in the connection to the past intrigued him. He went to the front desk and asked for Jeremy King. The attractive young woman behind the counter smiled at him.

"Mr. King is waiting for you in the restaurant, Mr. Sandbridge. The table against the wall, right inside the door."

She smiled again, this time more seductively. Richard noticed that she had a wedding band on her left hand.

"I'm a big fan, Mr. Sandbridge," she continued. "I think you write the most beautiful songs."

"Thank you. That's very encouraging."

He walked away without looking back and entered the restaurant. The place was empty except for a blond man sitting where the receptionist had said he would be. Jeremy King.

As Richard walked up, Jeremy put down the menu he was perusing, stood up, and stuck out his hand.

"Mr. Sandbridge, I presume. Jeremy King."

"Please, call me Richard," he said, sliding into the seat across from Jeremy. "What looks good today?"

"There's a hot roast beef sandwich au jus that sounds interesting, along with the usual assortment of lunch items."

The waitress came and took their drink orders. Richard was glad to see that Jeremy ordered ice tea. *So many Christians I go out to eat with are half in the bag by the time lunch is over. This guy is a nice change.*

They exchanged the usual pleasantries about the drive over and how Jeremy liked his room, and then Richard got down to business.

"As you may know, Jeremy, Charis Records has grown a lot in the past few years."

"That's for sure. Three monster hit records, the top Christian band in the country, and the hottest new writer-producer. You folks are what's happening right now."

"Yes we are, and we want to keep it that way. We've been looking at the market, and we—the board of directors and myself—have come to the conclusion that we need to be doing more than just selling records, cassettes, and compact discs. But let's not talk music, Jeremy. I came to talk to you about something else."

"Yes, I've been wondering about that."

Just then the waitress approached and asked if they were ready to order. She also had a record album with her—*The Best of Soul Circle*—and wasted no time. "Gee, Mr. Sandbridge, would you mind signing this for me? I just love 'Tonight.' I think it's the most beautiful song ever written."

Richard smiled at her "How did you know it's my song?"

"This is New York, Mr. Sandbridge. Every person you see working in a restaurant is probably in show business in one form or another. I happen to be a Christian singer-songwriter. I have all the records with your songs on them. You're bigger than Burt Bacharach."

"Well, thanks. That's most complimentary. So you're a songwriter. Got any good tunes?"

"I think so."

Richard pulled out a card. "Send me a cassette of your two best, along with an envelope with a return address. I'll give you my honest opinion. Hope that helps."

"Oh, thank you, Mr. Sandbridge!"

The waitress started to walk away with the card clutched in her hand.

"Miss?"

She turned back to them. "Yes, Mr. Sandbridge?"

"Aren't you forgetting something?"

The girl blushed and pulled her pad out of her apron. Jeremy and Richard both smiled as she stammered out the specials of the day. She took their order and left. Richard watched her go with a sad smile.

"The truth is I probably won't be able to listen to more than about thirty seconds of her songs, but you never know. Every once in a while you find something. There are so many young people here wanting to live the dream. If they only knew how hard it is."

"You didn't seem to have any trouble making it, Richard."

"You know, Jeremy, that's true. I don't really understand my success except that it's totally from the Lord. Someday, when we have time, I'll tell you my story. But today I want to talk about you."

Richard took a sip of water and then continued. "Let me just lay it on the table. We want to buy Kerusso Publishing and merge it with Charis Records."

Jeremy, clearly surprised at the idea, started to speak, but Richard pressed on. "Before you respond, let me finish. We want you too, Jeremy. Kerusso Publishing would become the literary arm of an umbrella corporation, with Charis Records as the music side. You would continue to run Kerusso just as you have been. You would receive cash and stock in the mother corporation in return for your company, and we would pay you a very competitive salary. In return, you keep publishing—not only the Amish material you've been working on but also standard Christian fiction and nonfiction books. We think we could attract some of the big-name Christian authors and teachers to our stable of writers. You would have your pick of great books to produce… I mean, publish."

Jeremy let out a breath. "Let me be sure I heard what you said, Richard. You want to buy Kerusso Publishing, bring it alongside Charis Records, and basically take over the Christian music and publishing markets. And you want me to run the publishing side?"

"You got it."

"Why me?"

"We like your style, and we like the focus you have on all things Amish. I'm not usually one to walk in the prophetic, but here's what I see. You've had great interest in the Amish fiction novels you've published, and our research shows that they have done very well for you. Am I right?"

Jeremy nodded.

"We're convinced that you have your finger on the pulse of the next big market in Christian books. Two of your Amish books are doing really well, and we think you can do a lot more of the same. And we will put our money where our mouth is to back up that belief. So now… what do you think?"

Jeremy was silent for a moment. "Well, it sounds really good. I've been wondering about the next step for Kerusso Publishing, and then here you come and drop it right in my lap."

"So you like the idea then?"

"I think it's a great idea, and the timing couldn't be better. I've been working with an author for some time now. She's the best writer I've come across in all the years I've been in the business. She's brilliant, she's deep, she's funny, she's beautiful, and most interesting of all, she's Amish. With the right promotional backing, I think she could become one of America's best-known authors."

"Has she published anything yet?"

"Yes, we just put out her first book about three months ago. It's called *Dear Jenny*. It's a compendium of articles she wrote for some local papers around Lancaster. She began by just telling stories about her parents and growing up Amish in Ohio, but pretty soon people starting writing in with questions about the Amish lifestyle, so the column became known as "Dear Jenny." Her name is Jenny Hershberger, and her book is starting to do very well regionally. And *Dear Jenny* doesn't even begin to show what this lady can do. She is absolutely brilliant. Wait until you read some of the book."

"Jenny Hershberger...Jenny Hershberger," Richard said. "Why does that name sound so familiar?"

"She's getting some press right now. Maybe you read about her somewhere. My point is that she is also a great fiction writer. She has a book that I worked on with her. It's the most amazing story about how she was rescued in the huge snowstorm that blew through Ohio in 1950. Nobody could find her parents, so an Amish family adopted her. Then years later it turned out that her mother was Amish. If I could get her to let me publish the book and then come out with a series, we might have some best sellers on our hands."

"Sounds like a really great story. You say it's autobiographical?"

"In an interesting way. She wrote it like a novel, but it's a true story—a real tear-jerker."

"Jenny Hershberger...Sounds great! I'd like to meet her."

"If we can work out this proposal, you definitely will."

◇◇◇

Jenny sat in the kitchen with the three men from her church. She was trying to stay calm, but her heart was beating hard inside her chest. The whole thing brought back memories of her meeting with Samuel Lapp and the tragedy that resulted. She didn't want anything like that to happen again. Then Jonas Plank spoke up.

"Mrs. Hershberger, we are aware of what happened with the former *bisschop* of Lancaster when you were in Ohio, and we deeply regret it. We believe your parents would still be alive if Samuel Lapp hadn't interfered with your family. So first of all, we want to ask you to forgive us."

Jenny felt a slow sense of relief at his words. "Of course I forgive you. I've come to terms with everything that happened in Apple Creek. But there must also be another reason you have come here tonight."

"*Ja*, Jenny, there is."

He looked at the other men and then continued. "We don't want you to be afraid. We have not come to bring discipline, but protection."

"Protection?"

"*Ja*. We're concerned about your well-being and your walk with the Lord."

"May I ask what brought this about?" Jenny asked.

The second elder spoke up. "We obtained a copy of your book and read it, and we find it to be delightful."

"Delightful? But I thought you had come…"

Jonas smiled. "To tell you we hated it? No, Jenny. It is *wunderbar*— quite charming. You give a true and accurate portrayal of the Amish life, and after talking it over, we have decided that it can only help the Amish community. You see, after the affair with Samuel Lapp, there was much misunderstanding about us among the *Englisch* around Lancaster. There were many accusations leveled at the Plain People because of the evil behavior of one man. It did us great harm. We want to live in peace with our neighbors, but many of them became suspicious of us. We were labeled as a cult by some."

"So how does my book help?"

"We feel that your book gives a real insight into our lifestyle, especially your detailed discussions about the roots of our faith. You have a wonderful grasp of the history of the Amish, even before we came to America. Your words seem to brush away many misconceptions about us, and because of your book, people are beginning to realize that we are really not any different from anyone else. The tensions that Lapp created seem to be easing. Instead of seeing us as aloof and secretive, people see, through your book, that although we may have separated ourselves from the world, that doesn't keep us from having our problems."

"So what is the concern?"

"You are a widow, living with an *Englischer*…"

"Bobby Halverson?"

The three men looked at each other and then nodded.

Jenny started to protest. "But he's like a blood relative. He was my papa's best friend—from the war. We're not living…together! He lives on my farm!"

Jonas smiled again. "*Ja*, we understand your relationship to Bobby Halverson. We also know that he is a good friend to the Amish. *Bisschop* Troyer in Wooster has nothing but the greatest respect for him. But there are many who do not understand a single woman living in what they see as questionable circumstances."

Jenny crossed her arms. "I'm not going to tell him to go away, if that's what you are asking."

"No, of course not, Jenny. We're not asking that."

Jonas looked to the others for reassurance. They nodded, so he continued.

"Our concern…what we think…"

He sighed and then got to the point. "We feel that you need a covering—a husband, to be specific. You're still young, and there are many eligible bachelors who would want to court you if you were open to that. We just think with that kind of protection, the people of our district would be more inclined to support your writing and your *Englisch* friend. But without a husband, it's easy for people to talk."

The old familiar irritation rose in Jenny. She did her best to control it because she saw that these men were not being judgmental, but caring. So she took a deep breath before she spoke.

"I have not considered taking another husband. To be honest, I was offered marriage several years ago, but it was outside the faith, and I could not do it. And I don't think the men of our district would want to court me if they really got to know me. I'm strong-willed and temperamental, and I know what I want. Not many men could put up with that."

"And it is for that reason we are most concerned, Jenny. The Bible tells us specifically that man was put as the head of the woman to prevent her from being deceived. And that is what we want to protect you from."

The whole conversation was becoming bittersweet to Jenny. She was beginning to feel anxious and hemmed in, so she compromised.

"I will consider what you are saying and put it to prayer. If *du leiber Gott* has a husband for me, I will ask Him to show me who it is."

Chapter Thirty-Two

Beyond the Veil

◇◇◇

Richard Sandbridge sat in his office with a set of headphones on, listening to Nadine Carbone's demo cassettes. The songs were all good, and two or three were simply outstanding. Deeny was a gifted lyricist and a terrific singer. She was an excellent addition to Cross & Crowne, but Richard could see her moving up to a solo career very soon. All she needed was time on the road to hone off some rough edges.

Besides that, she's really pretty.

The light on his phone flashed, and he came back to reality. He stopped the tape, flipped off the headphones, and grabbed the receiver.

"Yeah, Deborah?"

"Jeremy King on line one."

Richard pressed the button. "Jeremy, how are you?"

"Doing well, Richard, very well."

"So what have you decided about my offer?"

"I talked it over with my employees, and they're all for it, and I am too! I personally think it's a great idea, and I'm ready to go with it. I just have a few questions about logistics. For instance, do you want us to relocate to New York? There are some other details too, but that is definitely the big question."

"That's great, Jeremy! And, yes, we've already talked about the logistics. We decided if you want to stay in Lancaster, it would probably work. The drive is only two and a half hours. Of course, you'd have to come over here a few times a month to sit in on board meetings, but other than that, you would have pretty much free rein. I'm certainly not that tuned in to book publishing, so I won't be micromanaging you. I do want to learn it, though, so I'd like to visit from time to time."

"Sounds good, Richard. When can we meet?"

"Cross & Crowne are going back on the road in two weeks. I've got to get them in the studio to lay down some tracks, so we'll probably have to wait until after they leave. I know this sounds like the old 'hurry up and wait' routine, but I have to get some new songs started with these guys or they'll revolt on me."

"Perfectly fine, Richard. I've got some things I need to take care of here. Jenny Hershberger is starting to get some interest from some syndicators. There's a possibility we'll get her into some big papers in the Midwest—Ohio, Indiana, Illinois…you know, places with large Amish populations. So two weeks would work for me."

"Sounds good, Jeremy. I'll call you in the middle of next week and we'll set a time."

Richard hung up the phone and looked out the window of his penthouse office. *Why does the name Jenny Hershberger sound so familiar to me?*

At four thirty, Deborah buzzed to tell Richard that Nadine Carbone was waiting to see him.

"Send her in, Deb."

Deeny Carbone walked into Richard's office. Richard could tell that she had taken extra care to look nice. She had on a sleeveless spring dress that was color coordinated with the large rose tattoo on her left shoulder, and she was wearing some slightly elevated shoes. Her hair was pulled back from her face, and she wore just enough makeup to highlight her dark eyes and pretty features.

"Hey, Deeny, what's the occasion?"

"I just came from rehearsal with the guys. It's only a few blocks, so I thought I'd take a chance and come over. I'd really like to hear what you thought of my demo."

Deeny held her purse in both hands as though to hide behind it. Richard waved her to a chair.

"Okay then…I've got some bad news and some good news."

Deeny looked perplexed. "What's the bad news?"

Richard smiled. "The bad news is that you have a few stylistic habits you've gotten into with your lyrics that I'd like to help you with. And I want to work on the dynamics you use when you're singing. Your tendency is to over sing, and I think I can help you overcome that."

Deeny brightened. "If that's the bad news, then what's the good news?"

"The good news is you have some terrific songs. I really like all of them, but there are two that I really love. I think we can build some of the more up-tempo ones into the Cross & Crowne set and record them with the group. But the two I really love, I want you to do solo. You can play keyboards and I'll do the guitar tracks. We'll get Johnny Burris in on bass and Eddie Cottrell on drums. Oh, and I'd like to get Kenny Wilson to do the horns."

"Richard, those guys are the best in the business! They must cost a fortune!"

"It will be worth the expense. I think you have at least two hit records on your demo, maybe more."

Deeny sat in the chair for a minute staring at Richard. Then she put her face in her hands, and her shoulders began to shake.

"What, Deeny? What is it?"

Deeny composed herself, pulled a tisssue out of her purse, and dabbed her eyes.

"Nobody whose opinion I trusted ever said my music was any good, and I've been writing since I was a kid. My dad used to say my songs were terrible. Of course, he was drunk most of the time, so I learned to take his ranting with a grain of salt." Deeny flipped her hair back over her shoulder and dabbed her eyes again.

"This whole music thing has been really hard. I had to work my way up in a cheesy club band that didn't want to do originals. After I left them, I played the punk circuit for a couple of years, thinking I might get to showcase some of my tunes there. But the punk guys were bigger chauvinists than the club band, and they froze me out. When I met the Lord, the first thing that happened was getting this gig with Cross & Crowne. And they have been very noncommittal about my songs. So it's really nice to have someone…I mean, someone like you to encourage me."

"It's more than just encouragement, Deeny." Richard knit his fingers together and leaned forward. "The songs are really, really good. And I love that you don't compromise the message of the gospel. It's built in and comes through loud and clear."

Deeny smiled at Richard. "Thank you, Richard. That really means a lot to me."

Richard took a closer look at Deeny. She really was a pretty girl. Long dark hair, dark eyes, a sweet mouth, and chiseled features made her a standout in any crowd. Richard took a chance.

"Can I take you to an early dinner, Deeny?"

Deeny hesitated and then nodded. "Sure. That would be nice, Richard. Thank you."

The Cornerstone Restaurant was more than just a place for an early dinner. It was a four-star New York eatery, and Deeny's eyes widened when they stepped out of the cab.

"Wow, the Cornerstone! I've always dreamed about eating here."

"Come on then, Deeny. It's early, so we can probably get a table."

They went in, and the manager recognized Richard right away. "Mr. Sandbridge! Nice to see you! We have a table right over here for you and the young lady."

"Thanks, Max. This is Nadine Carbone. She's a new writer I'm working with. You'll be hearing from her soon. She has some wonderful songs."

Deeny smiled at Max and blushed. Richard was glad to see that underneath the girl singer facade, Deeny was tenderhearted.

They ordered their dinner and chatted. Richard found Deeny to be bright, articulate, and funny. It wasn't long before he was feeling very comfortable with her.

"So after you left home, you traveled with the club band you were telling me about?"

"That's right. We played every sleazy dive up and down the East Coast. We traveled in an old Volkswagen bus and a Chevy van that carried our gear. We'd stop in a town and get two motel rooms—one for me and one for the guys. One guy slept in the van so the amps wouldn't get stolen, and the other four guys tossed a coin for the beds. We played clubs where we would make a hundred dollars a night and dinner. Sometimes the owners wanted to pay us off in drugs. Back then it was okay. We were pretty out of it most of the time."

Richard visualized the band in their bus. *I remember something about a Volkswagen. Did I own one once?*

Deeny interrupted his reverie. "What about you, Richard? You haven't told me anything about yourself. Where do you come from?"

Richard smiled a sheepish grin and shrugged his shoulders. "I don't know."

Deeny cocked her head. She had a puzzled expression on her face. "Excuse me…did you say you don't know?"

"That's right. I don't know where I'm from."

Richard stirred his coffee without speaking while Deeny waited. Finally she pressed him. "Are you going to tell me what that means, Richard?"

Richard passed his hand in front of his eyes. An image came to him. *Fire and water! Fire and water!*

"Not tonight, Deeny. Maybe another time."

◇◇◇

Jenny Hershberger let the three elders out. She hadn't exactly bowed to their wishes, but they all seemed to have come to a vague understanding. Jenny would pray about being open to finding a husband among the local men, and the elders of the church would give her suggestions concerning men they considered eligible from time to time. They said their goodnights, and then Jenny closed the door and leaned against it.

I don't want to get married...especially not to some oaf who will make a drudge out of me.

She went to Rachel's room, quietly opened the door, and peeked in. Rachel was sleeping, her head resting on the pillow and her long dark hair cascading around her beautiful face.

I don't need anyone else. I have my daughter to love me, I have Lem to help me, and I have Bobby to comfort me. That's all I need.

She sighed. The sound woke Rachel, who stirred and then rolled over and looked at Jenny.

"Is that you, Mama?"

"Yes, darling."

"What are you doing?"

"Just looking in on my beautiful girl. You are growing up, Rachel. When did that happen?"

"I'll be fifteen soon, Mama, and then I'll be out of *schule*. But I want to keep studying."

"I know, Rachel. You're like me. You have an inquisitive mind and the same curiosity as your mama. But you also have your papa's way of seeing into the heart of things."

"I wish papa had never gone on that boat, Mama."

"So do I, Rachel. So do I."

The cab ride back to Deeny's apartment was quiet. They sat in the back without touching. Finally Deeny spoke.

"I'm sorry if I dug into something that is none of my business, Richard. Please forgive me."

"It's not your fault, Deeny. It's just something I don't like to talk much about. Just so you don't think me totally weird, I will tell you this. I'm a retrograde amnesia victim. I have no memory before about eight years ago. All I know is that I am a musician and a songwriter. I woke up one day in a hospital. I didn't know how I got there, and no one could tell me anything about my past. It's as though my life started eight years ago. That's all I know."

"So that's why you just seemed to burst onto the music scene."

"Yeah, that's an interesting story. It's also why I don't do interviews."

The cab pulled up in front of a brownstone on the upper East Side.

"Would you like to come up and tell me about it?"

Richard looked at Deeny. The streetlight outside cast her lovely face into shadows. For just a moment he considered going with her. Then he took a deep breath.

"You know, Deeny, a few years ago I might have said yes. But I can't, and you know why."

Deeny looked down. "Make no provision for the flesh?"

"You're a beautiful girl, Deeny. I hope we can get to be good friends. But I can't get involved with anyone. It just wouldn't be fair."

"But maybe I could help you, Richard."

"Maybe. But what if my past has something in it you would not want to be involved with? I think it's best we have a friendship and leave it at that."

Deeny reached out her hand, and he took it.

"Goodnight, Richard. I'll be praying for you."

Chapter Thirty-Three

The Visit

◇◇◇

Richard Sandbridge pulled up in front of Kerusso Publishing on Chestnut Street in Lancaster. The building was an old brick two-story retail space with French paned windows all along the front of both stories. Richard climbed out of his BMW, grabbed his briefcase, and walked through the front door.

The downstairs was basically a warehouse space with a broad flight of stairs in the back. Pallets of boxes were stacked everywhere. It was disorganized in an organized way that Richard liked. The clutter meant that things were happening at Kerusso Publishing.

A young man sat at an old wooden desk by the front door. Bills of lading and order forms littered his desk. He glanced up and then got up quickly and walked around the desk with his hand out.

"Mr. Sandbridge! How nice to meet you. I'm Tom O'Neil, the operations manager. Please excuse the clutter. We're very busy right now. We just got a shipment of *Dear Jenny* from the printer, and the guy just kind of walked in here and dumped them on me."

"I'd rather see the clutter than an empty warehouse, Tom. Nice to meet you."

"Jeremy…uh, Mr. King is upstairs in his office. Just make your way through those boxes and up that flight of stairs."

"Thanks, Tom."

Richard walked up the stairs and turned left at the top. Down at the end of a broad hallway he could see Jeremy sitting at his desk with a phone to his ear.

"Sure, Fred, I can get you two hundred copies. You sure you can sell that many?" Jeremy looked up, saw Richard, and waved him in.

"Fred, you know we have the best return policy in the business. If you can't sell them in six weeks, ship them all back…What? Well, I know they've been selling like hotcakes. Why do you think I'm so willing to give you a great return clause?"

Richard heard a voice on the other end of the line say something, and then Jeremy laughed.

"That's right, Fred. My mama didn't raise any fools. I have to go, but if you fax me over that order, I'll have Tom get those out today… Right! You too! Goodbye."

Jeremy hung up and stood to welcome Richard.

"Welcome to Kerusso Publishing, Richard. I hope you don't mind the mess."

"Like I told Tom, I'm glad to see it. Very encouraging. Makes me know that Charis made the right decision."

"Yes, I think so, Richard. Sales of *Dear Jenny* are starting to climb. I'm getting them into a lot of the chains, and some of the big book clubs are asking for hardcovers. I'm thinking that we're going to do really well on this book."

"We'll thank the Lord for that, Jeremy. So what's the plan for today?"

"I want to go over our records with you and give you our auditor's report. Then I'd like to take you over to see where we print the books. After that, lunch. There's a little place outside town that serves Amish food. You'll love it. And we can kill two birds with one stone."

"How so?"

"The restaurant is near a little town called Paradise. That's where Jenny Hershberger lives. I'd like to run by there and see if she's home. I want you to meet her."

"That sounds great, Jeremy. Let's get to work."

Bobby Halverson sat on the front porch of Jenny's house in a big overstuffed chair. Rachel sat on a stool next to him, reading. Lem walked around the side of the house and up on the porch.

"Hey, Bobby. I heard some wild turkeys gobbling down in the woods this morning. Want to go down before sunrise tomorrow and see if we can get a couple?"

"Count me in, Lem. Some roast turkey sounds mighty good."

Rachel looked up from her book. "Uncle Bobby?"

"What, honey?"

"Will you teach me how to shoot so I can go with you and Lem?"

A picture came to Bobby's mind of Rachel lying prone with a twelve-gauge shotgun pressed to her shoulder, her eye squinting down the barrel, and a look of concentration furrowing her brow. A powder burn blackened the side of her prayer kappe.

"You sure that's what you want to do?"

"*Ja*, I'm sure. Lots of Amish girls know how to shoot."

"You know, your grandpa was a crack shot. I asked him one time where he learned to shoot. He told me he had been hunting all his life."

Bobby turned to Lem. "What do you think, Lem? Reuben told me once that his folks hunted all over Pennsylvania and Ohio. I guess it wouldn't hurt for Rachel to carry on the tradition."

"Sounds good to me, Bobby. But you're the marksman, so you should teach her."

"Okay, Rachel, we'll get started this afternoon."

"Then can I come with you tomorrow, Uncle Bobby?"

"If you can stay quiet and do exactly as we tell you, you can come."

"Can I shoot at the turkeys?"

Bobby laughed. "We'll see about that, darlin'. We'll see about that."

Richard drove his BMW convertible down a tree-lined lane outside Lancaster. It was a beautiful day, and they had the top down. Jeremy pointed ahead.

"Take that next right, and about a half-mile down we come to the restaurant. I'm going to turn you on to some food you'll never forget."

In about five minutes they pulled up in front of the Friendly Farmer restaurant. Richard got out, stretched his legs, and then followed Jeremy inside. The place had neat handmade tables and a cozy atmosphere. A big buffet overwhelmed the middle of the room.

"The buffet is the way to go, Richard. They have a salad bar, the best local vegetables, chicken, ham, and beef. The lunch desserts are great. My favorite is anything with custard."

"Sounds good. Let's go."

After they ate their lunch, Richard and Jeremy sipped cups of coffee.

"You're kind of quiet today, Richard. Anything on your mind?"

Richard took a breath and glanced out the window. Then he took another sip and looked back at Jeremy.

"I was thinking about a conversation I had with Deeny Carbone the other night."

"Who's that?"

"Deeny is one of the singers in Cross & Crowne. She's a terrific girl, she's gorgeous, she writes great songs, she's gorgeous…"

"You said that twice. I guess she's gorgeous."

Richard smiled. "Yeah, I guess that's the problem. Can I share something personal with you, Jeremy? I mean, have we known each other long enough? I feel like we're getting to be friends. You're one of the few Christians I've met in this business who doesn't mix their faith with the desire to be famous."

"Whatever you say to me, Richard, will not go beyond these doors."

"Okay, I appreciate that. Here's the deal. The other night, Deeny and I were having dinner, and she asked me about my family. You know—where I was from and all that. I had been having a great time thinking that maybe something could come of this, and suddenly things got very awkward."

"So…was there a problem with that question, Richard?"

"Yes, a big one."

Jeremy looked at Richard expectantly.

"The thing is, Jeremy…I don't know."

"You…you don't know what the problem is?"

"No. The problem is, I don't know where I came from."

"How can that be?"

"I'm a retrograde amnesia victim."

"Retrograde amnesia? What's that?"

"I can only remember so far back in my life, and beyond that, nothing. For me the cutoff point is about eight years ago."

"What happened?"

"All I know is that one morning I woke up in a hospital. I don't know how I got there. My head and face were bandaged, and I hurt all over. I had no ID, and I couldn't remember my name. They told me they had found me wandering around downtown in Sandbridge, Virginia. I had a nasty knock on my head, and my face and hands had been burned."

"Sandbridge?"

"Yes, it's on the Virginia coast. And that's how I got my name. The police looked into it, but there was no way they could identify me. They came up with all kinds of scenarios, but my fingerprints had been ruined, so they had no clue about who I was. There were no missing-persons reports filed that matched my description. It was like I just dropped out of the sky or something. So they called me Richard Sandbridge."

"But how did you get into the music business?"

"Well, that's really an interesting story. When I was in physical therapy, the hospital was trying to figure out what to do with me. The counselor asked me if I was interested in anything. I told them I thought I could play guitar. After my fingers healed up, they brought me one. It was amazing because I just sat down and started playing. I knew one song."

"'Tonight'?"

"Yes, 'Tonight.' Everybody thought it was beautiful."

"But how did it get to be a hit?"

"I had to have some cosmetic surgery done on my face because of the burns. That's why I wear this mustache. I still have some scars around my mouth. The doctor who did my surgery had done some work on Larry Carroker, the lead singer for Soul Circle, after Larry was in that bad car wreck, and he had stayed in touch after the surgery. So the doctor knew the group was looking for some songs. He had heard me play 'Tonight,' so he recommended me to Larry. I showed Larry the song, he loved it and recorded it, and the rest is history."

"Richard, that's an amazing story. And you don't remember anything about your past life?"

"That's right. No parents, no place where I grew up, no girlfriend… nothing. That's why I don't do interviews. I'd have to make something up. The music press thinks I'm some kind of Howard Hughes recluse, but that's the way it has to be."

"So then you wrote 'Anna' for Soul Circle, and you had your second monster hit. So what happened next?"

"When I had the hit with 'Tonight,' I became good friends with Larry Carroker. He invited me to a few sessions. They asked my advice on production, and it turned out I had a good ear for producing and mixing. They let me sit in as assistant producer on a couple of tunes and loved the way the songs turned out. So they recommended me to some friends, and that's how I got to produce some other groups."

"So Charis called you?"

"Well, that happened after I met the Lord."

"Yes, Richard. You need to tell me your testimony."

"It turned out that Larry was a strong Christian. Over a couple of years, when I was getting started in the business, he helped me a lot. When we were hanging out, he would drop hints about his relationship with Jesus. One day I just called him on it, and he shared the gospel with me. It made absolute sense to me. It was like I was already a believer. I accepted Christ and started letting Him steer my career in the direction He wanted."

"And then Charis Records called you."

"That's right. They had just signed Cross & Crowne, but the band needed some songs and a producer. Charis had heard about my conversion, and since they were a Christian company, they thought I would fit. "Crown of Thorns" and "Turn to Me" were the result of that collaboration."

"Wow! That's all I can say. Wow! What an amazing story, Richard! So do you remember anything at all?"

"Sometimes. I get pictures, like flashes. For instance, Deeny was talking about touring with her band in an old Volkswagen bus. I had the distinct impression that I owned one sometime in the distant past. And my faith was the same way. After I accepted Christ, I got a Bible. When I read it, it was as though I already knew what it said. Some of that I chalked up to the work of the Holy Spirit, but sometimes it was just too real. I felt like at some point I had already spent a lot of time studying it."

"Amazing…just amazing." Jeremy shook his head then glanced at his watch. "Say, if we want to drop by Jenny's place, we need to go. It's just a few miles from here."

Richard and Jeremy pulled into the lane off Leacock Road. They drove down the long driveway up to the house. Richard took off his sunglasses and stared at the house.

"What a beautiful place, Jeremy."

"Yes, it is. Jenny inherited it from her grandfather."

Far off in the distance, they heard what sounded like gunshots.

"Sounds like someone's hunting."

Jeremy got out, walked up on the porch, and knocked on the door. There was no answer, so he knocked again. When nobody answered, he went off the porch and walked around the side of the house. In a minute he came back.

"I was hoping she was out in her garden, but there doesn't seem to be anyone home. I'll leave a note. Sorry you don't get to meet her."

"Me too, Jeremy. Me too."

Chapter Thirty-Four

The Proposal

◇◇◇

Jenny and Lem came home from their trip to the General Store. She grabbed some bags from the buggy and walked up on the porch. A business card stuck out from between the door and the jamb. She pulled it out. It was Jeremy King's card. There was a note on the back.

> Jenny,
> We came by, but you were gone. Call me.
>
> Jeremy.

Jenny wondered who the "we" was as she went inside.

Bobby and Rachel returned shortly after Jenny got home. Rachel was a mess. Her clothes were dirty, her *kappe* was askew, and her hair had lost most of its bun and was dangling down in long strands. She was filthy, but there was a huge grin on her face.

"Uncle Bobby taught me to shoot. It was the greatest fun, Mama, but my shoulder is so sore!"

Jenny smiled at her precocious child. "Lem told me you two were going to go shoot. I can see that Uncle Bobby must have had you crawling through the underbrush."

"Jenny, Rachel is a crack shot. I've never seen anything like it." Bobby leaned two guns against the wall. "I gave her a few pointers, and then she started knocking down everything she aimed at."

"Well, her father was an Eagle Scout marksman when he was in the Boy Scouts. And being around you and Papa, something must have rubbed off."

"Uncle Bobby said I could go with them tomorrow to shoot some turkeys. Can I, Mama?"

"If it's all right with Uncle Bobby, you can go. But isn't it going to be hard in a dress?"

"I was thinking I might wear some jeans, Mama."

"Rachel, you cannot even think about wearing jeans until your *rumspringa*. You are only fourteen and you need to dress proper Amish."

"But, Mama, it will be so hard to crawl around in this dress!"

"If you want to go, that is how you will dress. Perhaps you should just stay home."

"If I have to be stuck with such stupid rules, maybe I don't want to be Amish!" Rachel's voice rose.

"Rachel!"

Before Jenny could finish, Rachel stomped off to her room, leaving Jenny and Bobby in an awkward silence.

Jenny sat down at the kitchen table and rubbed her forehead. "Great! I thought maybe I'd get to wait on dealing with a rebellious teenager until she was a little older."

Bobby slid into a chair beside her. "Jenny, Rachel is a good kid. She seems to have her head on straight."

"Mostly, Bobby, but we actually have a real conflict going on that has strained things between us. When she finished *schule* this spring, she was told she couldn't continue. Amish girls and boys only go until the eighth grade. Rachel was heartbroken. She desperately wants to continue her education."

"And you've been having a fight over it?"

"Yes, Bobby, and it breaks my heart. When I finished school, I was working on a big project about the history of the Amish in Ohio. I wanted to keep going with it, and the local librarian offered me an internship so I could have everything I needed, but *Daed* was against it. Only after the elders intervened did Papa give his permission. So I was able to continue my education. Now Rachel wants to do the same thing, and I have to say no. I feel like a hypocrite."

"Why can't she keep studying at home?"

"I've suggested that, but she had her heart set on taking some classes in animal husbandry over at the community college. It's driven a wedge between us, and now, here I am, an Amish widow writing books, with my beloved *Englischer* uncle living on my place and a teenager dealing with her hormones who thinks her mother is crushing her dreams. It's a little *beunruhigend*…a little unsettling. Maybe the elders are right."

"Right about what?"

"I had a visit from the local elders. They think I am in a dangerous position."

"Dangerous?"

"Yes. The Bible says that a woman needs the covering of a husband, especially if she's going to be in a position to be deceived. They want me to start considering some of the local men who seem eager to court me."

Bobby gave a low whistle and leaned back in his chair. Then he spoke.

"Jenny, you are a different kind of Amish girl. You've been through hard times and good. You grew up in an Amish family and were raised by my closest friends. Then, at a very difficult point in your life, you found out that one side of your bloodline is *Englisch*, and the other is Amish. You married an *Englischer* who became one of the finest Amish men I ever met. So you have a built-in conflict. *Englisch* or Amish? Who are you, really? And now Rachel is getting to the age where she's sorting through the same questions. I think you may have to make a bigger choice than you really understand."

"What do you mean, Bobby?"

"I think your elders are right. I think if you stay Amish, you should marry again and live this life the way it has been lived for centuries— turn your back on the world and everything that's in it. But if you keep going with your books, I think there might come a day when you have to go out in the world a lot more than the Amish are willing to allow. And so you have to decide who you are and what God—"

"What God is wanting for my life?"

"Yes, Jenny…what God wants for your life."

On the way back from Paradise, Richard and Jeremy passed a large field. Some men were working in the field with a horse-drawn piece of equipment. It was moving down rows of green plants and digging them up. Something inside Richard made him pull over to the side of the road. He climbed out of his car and walked to the fence.

Jeremy got out and followed him. "What is it?"

"Those men, Jeremy. What are they doing? They're Amish, aren't they?"

"Yes, they're Amish, and they are digging potatoes. The horse draws the digger down the rows and the men follow after, bagging the potatoes. Why?"

"I don't know, Jeremy. I have the strangest feeling that I've been here before, standing at this fence, watching Amish men harvest their crops."

Richard stood a moment longer, and then he began to softly sing. "*Lassen Sie ihn, der gelegen hat, seine Hand auf dem Pflug nicht sehen sich um!*"

Jeremy stared at him. "How on earth do you know that song, Richard?"

Richard turned with tears streaming down his face. "I don't know, Jeremy. What does it mean?"

"'Let him who has laid his hand on the plow not look back!' It's an Amish song."

Richard's knees buckled, and he started to fall. Jeremy leaped forward and grabbed him.

"Richard, what is it?"

"I don't know, Jeremy, I just got very weak. Can you get me into the car? You'll have to drive."

"Sure…come on, my friend. Let's get you someplace where you can rest."

Jeremy helped Richard in, and then he got into the driver's seat and started the car.

"I'm going to take you to my apartment, Richard. You should stay there tonight."

"That's fine, Jeremy. I don't know what's happening, but I have a splitting headache, and I need to lie down."

Jeremy put the car in gear, and they drove off. Richard turned to look at the men in the field one more time. He pressed his face against the window. The glass was cool against his skin.

What was that, Lord? What was that?

The next day, Jenny went to Bobby's house and called Jeremy's office. She waited a few moments, and then Jeremy's secretary answered.

"Kerusso Publishing, this is Judy. How can I help you?"

"Jeremy King, please."

"I'm sorry, Mr. King isn't in the office. Can I take a message?"

"Would you please tell Mr. King that Jenny Hershberger called?"

"Oh, Mrs. Hershberger, I didn't recognize your voice. Jeremy is at home. He said if you called to give you that number. Do you have a pencil?"

Jenny wrote down the number and called Jeremy's house.

"Hello, this is Jeremy."

"Jeremy, it's Jenny."

"Jenny, how wonderful it is to hear your voice. How are you?"

"I'm fine. I'm sorry I missed you yesterday. You asked me to call you."

"Yes, I did, Jenny. I need to talk to you. It's very important. Can you meet me today?"

"I have some things to do this morning, Jeremy. Would this afternoon be okay?"

"Certainly. Where?"

"At the Friendly Farmer?"

"Yes, I was just there having lunch with a friend. In fact, that's what I want to talk to you about."

"Is that the 'we' you mentioned in your note?"

"Yes, Richard Sandbridge. I'll tell you more about it when we meet. Four o'clock?"

"Sure. See you there."

Jenny watched Bobby drive away, and then she walked into the Friendly Farmer restaurant. She looked around and saw Jeremy at a table by the window. He stood up and waved.

"Jenny, over here."

Jenny walked over and sat down across from Jeremy. He looked good, handsome as always, and obviously glad to see her.

"Do you want to get something first?"

"A cup of coffee, Jeremy. I'm really not hungry."

Jeremy held up his cup, and the waitress nodded and came over. After the coffee was served, Jeremy turned to Jenny and gazed at her.

"You look wonderful Jenny, beautiful and—"

"What did you want to see me about, Jeremy?"

"Oww!" Jeremy smiled and rubbed his forehead. "There's that hammer again. Honestly, Jenny, one of these days you are going to knock me right out of my chair."

Jenny laughed. "Okay, Jeremy. I'm sorry. I am glad to see you. But you know that it's hard for me to put up with fluff and flattery."

"Telling you that you are beautiful is a serious issue to me, Jenny. No fluff in it. But let's talk about that later. I want to share some things that are happening. Have you ever heard of Richard Sandbridge?"

"No, who's that?"

"He's a songwriter-producer and one of the principals of Charis Records."

"What's Charis Records?"

Jeremy laughed and took a sip of coffee. "Okay, I forgot. You don't listen to music or the radio or records, and you would know absolutely nothing about the recording industry. Charis Records is a Christian record company that records and sells Christian music. They've been around for several years but didn't really break out until Richard Sandbridge, an already established secular songwriter, became a Christian and moved over from his label to Charis. Since then, they have virtually taken over the Christian recording business."

"So how does that relate to you, Jeremy?"

"Richard has become the vice president in charge of artists and repertoire for the company and a main stockholder. Pretty much what Richard says is what happens at Charis. Richard came to me with a proposal. He wants to buy Kerusso Publishing."

"But that's your life!"

"Yes, but here's the other part. I'm going with the company. I'll stay on as president of Kerusso and become a stockholder in the umbrella company Richard set up. I get to run Kerusso exactly the way I always have, but now we'll have almost unlimited resources at our disposal. Richard is particularly interested in *Dear Jenny*. He also knows that you are a terrific fiction writer. He wants to put your book out as soon as possible."

"The book about Jenna's quilt?"

"Yes. With their promotion budget and our connections, we can make that book a national best seller. You would become very famous, my dear."

Suddenly Bobby's words rang prophetically in Jenny's heart. *"Jenny, I think you may have to make a bigger choice than you really understand."*

CHAPTER THIRTY-FIVE

The Offer

◇◇◇

JENNY CONSIDERED WHAT JEREMY WAS saying. His conversation was animated, but as he spoke, Jenny began to drift away. It was as though she were hearing Jeremy from far away, and his words were an echo in her mind. She began to imagine herself traveling about the country, but the woman she saw in her mind was wearing *Englisch* clothing and driving her own car. She lived in a fine house, and the phone was ringing—people wanted her, loved her, needed her. She was married again, and it was Jeremy, and they were embracing…and then it was as though Jonathan walked into the room…

"Jenny!"

She jerked back to reality to see Jeremy looking at her with a puzzled expression.

"What? I'm…I'm sorry, Jeremy, what were you saying? I'm afraid I drifted off."

"Jenny Hershberger, sometimes you can be the most frustrating woman!"

"What?"

"What I'm saying is very important to me, and it could be important to you too."

Embarrassment flooded over her like a hot shower. She tried to sound contrite. "Tell me again. I was very rude."

Jeremy gathered himself and started again. "Jenny, I want you to marry me! I can't be more plain than that."

Something inside Jenny twisted like a snake. "We've talked about this before. If I marry you, I have to leave the church, and I—"

"Jenny, can't you just be honest with me for once? You keep putting up smoke screens. Do you care for me or not?"

Jenny looked down at the table. "I care for you a great deal. You are generous and kind, you love the Lord…"

"So if you care for me, what should stop us from being together? Some religious mumbo jumbo?"

Jenny started to speak, but Jeremy silenced her. "Let me finish. I'm going to speak as plainly as I can. You may not like me after I say this, but you will at least know that I care for you enough to tell you the truth."

"Jeremy, please! I don't want to go where you want to take me. I know what you're going to say—"

"Do you? Do you, Jenny? I want you to face up to something. You were very happy to be Amish when you lived with your parents in Apple Creek, or so you thought. But the truth is, you struggled all your life with the uncertainty of your past. Then Jonathan came along, and you fell in love with him. You would have gone away with him without a moment's hesitation. You would have left the Amish religion behind and lived your life with Jonathan in perfect contentment. Then you found out you were half Amish by birth, and again you were torn. But Jonathan saved you from having to deal with the questions when he became Amish. So you had your cake and ate it too."

Jeremy paused and looked at her until she met his gaze.

"And now, Jenny Hershberger, you have the same two paths set before you again. And you're struggling because you don't have absolute certainty of what God really wants you to do. This is what I know. In your heart you're not as Amish as you think you are. I think you would leave the church for the right reason. And I think that if you were really honest with yourself, you would admit that I could be a big part of the reason you would leave!"

There! It was out in the open! It was the thing that Jenny had been wrestling with all her life—the question that pestered her like a little dog barking at her heels. It was the unspoken dilemma that gnawed at her in her dreams, the shadow that lurked just around the corner... was she really Amish?

Jenny's whole life came flooding in on her. Loving memories were set against her deepest fears, hope for the future crashed against the agony of loss, glory fought with tragedy. Jeremy's words were like a maelstrom, and she was going down. She felt as if she were drowning.

"I don't want to deal with this, Jeremy! Please, this is too hard."

But Jeremy kept boring in. "Jenny, I'm your friend. But more than that, I love you with all my heart. I've loved you for seven years, like Jacob loved Rachel. I want you to be my wife. I want you to live in freedom. I know you love God, and He is what you need—not some outward dress or behavior that you think will make you holy but cannot. You're not under the Law, Jenny. You're under grace. Until you accept that, being Amish is hanging like a great millstone around your neck. You've got to make the choice, Jenny."

"But I love the Amish way, Jeremy. It's my whole life. It's everything to me..."

"Come on, Jenny! I love the Amish faith too—I grew up in the church, remember? But after I got over the absolute agony of being pushed out by a liar, I found that God had been working for the best all along. I am where I am supposed to be. And it hasn't drawn me away from my faith or robbed me of my salvation."

"But I'm afraid, Jeremy. It's all I know."

"You're afraid because you think the elders are right. You're afraid because you think you can lose your salvation if you're not Amish. And I can tell you, that's just not true. 'By grace you are saved, through faith, and that not of yourself. It is the gift of God.'"

Jenny remembered Jonathan's words, spoken to her so long ago. *The Amish church doesn't save us, Jenny. It's our relationship with Jesus that saves us.*"

Jeremy spoke again, and his words were gentle. "Please, Jenny. I know you've prayed about this before, but you always had the excuse that you were Amish and I'm not. Now I think you have to honestly face up to a choice that has been the great struggle of your life. And if you really pray about which path you will walk down instead of praying about me, I think you'll find the answer."

Jenny focused on his face. *He is kind, he loves God, and he loves me. What more can I ask for?*

She sighed and then said, "Jeremy, you've asked me to pray about this before. I thought I had worked it all out with God. I thought I could just go on being Amish and life would be perfect. But it's not perfect, Jeremy. It's full of tragedy and doubts, fear and uncertainty. And you're right. The question of who I really am has plagued me all my life, and I need to resolve it, once and for all."

Jeremy took her hand. "I've waited for a long time and I need you to choose. Kerusso Publishing and Charis Records are having an event in three days. Richard Sandbridge and I are announcing our merger. It's going to be a celebration. I would love to announce our engagement at that event too. If you can't say yes by then, I will know you've made your decision, and I'll let it go and never speak of it again. If we are to be married, I need you to be with me one hundred percent. Will you give me your answer in three days?"

Jenny knew that what he was asking was right. She needed to move on with her life, however it might turn out.

"Yes, Jeremy. I will tell you in three days."

It was dusk in Paradise. Jenny sat in her mama's old porch swing, watching the sky turn from pink to orange to indigo. As the light began to fade, the crickets picked up their courting song in the shadows around the house. Jeremy's question echoed in Jenny's heart.

"Will you give me your answer in three days?"

As Jenny pondered and prayed, she heard the sound of a horse-drawn buggy coming up the driveway. As the buggy approached, she could see that Abel Ramseyer, the new Lancaster *bisschop,* was driving. Seated next to him in the buggy was a man who looked familiar. The *bisschop* checked his horse at the gate, and the two men climbed down and walked up the path to the porch.

"Guten abend, Jenny."

"Guten abend, Bisschop Ramseyer."

The other man took off his hat. The *bisschop* turned and placed his hand on the man's shoulder.

"This is my friend, Isaac Augsburger."

Jenny stood and greeted the men with a handshake. The *bisschop* looked uncomfortable, but Isaac was personable and friendly. The *bisschop* spoke.

"We were driving by and I was…uh, remembering our conversation of last week, and…uh…I…"

Isaac laughed and broke in. "Abel isn't doing well with this, is he Mrs. Hershberger? I'm an old friend of Abel's. I've lived in another district for many years, but since my wife passed on, I'm moving back here to Paradise…the community I was raised in."

She smiled and motioned toward the door. "Won't you come in?"

The *bisschop* nodded, but Isaac put a hand on his arm. "It's a nice evening, Jenny. Do you mind if we sit on the porch?"

Jenny pointed to the chairs set beside the swing. The three sat together in the cool of the evening. After a while Isaac spoke.

"I've come with Abel to make my case to you…Jenny."

"Your case?"

"Yes, my case. I understand you lost your husband some time ago… so you understand what it means to lose….someone you love."

Jenny had sensed what this was all about as soon as the men pulled in the driveway. But the still-fresh hurt on Isaac's face and in his voice touched Jenny deeply. She would listen.

"*Ja*, Isaac, I do understand very much."

"Well, then." Isaac let out a breath of relief. "Since we both know the…loneliness of the widowed life…there's no sense in beating around the bush, is there? The fact of the matter is that I've come to ask your permission to begin courting you."

Jenny smiled. "I had a feeling that this was not just a social call, *Bisschop*."

Abel shifted in his chair. Jenny put her hand on his arm.

"Don't worry, *Bisschop*, I am not upset with you. We have discussed this matter."

"Yes, Jenny, we have, and to me, this marriage would be the answer to our concerns. I've known Isaac since he was a boy. He is honest, hardworking, true to the *Ordnung*, and a decent, kind man. You would do well to consider his offer."

He paused and then went on. "The elders and I have given this much thought, Jenny. We feel that you have come to a crossroad in your life. The Amish way is simple and straightforward. You either live it or you do not. You cannot be in the world and of it too. You cannot serve two masters. We do not wish to control you. You must make the choice for yourself. But we feel that you cannot go on with one foot in the world and one in the Plain way. It is too hard."

Jenny sat silently for a moment. Then she spoke. "What about my book? I thought you said you liked it."

"*Ja*, it is a good book, and we feel it has served a purpose, as we explained. But we have also seen that the danger of being drawn away from our ways is too great if you continue writing. The Amish do not seek notoriety. We do all we can to remain apart from the world. We feel that you should give up your writing, marry Isaac, and return to our ways with all your heart. That is what we wish for you."

Jenny listened hard for the voice of God in this. Then she said, "You're right, *Bisschop*. It's a question I've struggled with all my life. And now it seems the Lord has at last set two doors before me. One leads to the safety and simplicity of the Amish way, the other to the fulfillment of a gift I believe God gave to me to bless others. But it seems I cannot have both."

Jenny rose from her chair with a sigh. The two men stood with her.

"I need to consider your words. I must seek the Lord. So I will say this. I will give you my answer in three days."

Chapter Thirty-Six

Questions

◇◇◇

So now the great crisis of Jenny's life was upon her. All her days it had been hidden in her heart, and now at last the Lord had drawn it out and laid it before her. She lay upon her bed in the midnight hour, sleepless and with one thought on her mind.

Choose this day whom you will serve.

The question was clear, but the answer was not. Was staying Amish what the Lord wanted for her, or did He want her to pursue the gift He had given her? Why couldn't she do both? She did not know the answer, and the heavens were like brass above her. The gentle voice of the Spirit was strangely silent. When Jenny went to bed that night, she felt as if she were being crushed between two great stones. She longed to go to Jerusha and seek her *mudder's* wise advice, but her mama was gone and no one else was there to help. It was for her alone to decide.

Choose this day whom you will serve.

Finally, too restless to sleep, Jenny rose from her bed. She put a shawl around her shoulders and slipped outside. The screen door creaked softly behind her as she went out onto the porch. It was perfectly still outside, that time of the night when the old day has passed and now all nature is taking a breath before traveling on into the next morning. The moon stood still in the heavens high above her, almost full. The soft light illuminated the yard around her house, and she stepped down into the front yard. The silver grass was cool beneath her bare feet, and she stood and waited as though earth and sky would give her the answer. Night sounds began to filter into her hearing—a frog croaking, the hoot of an owl in a tree near the pasture. In the far reaches of the night a train whistle lingered mournfully. It seemed that all her life was hemming her in, corralling her step-by-step toward this great battle in her soul.

She had a choice to make, and though she felt helplessly caught on its horns, she knew that in the end there was only one answer that would serve the purposes of God. Everything else would take her down side roads that might eventually bring her safely to the end of her days but would keep her from the fullness of God's plan for her life. She knew this without knowing the answer. And the enormity of the consequences weighed hard upon her spirit.

Jenny went around the side of the house into her garden. Beyond the garden gate was the path that led out onto her land. Her land! This place—the houses, the barns and fields—was a reminder that she had a place in the great scheme of things, an identity that had been passed down to her by her Amish *grossdaadi*…

…*as a memorial to the blood of my people, which flows in me.*

She went through the gate and started up the path toward Bobby's bungalow. The trail was well worn with no stones to bruise her feet. Still, it felt like the road to Calvary. Did her cross stand on that hill ahead of her?

As she looked ahead, she saw a tiny glow in the darkness. For a moment she wondered what it was, and then she realized that Bobby was up too, smoking a cigarette on his porch. She went on up the path and stopped by the gate into his tiny yard. Bobby spoke out of the darkness.

"Hello, Jenny. Can't sleep?"

"No, Uncle Bobby, I can't. I…I have a lot on my mind."

"Got some choices to make, little girl?"

"*Ja*, and they are very hard choices. My whole life seems to be hanging on this moment, and I'm afraid that choosing the wrong path will send me plunging over a cliff of my own making."

"And no one can make the choice for you, right?"

"*Ja*. It feels like the Lord stripped everything away from me to bring me to a place where my life is resting on what I alone decide. My mama and papa are gone, Jonathan can't help me…"

"Come sit a while, Jenny."

Jenny went through the gate and sat down by Bobby. He took a drag on his cigarette and looked over at her. The moonlight illuminated his face, and Jenny could see the kindness in his eyes. He reached over and patted her awkwardly on the shoulder.

"I don't have a way with words like you do, Jenny. I've always had a hard time articulating what's inside me. So bear with me for a minute."

"You're a man whose advice I trust. I'm ready to listen," Jenny said, settling in.

"I was there the day your sister, Jenna, died. I carried her to the hospital in my arms, and when the doctor told me she was dead, I never thought I would ever love a child again the way I loved her. But then you came along. Ever since the day your dad and I found you with Jerusha in that old cabin, you've been linked to my life. I've watched you grow and struggle, I've seen the challenges you faced, and as you grew up, you became like my own daughter."

Jenny put her head on Bobby's shoulder. His arm crept around her.

"I know the choice you have to make, and I know it's not easy. But whatever you decide, I will stand with you. You're not a girl anymore, Jenny Hershberger. You're a strong, lovely, brilliant woman who I'm very proud of, and I have no doubt you'll make the right decision. I just want you to remember one thing. When your dad and I were on Guadalcanal, we had to make many decisions in an instant that dictated whether we lived or died. But the hardest thing I ever learned came at the most unexpected moment.

"We were resting in an abandoned Japanese camp. They had all run off when we approached, and they left everything behind—even their dinners were still on the table. Compared to how we had been living the last few weeks, the place seemed like paradise. After we ate, we sat around, just shootin' the bull like Marines do. It almost seemed like we were back stateside. It was quiet and still, no war going on. We let our guard down. One of the guys stood up to stretch, and a sniper shot him right in the head. He was dead before he hit the ground. I learned in that moment that we have to be the most careful when we think we are the safest."

Jenny realized the wisdom in what Bobby was saying. And then a great clarity burst upon her mind. This choice that was before her would define every other moment of her life. It was a God-given moment of destiny that she couldn't shy away from. She knew that it was important that she seize it without fear because everything that would come after would be changed when she chose. But still she waited.

"Thank you, Uncle Bobby. That's a great help to me."

They sat together without speaking again until the first light of dawn began to peek over the hills away in the east. Then Jenny kissed Bobby on the cheek and went back to her house. In her room, she sat at the desk and took out her journal. She paused a moment and then began to write.

Sometimes I think life is like a rushing river that begins its
journey high in the mountains, tumbles down over jagged

rocks, rushes headlong over cliffs, and pours booming through nameless chasms until at last it escapes the harsh stone walls to the broad plain spread before it, flowing deep and quiet through lush meadows between banks that hold it tenderly.

On the way to this place, we usually make choices quickly and without thinking, like those a boatman makes as his vessel poises on the brink before it plunges headlong into the rapids. We look back on these instantaneous choices and understand, with a quiet shudder in our soul, the eternal enormity of a moment.

But even so, the choices we make as we drift in the place of safety and security can be the most consequential. For every soldier knows that in the lush growth beside a quiet river, or beneath the deep underbrush of a peaceful forest, the enemy is most likely to be hidden.

Now I must choose, and although the choice will not determine whether I live or die, it will indeed establish all the rest of the days of my life. And once more I come to a moment when I must surrender again to the One who has always guided me, for I cannot decide in my own flesh, but I am assured that I will know these things by His Spirit.

She looked at what she had written and then closed the book and rose to the work of the day. In her heart she ceased to strive because she finally knew that if she simply trusted the Lord, He would help her know what to do. One step at a time.

◇◇◇

Richard Sandbridge drove his BMW along the Long Island shore. It had been a long time since he visited the coast. He didn't like the ocean. Something about the endless gray-green swells disturbed his sense of balance. He thought it must be the interminable movement, the rushing away to unknown places to break, unheard, upon some distant fog-bound coast that seemed so unplanned to him. Since the day he awoke in the hospital, he had tried to do everything he could to bring order to his life because his memory was missing so many parts. He often felt as if he were taking a jigsaw puzzle out of its box and working feverishly to solve it, only to find in the end that most of the critical pieces were missing or from another puzzle entirely.

He pulled his car into one of the public parking lots along the beach, turned off the engine, and got out. The wind was chill, and the blowing sand stung his face. He stared out at the open water.

Why do I hate the sea?

The day was cold, and not many cars were in the parking lot. Richard was lost in his thoughts. Ever since his experience watching the Amish men dig potatoes, his waking moments had been filled with unrecognizable fragments and pieces, like the old psychedelic light shows back in the sixties at the ballrooms in San Francisco.

How do I know about the ballrooms in San Francisco? I've never even been there…or have I?

One very disturbing picture kept thrusting itself into his consciousness—the face of a man with a long greasy ponytail and a three-day beard. The man was looking up at him and saying words he couldn't make out—something about going home. And then the man died. And then a long, terrible journey and the Amish men again and through it all, the feeling that something enormous was missing from his life.

Lord, will you help me? I can't go on this way. Who am I, Lord?

"Hey, buddy, got a light?"

The voice broke in on him. Richard turned to see an unkempt man standing next to him with a cigarette between his lips.

"Sorry, pal. I don't smoke."

"Well, how about some spare change? I could use a beer."

Richard looked at the man and then reached into his pocket. As he glanced down he didn't see the short piece of pipe that came out of nowhere and crashed into the side of his head. After that he didn't see anything.

CHAPTER THIRTY-SEVEN

Jenny's Choice

◇◇◇

Fire and water, fire and water and the sea—the endless sea. He was drifting, drifting in the middle of the raging sea. The wind tore the tops off the waves, and the driving foam stung his face like lashes from a whip of ice. The freezing, killing water crashed down on him from all directions. Something flew through the air and struck him in the head, and there was no sense to any of it, no meaning. Terror gripped him.

And then he heard a voice and wasn't afraid anymore…

"I will never leave you or forsake you. Lo, I am with you always. Rise up and walk."

Richard groaned.

"Richard? Richard?"

The voice seemed to come from far away—through the fire, through the water…and then the mist cleared, and he opened his eyes and saw Jeremy's face.

"Jeremy?"

"Richard, thank God!"

"Where am I, Jeremy?"

"You're in a hospital in Far Rockaway."

"What happened?"

"You were mugged out at Jones Beach. The guy robbed you and stole your car, but some witnesses called the police. The State troopers caught him about a mile down the road."

"Did he hit me?"

"Yes, he cracked you a good one with a pipe. You've been out for a whole day."

"How did you find me?"

"Your office called me as soon as the police identified you. I've been here since this morning."

"What day is it?"

"It's Wednesday."

"Tonight's our announcement party!"

"That's right."

"I've got to get dressed, Jeremy. You've got to take me to my apartment so I can get ready."

"Richard, you're in no shape to go. We should call it off."

Richard grabbed Jeremy by his shirt and pulled him down. "No! You don't understand. I have to go."

◇◇◇

Even though the answer wasn't yet clear to Jenny, she spent her morning in peace. All she knew was that she needed to do her best to follow the leading of the Spirit. And then, around eleven, she saw Abel's buggy coming up the lane. For a moment she wanted to run away and hide, but she steeled herself.

"Lord, I trust You to give me the words to say."

In that instant her course of action became clear. She didn't wait for the men to come in, but rose up and went out to meet them. She stood by the gate as the buggy came to a halt.

"*Gut Mariye*, Jenny."

"*Gut Mariye*, Abel, Isaac."

The men started to get down, but Jenny waved them back to their seats. "There's no need for you to come in. I have made my decision."

Isaac leaned forward in his seat.

"Isaac, I know you to be a good and righteous man. I know you would be a good husband. But I cannot marry you. I do not love you in that way. I would be untrue to myself and to you if we were married. You deserve to be loved completely, and I cannot do that."

"But marriage for the Amish need not be about love, Jenny. It's built on the needs of our community and our faith first."

"*Ja*, Isaac, I have heard that. But I need something more."

Isaac pressed his case. "But love could grow between us, Jenny. Could you give it a chance?"

"I'm sorry, Isaac. I know this is the decision I must make."

Abel spoke up. "And what will you do in regards to your place in the church? Do you think you can go out into the world and still be true to the Plain way? I'm deeply concerned for you, Jenny Hershberger. I do not think it can be done. You cannot serve God and mammon."

"I appreciate your concern, *Bisschop*. I don't know the answer to that part of the question. I have a strange feeling that I will know by tonight, but at this moment, I can't say."

Isaac tried once more. "You are sure, Jenny? You will not reconsider? I can give you more time if you need it."

Jenny walked over to the side of the buggy. She took Isaac's hand and looked up at him.

"You're a good man, but even if you gave me a year, my decision would be the same. Do not be angry with me. I must do what I believe the Lord is telling me."

Isaac sighed. "As you wish, Jenny. As you wish."

He nodded to Abel, Jenny released his hand, and the *bisschop* cracked the reins. The horse started up, and the buggy moved off. As Jenny watched it go, fear rose in her heart.

Did I hear You right, Lord? Am I giving up everything I know because I think I have heard You? Lord, this is too hard.

And then she heard the gentle voice.

"And thine ears shall hear a word behind thee, saying, This is the way, walk ye in it, when ye turn to the right hand, and when ye turn to the left."

Then Jenny knew what she must do.

Bobby looked at Jenny with a wry smile on his face.

"Are you sure, Jenny?"

"Yes, Uncle Bobby. But I need you to take me into town first. I have to go to the department store and do some shopping. Then we'll go."

"Okay. What about Rachel?"

"She went to Lem's house. They have a cow that's about to calve, and Rachel wanted to help. She'll stay there tonight."

"Let's go then."

Bobby and Jenny walked out to Bobby's pickup, climbed in, and headed for Lancaster.

Richard's head was pounding, but he was determined to go. The doctor had protested, but Richard was adamant. He signed the release papers as the doctor shook his head in warning.

Richard turned to Jeremy. "Will you take me home, or must I call a cab?"

"You're a stubborn man, Richard," Jeremy said, shaking his head. "But there will be no need for a taxi."

The two men went out to the car, where Richard winced as he climbed in. Jeremy drove the car out of the hospital garage and headed toward Manhattan and Richard's apartment. The sunlight was bright and hurt Richard's eyes.

"Do you have any sunglasses, Jeremy?"

"There's a pair in the glove box."

Richard fished around until he found them and then put them on. They were a very large pair of Carreras that covered most of his upper face, but they blocked the light. The pain in his head started to subside.

When they got to Richard's apartment, Richard went into the bathroom to find a bottle of aspirin. He looked at himself in the mirror. A large bandage covered the side of his head.

That's the same side I was bandaged on when I woke up in the hospital the last time…

Gently he pulled the tape until the cumbersome dressing came off, and then he searched around in the cabinet until he found some new tape and a smaller gauze pad. He made a dressing and covered up the stitches that ran in a line from the end of his eyebrow toward the top of his ear.

The guy really clocked me.

As he looked in the mirror he heard a voice, strident and whiney in his ear.

"Candyman, my main man, what's happening?"

Startled, Richard looked around, but no one was there. He shook his head.

I mean, he really clocked me. Now I'm hearing voices!

Just then Jeremy called from the other room. "How are you doing, Richard?"

Richard didn't answer.

"Richard?"

Richard wondered who Jeremy was calling. Then he remembered. *Richard? Oh…I'm Richard.*

He answered Jeremy. "Fine, Jeremy…I'm fine."

Jeremy walked in with a concerned look on his face. "Are you sure you want to do this?"

"Yes, we need to go. But you have to hang pretty close because my brains are a little scrambled."

"Okay, pal. Whatever you want. And by the way, there might be another announcement tonight."

"What's that?"

"I've asked Jenny Hershberger to marry me."

Richard frowned. That didn't seem right. "Isn't this the third time?"

"Yes, but this time she has promised to give me an answer. I think she's finally ready to see things my way."

"Okay. Well, good luck."

Jeremy smiled. "I'm trusting the Lord that she'll do what He wants her to do."

As soon as Jenny walked out of the dressing room at the department store, Bobby stared in amazement. She wasn't wearing her Amish clothes. Instead, she had on a simple sleeveless black dress cut just below her neckline. The hemline dropped modestly below her knees. Her golden-red hair was released from the confines of the bun and cascaded softly down around her shoulders. She smiled shyly at Bobby, and her lovely violet eyes flashed.

Bobby shook his head. "All I can say is, wow!"

"The last time I wore *Englisch* clothes was when I ran away with Jonathan. I must say this feels very awkward."

"Well, you look great. Any reason why you're going dressed this way?"

Jenny shrugged. "I'm not sure, Uncle Bobby. I hope I'm hearing this right."

She handed him a bag with her other clothes in it. "I just need a couple more things—a purse and a white sweater. I hear it gets cold in Manhattan."

They finished shopping, and before Bobby put her old clothes in the truck, Jenny took her *kappe* out of the bag and put it in her purse. Bobby looked at her quizzically.

Jenny shrugged again. "I just feel better if it's close."

Bobby helped her into the passenger side and then walked around and climbed in.

"You sure about this, Jenny? It's a big change. Is it what you really want?"

"I don't know, Uncle Bobby, but if I'm to give Jeremy an honest answer, I have to find out what his world is really like."

"Okay, let's go."

The truck roared away from the curb and headed out Highway 222 toward New York City.

Jeremy and Richard arrived at the club where the announcement party was being held. The place was a beehive of activity. Cross & Crowne were slated to play a set after the announcement, and their roadies were busy setting up the band's gear. The caterers were putting up a long buffet table, and delicious smells drifted out of the kitchen. Gary and Deeny were sitting at the grand piano going over a vocal harmony. When Richard walked in, they both got up and came over. Gary pointed at the bandage on Richard's head.

"You going to be okay, Bro?"

"I'm just fine, Gary, thanks."

Deeny took Richard by the arm. "Are you sure, Richard? You look a little pale."

"Thanks for your concern, guys. I really appreciate it. But this is too big of a deal to call off now. So with your help, we'll get through the business and then I'll just sit back and listen to you play. I'm sure it's going to be an exciting evening."

As he started to walk away, a voice spoke plainly in his ear. *"Let him who has laid his hand on the plow not look back! Press on to the goal! Press on to Jesus Christ! The one who gains Christ will rise with Him from the dead on the youngest day."*

Richard turned around. "What?"

Gary and Deeny looked puzzled. Richard stared at them.

"Didn't you just say something to me?"

The two shook their heads.

"My mistake."

Jeremy was giving some instructions to the staff, and Richard started to walk over toward him. And then he heard the voice again.

"And thine ears shall hear a word behind thee, saying, This is the way, walk ye in it, when ye turn to the right hand, and when ye turn to the left."

Richard turned, but no one was there.

Chapter Thirty-Eight

Only by Grace

◇◇◇

Bobby's truck roared down the road toward Manhattan as Jenny sat in silence.

It's odd how life works out. Here I am, driving to New York to find the answers to all my questions...again. Some things never change.

She thought back to the day when Jonathan had agreed to help her find her birth mother and they had driven out of Apple Creek in his old Volkswagen van. When she remembered the vehicle, she giggled.

Bobby looked over. "What's funny?"

"I was just thinking about Jonathan's old van. That's what I was riding in the last time I went to New York. Well, at least we were headed in that direction."

"You mean the van with Timothy Leary collaged on the front and Guru Garagekey plastered on the door?"

Jenny giggled again. "Yes. Jonathan took himself so seriously. But he was actually a bit ridiculous."

Bobby shook his head. "Well, he sure turned out to be a great guy."

Jenny was quiet. Cars whizzed by them in the opposite direction, heading west. She counted telephone poles for awhile. Finally she spoke.

"He was a wonderful man, Uncle Bobby. I know we didn't see you often when we lived in Paradise, so you didn't get to really notice, but he changed so much. He loved the Lord with all his heart. He was a good husband and a wonderful father."

"You still miss him, don't you, Jenny?"

"*Ja*, I do. I miss him every day. He was my one true love."

"Nothing worldly about loving someone with all your heart, Jenny. Sometimes I wish I had found that kind of love in my life."

"Weren't you married once, Uncle Bobby?"

"Yes, but that was a long time ago. It just didn't work out. After that, I just kind of wandered in my life."

"I don't think you wandered, Uncle Bobby. You were sheriff for twenty-five years. That was important. And that wasn't all."

"What do you mean?"

"I think you had a very specific task in your life, one that was given to you by God, beyond your calling to be a sherriff. I think you were assigned to bless my family…you know, like a guardian angel. You were with my *daed* in the war, and you helped him to come home. Then when my mama was lost in the storm, you kept searching until you found her. And then when I was in trouble in the woods, you rescued me. And you had an even bigger part in finding my biological mother. And now it's you who are helping me to…"

"To what, Jenny? Aren't you going to New York to tell this guy you're going to leave the church and marry him?"

"I…I don't know. I guess so. When I turned Isaac down, I guess I assumed I would be leaving the church. Why else would I be wearing these clothes?"

"I can't tell you that. But I do know this about what you just said…I mean about me being like your guardian angel. I think maybe God did send me to help your family. Knowing Reuben and Jerusha and you and Jonathan and now Rachel—that's what has given my life meaning all these years. Strange, isn't it?"

"Not so strange to me."

They sat in silence again as the miles rolled away behind them. Bobby reached into the pack in his shirt pocket, pulled out a Camel, cracked the window, and lit up.

"So, Jenny. If we get to New York and you decide not to accept this guy's proposal, then what?"

Jenny shook her head. "I don't know, Uncle Bobby. I don't know."

"Testing…one, two, one, two…Glenn, can you bring me up in the monitor, please?"

Deeny Carbone was testing her microphone. There was a momentary squeal as the audio engineer cranked it too far. He yelled from behind the board, "Sorry about that, but I've already got it almost maxed. You guys will have to turn down your amps a little."

While that was happening, the lighting crew was making sure that the three main singers of Cross & Crowne were bathed with lights and there were no dead spots on the stage. Charis Records was going to make sure the announcement party came off professionally. Jeremy King was watching the whole thing in awe.

"Wow, I had no idea there was so much preparation involved in getting a band ready to perform. Do they go through this at every show?"

Richard looked at Jeremy. "What?"

"Do they do this before every show?"

"Oh…yeah, this is standard operating procedure. There's so much equipment, and so many things could go wrong."

"I guess it's a far cry from guys like John Fischer or Randy Stonehill singing Jesus folk music at little coffeehouses back in the sixties. When did it change?"

Richard smiled. "Well, I don't know a lot about it since I don't remember too much about those days."

"Oh, yeah. Sorry, I forgot."

Richard grimaced and rubbed his forehead.

"Are you all right, Richard?"

"I've got a splitting headache. The lights and the volume are kind of getting to me. I think if I want to make it through tonight I'll go take a nap back in one of the dressing rooms."

"Do you need any aspirin?"

"No, I brought some from my apartment. Say, Jeremy, the rest of the guys from Charis Records will be showing up about an hour before the announcement. Would you meet them for me and get them settled...you know, make sure they get pointed at the buffet? And a whole contingent is coming from the media. Make sure the box office has their press passes. Then come get me in time to freshen up a bit."

"Consider it handled, Richard."

The old Ford truck crept up Third Avenue looking for East Sixty-Second. Cabs were zipping by, and the cars behind Bobby were honking belligerently.

Bobby glanced at Jenny. "I don't think we're in Ohio anymore, Toto."

Jenny grinned. "This isn't Paradise, that's for sure."

Finally they reached the cross street and turned left. Jenny checked the address Jeremy had given her.

"It's twenty-five East Sixty-Second, Uncle Bobby."

They pulled up at the address. The club was in an old brick building with modern awnings attached over the barred windows. The sign above the door was simple and elegant. *Paradisio*. A strange chill went down Jenny's spine.

"Maybe I was wrong, Uncle Bobby. Maybe we are in Paradise after all."

Richard Sandbridge lay in the darkened dressing room. The pain in his head was becoming more intense.

Maybe I should have stayed in the hospital.

The room began to swirl, and Richard felt a little sick. He closed his eyes. Then suddenly he was in a van, an old van…

Another car passed going west, followed by a string of cars. He could see the waves of the lake lapping against the bare dirt shore. A dead stump sticking up out of the water came into view. Then the clouds over the lake opened up a bit, and the dim new moon faintly lit the bleak landscape, touching the waters of the lake with a ghastly illumination. The starkness of his surroundings and the events of the past few days crowded in on him, and fear gripped him. He saw Shub's eyes, dead, like this horrible place, and he almost ran off the road. His breath was coming in gasps, so he pulled over to the side of the road.

Get it together, Johnny! Do something! Get a grip on yourself.

Richard jerked awake. The vision had been so real. Where was that? Who was Shub…and who was Johnny?

Bobby rolled down the window when the young man in the tuxedo knocked on it.

"Can I help you, sir?"

"Yes, we are supposed to go to a party in that club, but there's no place to park."

The young man looked at the truck and smirked. "You won't find a parking place until you get to New Jersey. We do have valet parking, but I'm not sure any of our attendants would want to drive this hunk-a-junk over there."

Bobby reached out through the window, took hold of the young man's lapel, and pulled him close.

"I didn't live through World War II and twenty-five years as a cop to be tweaked by a smart-aleck kid on the streets of New York. Now you give me exact instructions on how to get to your 'val-ay parking,' or I might make you show me in person—from the back of the truck."

The young man's demeanor changed noticeably. "Yes…yes, sir! It's right around the corner. You'll see the sign for *Paradisio* parking. Just give them this."

He handed Bobby a ticket. "And if you'd like, sir, I can escort the young lady inside until you return."

"Much better attitude, son. You do that."

Richard got up and went into the bathroom. He reached in his pocket, grabbed the aspirin bottle, and shook four out into his palm. He looked up into the mirror. The man he saw there was not him. The face was different; the hair was long and the clothes…

A thin cotton embroidered shirt, torn bell-bottom jeans, and green suede Beatle boots…a leather-fringed jacket…he stared at his pale complexion…I've got to get out more…

Richard blinked his eyes. He was back, but he was beginning to feel unnerved.

This is getting way too weird. I should just forget this and go home.

There was a knock on the door. "Richard? Are you ready?"

"Jeremy. Do me a favor and get the band to play a couple of songs. Then we'll do the announcement. I'll be out in a few minutes."

"Okay, Richard, I'll take care of it."

Jenny walked into the club. The place was dark except for a brightly lit stage, where a few people were doing what looked like last-minute arrangements. A spotlight projected a message on a curtain behind the stage—Charis/Kerusso, Christ in the Arts. Jenny didn't understand what that meant. As she stood and wondered, she heard a voice say her name.

"Jenny? Is that you?"

Jenny turned to see Jeremy walking toward her. He stopped in front of her and stared. "You…you look so different."

She clutched her purse. Suddenly she felt as local as…*a fish in a tree? Jonathan used to say that.*

"Don't you like it, Jeremy?"

"Of course I do! You look…absolutely amazing. Wonderful. I…"

Jenny blushed, and then she remembered Bobby.

"Jeremy, can you make sure that my uncle, Bobby Halverson, gets in? He drove me."

"Sure, Jenny. Just wait here for a minute and I'll put him on the guest list."

Jeremy walked away, and Jenny sat down at a table. She looked around her at the crowded room. The place was awful—the stage lights and the darkness and people with no faces talking loudly…she was overwhelmed by it. As she sat there, a man came out on the stage and grabbed one of the microphones. Behind him some men with instruments came out and began plugging in. A very pretty girl with long dark hair sat down behind the grand piano. The man spoke.

"Welcome, everyone. Tonight we launch what we hope will be a new season for the gospel in the arts. All of you are here because you love the Lord and you want to see His name lifted up in the music industry and through book publishing. But before we get to our big announcement, we are going to have these guys open the evening with some of their songs. Here they are…Crossss aaaandd Crownnnne!"

The people in the club began cheering and shouting. Suddenly there was a huge roll of the drums and a loud, frantic-sounding solo from the guitarist, who twitched and swayed and then struck a triumphant pose with his last note. The band powered in with the first chords of the song, and the room was filled with ear-splitting sound. The singers stepped to the microphones and began to sing. It was something about "long ago in Jerusalem," but Jenny couldn't understand the words. The noise was deafening. She put her hands over her ears and got up. Jeremy came back and saw her standing there with a stunned look on her face.

"Jenny, what is it?"

She could barely hear him. She had to shout back at him.

"I can't…I can't, Jeremy. This won't work. I've got to go."

She turned and headed for the door. Jeremy ran after her.

Chapter Thirty-Nine

The Song

◇◇◇

RICHARD STOOD AT THE DRESSING-ROOM SINK, filled his hands with cold water, and splashed it on his face. He could hear the band playing, and the volume did nothing to soothe his throbbing head. He dried his face and then looked around. The sunglasses were on a small table by the couch. He grabbed them and put them on. He felt a sharp, stabbing pain in his head that almost knocked him to his knees. He reached out toward the door…

He walked to the fence and stared at the scene. There were men of all ages in the group. An old man with a long white beard operated the cutter. Behind him younger men with dark beards drove the horse teams as boys walked alongside them. It seemed that the men were teaching the boys as they moved through the field, pointing to the row of hay and calling the boys' attention to the teams of horses and machines as they walked…

The long file of machines turned the corner of the big field and came along the fence line…some of the men were singing.

"Lassen Sie ihn, der gelegen hat, seine Hand auf dem Pflug nicht sehen sich um! Presse zur Absicht! Presse Jesus Christus! Derjenige, der Christus gewinnt, wird sich mit ihm von den Toten am jüngsten Tag erheben."

And then Richard was crying out on his hands and knees. "What does it mean? Oh, God, what is happening to me?"

"Let him who has laid his hand on the plow not look back! Press on to the goal! Press on to Jesus Christ! The one who gains Christ will rise with him from the dead on the youngest day." Rise up and walk, My son. Your faith will make you whole.

Richard pulled himself up. He took a deep breath. He had to get out of this room. He opened the door and went out into the hall. The backstage area opened directly onto the stage. He stood while the band finished their song, and then he opened the curtain and stepped out onto the stage. Gary had just turned to check his amp, and he saw Richard standing there. Quickly he stepped over to the piano, whispered something to Deeny, and then turned back to the microphone.

"Ladies and gentlemen, tonight we have a very special guest. We are going to ask him to sing for you the song that started his career and ultimately led him to Christ and to Charis Records to be our producer. Would you please welcome…Richard Sandbridge!"

The audience burst into loud and sustained applause. Richard felt a sense of desperation begin to crawl over him, like a fever chill. Then he heard another voice.

Play the song. Today is the day of your salvation.

Peace like a river washed over him. In a daze he moved to the piano. Deeny got up and made room for him. As he sat down, the keyboard looked strange and unfamiliar. He wanted his guitar, but then his hands were on the keys and he was nodding to Gary. The first chords flowed from his hands, and the band joined in. The sax player lifted up the familiar melody to the intro.

Jenny rushed out the door of the club with Jeremy close behind her. He caught up and grabbed her arm, spinning her around to face him.

"Jenny, where are you going? I thought…"

Jenny looked at his strained face, and then like a beautiful ray of sun breaking through dark clouds, the answer came to her.

"I can't, Jeremy."

"Can't what, Jenny?"

"I can't marry you. Don't you see?"

"No, I don't see. Help me understand, Jenny."

Behind her, Jenny heard footsteps on the sidewalk. She looked and it was Bobby.

"Everything all right, Jenny?"

"Just give me a minute, Uncle Bobby, and then we'll go."

She turned back to Jeremy. "I can't marry you because I don't love you. At least I don't love you that way. You deserve a woman who will cherish you, who will love you completely, who will be one heart with you. And I can't do that."

"But why, Jenny? I don't understand."

"When I was in the hospital the day my parents died, my papa passed first. But the monitor on his heart kept beeping. And then I found out why. He and my mama were holding hands, and my mama's heart was beating through him. And then their life and their love became so real for me. They were two lives that shared one heart. They had truly become one flesh. And I saw that it was a gift that God gives rarely, but when He does, it is to be honored and cherished and treasured, for I believe He only gives it once."

"But—"

"I had it, Jeremy, don't you understand? I was one flesh with Jonathan. We were two lives with one heart, and there can never be another for me. I can't marry you. That's all I can say. I can't marry you."

Inside the club, the music changed from loud to soft. Gentle chords drifted sweetly out the door as a lyric saxophone danced a sweet melody above them. And then a beautiful, clear voice lifted over the chords, and words that she never thought to hear again broke upon her senses.

Tonight, I whisper in your ear,
I always want you near.
Tonight, kiss me tenderly,
Come so easily,
Into my heart, tonight.

Jenny's breath caught in her throat.

A lover's symphony,
The sweetest harmony,
And all that I can be
Is here with you tonight.
I'll do the best I can
To be your loving man,
And everything I am
Is here with you tonight.

With each line she heard, a deeper shock pierced Jenny's heart. She turned and stared at the door.

"That song…"

In a trance, Jenny moved toward the door. Jeremy looked after her and then to Bobby.

"What's happening?"

"I don't know, Jeremy," Bobby said.

Jenny walked through the door and back into the club. Bobby and Jeremy went after her. It took a moment for Jenny's eyes to adjust. The bright stage lights were almost blinding, and she could barely make out someone sitting at the piano, singing a song.

Tonight I sing this song of love,
You're the one I'm dreaming of tonight.
Kiss me tenderly,
Come so easily,
Into my heart tonight.

As the band picked up the melody, Jenny walked slowly through the club. She didn't see the people. She only saw a man sitting at the piano—a man with shoulder-length dark hair and sunglasses. She couldn't see his face because he was turned away from her as he played. She kept moving forward until she stood directly behind him. His clear voice lifted up, like an angel singing…

> A lover's symphony,
> The sweetest harmony,
> And all I want to be
> Is here with you tonight.
> I'll do the best I can
> To be your loving man,
> And everything I am
> Is here with you tonight.

The words…Jonathan's words…it was the song he wrote for her. She stood in wonder as the man came to the last verse. And then she lifted up her voice and sang with him, for she knew the song by heart.

> Tonight, I sing this song of love.
> You're the one I'm dreaming of.
> Tonight, kiss me tenderly,
> Come so easily
> Into my heart tonight.

As the band played the last chords and stopped, the man slowly turned. The lights glared off the sunglasses and Jenny still couldn't see his face. She spoke.

"Where did you get that song?"

The man turned his head to the voice. "I wrote it."

"No, you did not. My late husband, Jonathan, wrote it."

The man recoiled as though he had been slapped. "Jonathan?"

Jenny moved closer. "Who are you?"

"I'm…I'm Richard…Richard Sandbridge. I wrote…I wrote…"

Jenny reached up and gently removed the sunglasses. The face…so familiar, but different. The mustache…the…oh, Lord! The eyes! The eyes…the wonderful sea-blue eyes, just like her papa's. The eyes that drew her in and in until she was one with him.

"Jonathan? *Jonathan?*"

The man looked puzzled. "No, I'm…I'm Richard…Who are you?"

"Jonathan, it's *me*. It's your Jenny."

Richard reached out, his hand shaking. "Jenny?"

Jenny took her hair and rolled it up into a bun. She grabbed a pin out of her purse to hold it. Then she lifted out her *kappe* and put it on.

"Jonathan, it's your Jenny. It's me."

He stared at her, and then the light of recognition broke upon his face. Both of his hands reached out. Jenny took them in hers. The old shock ran up her arms and into her heart.

"Jenny! Where have you been? It was so dark…oh, Jenny…"

Jonathan moved off the bench and stood before her. Jenny reached out and touched his face, gently, oh so gently, and then she was in his arms and he was holding her and his strong arms were around her and…

"Oh, Jonathan! Jonathan!"

Bobby Halverson walked up behind them. He stood there for a moment, staring at Jonathan and Jenny. And then he put his hands gently on their shoulders and smiled.

"Let's go home."

> And now the circle has come all the way around to its end and closed again. And all that was undone is born fresh and new in my heart. I am home, I am safe, and Jonathan is home with me, here in Paradise. My hopes have been fulfilled, and my prayers have been answered. *"O the depth*

of the riches both of the wisdom and knowledge of God! how unsearchable are his judgments, and his ways past finding out!"

And as this great joy fills my heart, I see the plan of God with such clarity. The future runs away before me like a great broad river flowing down to the ocean, and the past stands like the memorial stones in the waters of the Jordan. And I see that the roots of my faith are bound to the roots of my life, unbreakably mingled, and I know that we, Jonathan and me, are Amish, and we will always be Amish. And we rest in the arms of those who went before us and were faithful and loved us, and I remember them and the memory keeps me here, where I belong.

These memories are moments of the purest joy that often find me when I am most in need. They come when I am burdened by the troubles of the day, or wound tight in the snares of the world, or numbed by an undeserved wound. An isolated thought or a fragrance or an unbidden reminder will creep into my heart, and in an instant I will be transported on spirit wings to my beloved home in Apple Creek, Ohio.

In my mind's eye I see Mama, sitting at the quilting frame, a small smile playing about her lovely face as she allows God to move through her heart and hands to bring forth such beauty that just remembering it is enough to steal the very breath from my body and leave me gasping in wonder. There is my papa, the smile behind his eyes keeping me warm and safe as his strength and love protected me all my life.

Outside the sky is painted with God's brilliant palette of purples and pinks, and the smell of the fields is an intoxicant of the purest measure to my soul. How I loved those days! How they live in my heart and my memory, bringing me the beauty of another time that was unsullied and without blemish. How can I tell you of the love that rises in my heart, the joy that springs forth with each remembrance? No, I cannot. For unless you have been there, unless you have the same yearning in your very being, you cannot know of what I speak. And so I hold these times in my heart. They are mine, mine alone. They are my Apple Creek dreams.

Epilogue:
Among the Trees of Eden

◇◇◇

THEY SAT TOGETHER ON THE front porch of the old farmhouse—the little Amish woman and the tall writer. Cups of tea sat on the small table in front of them, and a warm summer breeze heralded the coming of another beautiful evening in Paradise, Pennsylvania. The writer had come all the way from California to meet her, and now they were talking as if they had known each other for years.

"So what happened after you found Jonathan?"

"I brought Jonathan home to Paradise. It took him a long time to remember his life leading up to the explosion on the boat, but with the Lord's help and a lot of love, he eventually recollected most of it."

"Was it hard for him to come back…I mean, to being Amish, once he had so much success in the music business?"

"*Ja*, he did struggle with that, especially on the days when he got confused."

"Confused?"

"Jonathan sustained a serious injury when the boat exploded. Then he drifted on a piece of wreckage for almost two days, and after he washed ashore, he wandered the streets of Sandbridge for a whole day in the storm before anyone found him and realized he needed help. A few days before I came to New York for the announcement party, he was injured in an attack by a mugger. It all had a lasting effect on his health. Some days he thought he was Richard Sandbridge. Those were the hard days. But in spite of that, thank the Lord, we had thirty wonderful years after I found him."

"Had?"

"Yes, Jonathan passed two years ago. His injuries finally took their toll. He had a hemorrhagic stroke one afternoon while he was cutting hay. He was in the field behind the house, and I heard him call me."

The writer looked at Jenny. She was looking somewhere far away.

"He died in my arms."

"What about Rachel?" the writer asked.

"It was hard for Rachel when her papa came home. She was fourteen, becoming a young woman, and Jonathan had missed such a big part of her formative years. They were at odds for a long time. I think Rachel had finally reconciled herself to Jonathan being dead—she had moved on. And then when he came home, she had to learn that relationship all over again. I think she felt like he came between her and me. Eventually they found what they once had when Rachel was little, but it took a long time."

"And Bobby Halverson?

"Bobby is still here with me. He lives up there in the bungalow on the knoll."

She pointed past the barn. The writer could see the small house through the trees. An old pickup was parked in front of it.

"He's ninety-four now, but he's as fit as a fiddle and a great comfort. He's been family to me since I was four years old. He's helped me through some very hard times."

"And what about your books? Jeremy King told me you had written some wonderful books."

Jenny looked at the writer, and a strange look passed over her face.

"*Ja*, the books. Well, Jeremy would be interested in those. After all, he helped me write the first one, and he is a publisher."

Jenny paused again as though she were hearing something the writer could not. And then she stood and motioned to him.

"Come with me."

They went into the house and up the stairs to the second floor. Jenny opened the door to one of the rooms. Books and papers were piled on the floor, and shelves on every wall were stuffed full. Under a long window on the front wall stood a beautiful desk made of pale wood. The top of the desk was strewn with papers and notebooks with an old Underwood typewriter in the middle.

Jenny ran her hand over the wood. "My papa made this for me when I first became serious about writing."

In the corner of the room stood an old cedar chest. Jenny knelt in front of it and opened the lid. The scent of cedar and lilacs filled the room. Jenny reached into the chest and pulled out several bundles tied with string. She laid them on the floor, and then she reached into the chest and took out a larger bundle that was at the bottom. She stood up.

"Could you pick those up for me?" she asked.

The writer stooped and picked up the bundles. There were six of them. Jenny cleared a space on a low couch and motioned to him.

"Put them here."

Then she opened the first bundle. It was a manuscript, typed in old-style courier font.

"This is the story of the quilt and how my mama made it so she could run away from God."

She pointed to the others, one by one.

"This is the story about how Jonathan and I met and married and came to live on this farm, and this is the story of Jonathan's...his death and resurrection, so to speak, and how I came to be a writer."

"What are these others?" the writer asked.

"These stories are about the women of my family, going back to the beginnings of the Amish faith in Switzerland. And one of these is the story of my Rachel and her husband, Daniel, and the great trial they faced before...well, you read it."

"You're letting me read these?"

Jenny ran her hands over the books. "When I came back to Paradise with Jonathan, the Lord made it very clear that this was my home and my life. I am Amish, my ancestors were Amish, and here is where I belong. But He allowed me to write these books. I did not know why until you came today. I am giving them to you."

"*Giving* them?"

"*Ja.* I read your book. It was well written and honest. I believe the Lord wants these stories told, but not by me. Jeremy tells me you are trustworthy, so I'm giving them to you. I want you to take these books and rewrite them, your way. I want you to tell the stories in your own words. I believe the books will bring healing to many people as they have to me."

The writer stood with the first manuscript in his hands. He knew he had been given a great gift.

"I'll tell the stories as you have written them."

Jenny patted him on the shoulder. "I know you will."

Then Jenny laid the large bundle on the couch and unwrapped it. She took out what was inside and unfolded it. It was a beautiful quilt, unlike any other Amish quilt the writer had ever seen. The cream-colored backing was stitched to a stunning blue silk piece. In the center of the blue section was an incredible red rose. The hundreds of petals were cut perfectly, and the whole quilt was a masterpiece. The soft afternoon light coming through the window made the rose shine with a wonderful luminescence.

"This is the Rose of Sharon quilt—the most beautiful quilt my mama ever made. But it is more than a quilt. It's as though God wrote the story of my family here with His own hand. All of these stories I'm giving you were written because my mama made this quilt. Remember that when you tell them."

The writer stared at the beautiful quilt. The deep red was indeed like a rose…or—and the words sprang unbidden to his mind—the blood of Christ.

Jenny pointed to the rose. "That is Jenna's story. Mama named the quilt after Jenna, her little Rose of Sharon."

She turned the quilt over and showed him the exquisitely repaired corner and the faint stains.

"The quilt got stained and ruined when my mama was carrying me through the great storm. This corner was torn when she pulled the lining out to start the fire that saved my life. When I was searching for Mama Rachel and in great danger, the Lord told my mama to repair the quilt. As Mama restored it, He showed her how to pray for me. This part is my story."

Then Jenny turned the quilt back over and pointed to something in the very center of the rose. The writer had to take his glasses off to see the tiny key-shaped piece of red silk stitched almost invisibly there.

"My mama didn't know it when she sewed this on, but this is Rachel's story. You'll find that among the manuscripts."

Jenny spread the quilt out on the floor. It was beautiful—the Rose of Sharon quilt.

"And the whole quilt…it is my mama Jerusha's life, it is who she was, so creative, so beautiful, so warm, and so caring. I was blessed to have her. She was *ein Geschenk vom Gott*…a gift from God."

The writer glanced at Jenny. Again he had the feeling that she was looking somewhere far away.

"And what will you do now, Jenny? Will you write any more books?"

"No. That part of my life is over now. I will stay here in Paradise and grow old and pass and go to be with Jonathan and my mama and papa and my sister, Jenna, and all who have gone before. And my legacy will go on in these books, in this quilt, in my grandchildren, and in this farm. God has restored me to the garden, and I am content to live here among the trees of Eden."

Later, after they said their goodbyes, the writer drove away. He was going west, and the sun was setting. He stopped partway down the driveway and looked back. Jenny stood on the porch, watching. Her *kappe* was slightly askew, and the rebellious curls, now gray, fought to escape. And then the evening breeze picked up, and the golden light of the setting sun touched the leaves of the trees, and they began to dance and then flamed into fire. And he knew that all was well in Paradise.

Discussion Guide

◇◇◇

Dealing with the Death of a Loved One
In chapter 1, Jenny is dealing with the death of her husband, Jonathan. Lives are often transformed by such loss, but these changes do not necessarily need to be for the worse in the long run. Jenny is grieving. You may have had the same experience.

1. What are the initial effects of Jonathan's death on Jenny? If you have suffered the death of a loved one, did similar things happen to you?

2. Grief is about more than your feelings—it also shows up in the way you think. How did grief change Jenny's thinking? How did it change the way she felt about things around her? Did you relate to her? Why?

3. Jenny had to decide how to talk with Rachel about death and dying. How did she handle it? How would you handle it?

4. Does knowing Jesus Christ change your perspective about death and dying? Have you ever shared that perspective with unsaved loved ones and friends? If so, how did you do it?

Scripture reference: Hebrews 2:14-15

The Importance of Family in Troubled Times

When Jenny returns to Apple Creek, she is an emotional and physical wreck. A loving family is critically important in times of trial or suffering.

1. If you have endured a devastating loss, did you seek solace among your family, or did you isolate yourself and try to make it on your own?

2. Jenny discovered she had to develop an identity that did not include Jonathan. How important was that to her healing? Why?

3. Jenny involved herself in everyday, mundane things until she found her center again. Was that important? Is that something you would try to do if you were grieving? Why?

4. Jenny discovered the gift of writing, and it became the focus of her life. Have you ever experienced a new beginning after a time of loss?

Scripture reference: Joel 2:25; Isaiah 58:12

Choices

Toward the end of the book, Jenny must make a decision. Her choice will be dictated by her head or by her heart.

1. Have you ever had to choose between something you felt was the leading of the Lord and something that was practical and safe?

2. How did you choose?

3. Did it affect the direction of your life profoundly or minimally?

4. Was the outcome positive or negative?

Scripture reference: Acts 21:13-14

About Patrick E. Craig

Patrick E. Craig is a lifelong writer and musician who left a successful songwriting and performance career to follow Christ in 1984. He spent the next 26 years as a worship leader, seminar speaker, and pastor in churches and at retreats, seminars, and conferences all across the western United States. After ministering for a number of years in music and worship to a circuit of small churches, he is now concentrating on writing and publishing both fiction and nonfiction books. Patrick and his wife, Judy, make their home in Northern California and are the parents of two adult children and have five grandchildren.

Praise for the first two books in Patrick Craig's Apple Creek Dreams Series
A Quilt for Jenna and *The Road Home*

◇◇◇

"Patrick Craig writes with an enthusiasm and a passion that is a joy to read. He deals with romance, faith, love, loss, tragedy, and restoration with equal amounts of elegance, grace, clarity, and power. Everyone should pick up his debut novel in Amish fiction, turn off the phone and computer and TV, and settle in for a good night's read. Craig's book is a blessing."

Murray Pura
author of *The Wings of Morning* and *Ashton Park*

"A good storyteller takes a fine story and places it in a setting peppered with enough accurate details to satisfy a native son. Then he peoples it with characters so real we keep thinking we see them walking down the street. A great storyteller takes all that and binds it together with, say, a carefully constructed Rose of Sharon quilt and the wallop of a storm of the century that actually happened. *A Quilt for Jenna* proves Patrick Craig to be a great storyteller."

Kay Marshall Strom
author of the Grace in Africa and Blessings in India trilogies

"A touching tale of three people who have lost their way. In *A Quilt for Jenna*, Patrick Craig deftly contrasts the peaceful Amish lifestyle with the harsh World War II Guadalcanal battlefield, tied together with a lovely message of sacrifice, humility, and forgiveness. I was entranced."

Sarah Sundin
award-winning author of *With Every Letter*